MW01181723

Highland Wolf Pact: Compromising Positions

By Selena Kitt

eXcessica publishing

Highland Wolf Pact: Compromising Positions © 2015 by Selena Kitt

All rights reserved under the International and Pan-American Copyright Conventions. No part of this book may be reproduced or transmitted in any form or by any means, electronic or mechanical, including photocopying, recording, or by any information storage and retrieval system, without permission in writing from the publisher.

This is a work of fiction. Names, places, characters and incidents are either the product of the author's imagination or are used fictitiously, and any resemblance to any actual persons, living or dead, organizations, events or locales is entirely coincidental. All sexually active characters in this work are 18 years of age or older.

This book is for sale to ADULT AUDIENCES ONLY. It contains substantial sexually explicit scenes and graphic languge which may be considered offensive by some readers. Please store your files where they cannot be access by minors.

Excessica LLC
486 S Ripley #164
Alpena MI 49707

To order additional copies of this book, contact:
books@excessicapublishing.com
www.excessica.com

Cover art © 2014 Taria Reed
First Edition 2015

Warning: the unauthorized reproduction or distribution of this copyrighted work is illegal. Criminal copyright infringement, including infringement without monetary gain, is investigated by the FBI and is punishable by up to 5 years in prison and a fine of $250,000.

Chapter One

Scotland
Middle March – Near Castle MacFalon
Year of our Lord 1502

If she hadn't caught scent of the man, she never would have ended up in the trap.

Kirstin cursed the stranger as she struggled, strung halfway up the side of a huge oak tree, the limb holding her weight moving only slightly as she snapped and pawed at the net. She had caught his scent and had followed her nose to the edge of the wood, where it ended in a clearing. In the middle of the clearing was an enormous burial cairn. This was where the man knelt, one bare knee on the ground, his elbow up on the other, forehead pressed to his closed fist.

She had believed him to be praying, too distracted to notice her, so she had crept forward, curious. That had been her mistake. The movement had caught the attention of the man's horse. The big, black animal had thrown its head and yanked at the reins, tied to a stake on the ground, pawing the grass as it caught her scent. Kirstin's fur had prickled, standing on end, as the man turned his head to look at her.

He was a Scotsman—his plaid gave that much away. He didn't call out or move for a weapon when he saw her, as she expected a man might, when faced with a wolf in the early morning light. The man easily could have drawn the bow he had slung over his back, although if he moved, she would have been gone faster than he could cock an arrow. But he stayed still, his gaze meeting hers across the dewy grass.

And there was something about those eyes...

The moment their gaze locked, Kirstin felt it. Something crackled, like lightning flashing through storm clouds. The horse continued to whinny and paw his big hoof at the ground, but the human and the wolf didn't move. They just looked at each other, sizing each other up. If she had been a regular wolf, she probably would have instantly turned tail and run. But if she had been a regular wolf, she never would have followed the scent of a human this close in the first place.

Her tail twitched and her nose wrinkled when she caught his scent again as the wind shifted. He wasn't afraid. She would have smelled that—it was a tinny, copper scent, similar to blood, a mixture of sweat and adrenaline. The man whose eyes searched hers across the clearing wasn't afraid—although he should have been. She wondered at it, cocking her shaggy head and whining softly at her own confusion.

That's when he spoke.

"Are ye a wulver, then?" he called in a thick, Scottish brogue. He didn't make a move, didn't reach for a bow or a sword, but his words frightened her far more than any weapon would have. If this man knew the difference between a wolf and a wulver, and even suspected she was the latter, she was in far more danger than she thought. But then she remembered, she'd tied her own plaid around her neck before she left the den, and it was tied there still.

She had turned tail and run, even though he'd stood, calling after her, "Halt! Come back!"

If only she hadn't followed his scent. If only the horse hadn't noticed her and alerted his master. If only she hadn't taken off running. Or mayhaps if she had run the other direction, through the clearing instead of back into the woods. If she had only stayed home, snug in her den, taking care of her pack the way she always had...

But she couldn't lament this last.

Because while most of her pack was safe back in the den, their pack leader was at Castle MacFalon, sitting by his brother's bedside, waiting to see if he'd recover from wounds that would've instantly killed any mortal man. The warriors had returned to their den, exhausted, hungry, with a tale so horrifying, Kirstin didn't even want to imagine it.

But it was all she could think of as she took off running through the woods, following their scent on the trail. It would take her to the borderlands, back to Castle MacFalon, where one of her pack lay dying...

Not dying. She twisted in the net, glimpsing the ground below. It was going to be quite a hard drop to the forest floor. *He's not going to die. Not if I have anything to say about it.*

But she wasn't going to be able to do anything if she didn't get out of this damnable net. Kirstin twisted her big, furry head to see if any hunter was around. Had the man kneeling in the clearing been the one who laid this trap? She wondered. If so, he had seen her. He had watched her turn and run back into the woods. Straight toward the hidden net.

Kirstin felt a howl rising in her throat, nearly uncontrollable, at her sudden lack of freedom. Adrenaline coursed through her and she turned the howl into a low growl, forcing herself to be still, to stay calm. She couldn't let her animal side take control, even if she was in wulver form. She had to stop, to think, to get herself out of this. She would have to change into human form, find the dirk she had sown into her plaid, and cut herself free.

Before the hunter found her.

"Easy, lass."

The voice came from below and she froze, hackles rising, bladder tensing in her belly. He must have come from downwind, quietly tracking her, to appear so suddenly without her knowledge. She couldn't see him, but she knew the man had a bow. She'd seen it slung across his back. He had a dirk hidden under his plaid, like any good Scotsman would. He could, right now, have an arrow aimed at her side.

"I'm not gonna hurt ye." He spoke softly, from right beneath her.

She twisted in the net, trying to see him, and couldn't, but she could sense him. Smell him. It was the same scent that had caught her attention as she followed her pack's trail, the one that had intrigued her enough to leave the path and head toward the clearing.

"I hafta come up t'free ye," he explained. He'd come into the woods quietly, on foot. She didn't scent his horse at all. "I'm afeared somethin's caught. The trap will'na let go from 'ere."

His voice moved below her and she caught a glimpse of him out of the corner of her eye. She gave a low growl, baring her teeth. It was pure instinct. The man came up the trunk on her left side, climbing fast and efficiently. Kirstin twisted in the net, snapping at him as he got nearer.

"Easy, lass, I mean ye n'harm," he soothed.

He was already above her, standing on the branch the net was strung from. Then he sat, edging his way slowly toward her, leaning over so he could reach the place where the rope that held the net stretched taut over the branch.

"Ye mus' be from t'wulver den?" He talked softly as he worked.

His hands were big, untangling the rope, which was tensed with Kirstin's full wulver weight—almost double her human one. He had dark, shoulder-length hair that swept across his cheek, and he used his other hand to push it out of his eyes.

"Did ye come t'help Laina and Sibyl, then?" He stopped when he heard Kirstin whine softly at that. He cocked his head and looked at her. Up close like this, the steel in his eyes had softened, like storm clouds parting to reveal a deepening, blue sky underneath. He seemed to understand her response, almost like he'd read her thoughts. "Darrow's healin' more e'ery day. Sibyl says she thinks he's comin' outta t'worst of it."

Just hearing those familiar, beloved names made Kirstin's heart beat faster. Could it be true? Was this man a friend of the wulvers? If he knew Sibyl, Laina and Darrow, should she trust his words? But it wasn't his words, it was his actions that swayed her. The man was up in a tree, trying to free her. What really convinced her, though, was his lack of alarm. She didn't sense or scent any fear in him at all.

"We'll get ye down from 'ere and I'll take ye back t'Castle MacFalon." The man's brow creased as he tried to solve some problem with the trap she couldn't see from her vantage point. He glanced at her and half-smiled, a dimple appearing in his cheek. "I'm Donal MacFalon, by t'by. Laird of the MacFalon Clan. 'Though I'm t'first t'admit, I'm still gettin' used to the title."

Donal MacFalon. The wulvers had come home talking about him. She had listened to their tales in the dining hall, where the wulver women fed their travel-weary warriors a hot meal, and remembered the way they'd spoken of Donal MacFalon. Unlike his brother, this was a man of integrity, they said. And like his father before him, he would honor the peaceful pact made between man and wulver.

She really could trust him, then. At least, as much as she was likely to trust any man.

Kirstin whined softly, reaching out toward him with a paw. She could just reach the soft leather of his boot and she tapped it gently. Donal looked down at her and smiled when he met her eyes again. There were no storm clouds in those eyes at all now. Just a deep, sparkling blue, as reflective as the lake in the wulver valley.

"Yer safe, lass," he assured her with a slow nod. "I apologize fer the trap. Alistair—me brother—was set on catchin' all t'wulvers and killin 'em..."

She growled at this—although she knew the man's brother, Alistair, was dead. He'd been the one responsible for Darrow's wounds.

"Aye, 'tis jus' how I feel 'bout it." Donal made a face. "It'll likely take us months t'find all the traps an' take 'em down."

Kirstin yipped in surprise, a high pitched sound, when the rope holding the net lengthened, but just for a moment. Then it went taut again.

"Oh fer the love'a—" He struggled with the rope, his body swaying on the limb, and Kirstin prayed he wouldn't fall to his death.

Then she heard it. It wasn't far off, coming from deeper in the woods—the sound of men. It wasn't just one, but several. She glanced at Donal, but he was busy trying to finagle the trap and hadn't heard anything. Of course, he was human—his sense of hearing and smell were seriously impaired compared to hers.

She whined softly, looking at the man, Donal, wondering how to tell him. Mayhaps they were his men, heading this way? She hoped so. The might be able to help him get her out of this damnable trap, because she wasn't sure he was going to be able to do it on his own.

"Easy, lass," he said again, softly, as he maneuvered the rope. "Almost there."

She whined louder, reaching out with her paw to touch his calf. He glanced down, frowning, lifting his gaze to meet hers.

"What is it?"

Kirstin turned her head in the direction of the men. She could hear them clearly now. Couldn't he?

Donal held his hand up, cocking his head. He'd heard them. Good! He moved quickly and almost silently, easing his way up higher in the tree. Using the leaves as cover, he nearly faded into the tree itself in the greens and blues of his plaid.

Kirstin panicked. She was caught in a trap with men heading her way. The howl rising in her throat was irrepressible. Twisting in the net, she pawed and snapped at it, determined to free herself, even if it meant falling to the forest floor below.

"Easy, lass, easy!" Donal soothed, his voice low and soft. "I'll not let 'em hurt ye. I promise ye!"

She whined, turning her head to look at him. She could see him through a thick, Y-shaped branch, his head appearing above it. Did she dare trust this man? Her instinct to escape was strong, almost overpowering.

"I promise ye," he said again, giving her a slow, firm nod. "No harm'll come to ye on m'watch."

Kirstin heard them coming closer, along the path. Not his men, then, or he wouldn't be hiding. So who was it heading through the forest in the early morning light? Hunters?

She whined again, thrashing in the net.

"Shh!" Donal put his finger to his lips, shaking his head as he stood behind the thick tree limb.

Kirstin tried. She stilled, smelling them now—five men, heading their way. She made herself go limp in the net, turning her head so she could see Donal, see his eyes. He wasn't afraid—but he had a concerned knit to his brow. He didn't expect anyone coming through the woods on his land then. She saw he had his bow in his hand and he stood there, frozen, waiting.

Kirstin heard an arrow being knocked—and it wasn't Donal's. She wanted to warn him, to give him a chance to defend himself, but there was no need. He spoke before the other bow was drawn.

"If ye draw that arrow, I hope ye're a better archer than ye're a hunter." Donal's own bow was aimed in the direction of the interloper. "If I have t'drop from this tree a'fore I finish what I came up 'ere t'do, one of us'll be dead a'fore supper—and I do'na plan to miss the crispy skin of the swine I dragged in from t'woods t'mornin' a'fore last."

Kirstin heard another bow draw, this one from a different spot on the forest floor behind her, and she knew then that Donal was in trouble. She glanced up at the laird, seeing him preparing to launch himself from the tree, when a voice stopped him.

"Laird MacFalon, feel free to finish your task, free your quarry, and exit your perch."

Kirstin growled, feeling the hackles on the back of her neck rising. The voice was smooth, confident, even slightly amused—but she didn't trust the man it came from. She didn't know why—it was just instinct, but she trusted her instincts. Maybe it was just because the accent was so different from their own Scottish brogue. This man was English and spoke in the clipped way she was used to hearing from the Englishwoman, Sibyl, who had recently been living with them in the wulver den.

"I promise, this pair of mongrel poachers will hinder you no further," the Englishman assured them from below. "And, at your word, they'll hinder this world no longer either."

Don't trust him. Kirstin wanted to tell Donal, but she had no voice. Instead, she gave a low whine that turned into a growl in the back of her throat.

"Aye, thank ye, stranger." Donal frowned at Kirstin, hearing her animal warning.

The Scotsman was at a disadvantage, and he clearly knew it. He had to trust the Englishman, given that he had not only one, but two, arrows pointed in his direction, likely at very vital parts of his anatomy. Kirstin had a feeling that, whoever was below—especially if they were the poachers who had set the trap in which she was now ensnared— would rather have Donal dead before he left the tree than face him on level ground.

"Spare the curs, Lord Eldred," Donal called down. So he knew the man, then? But he'd called him "stranger?" Kirstin wrinkled her nose in confusion. "If they're honest poachers, they're hungry, and their wives and bairns will be as well. An empty belly's an ailment that spread quickly under m'late brother's watch—and t'will be cured under mine. As England's good King Henry's shown, there's none more loyal than those given mercy and a full belly—when warranted."

"You already have the makings of The MacFalon." The Englishman chuckled. "And your instincts are correct—I am Lord Eldred Lothienne, at your service."

So the laird had been guessing at the man's identity then, Kirstin realized, looking up at the Scot.

"Easy." Donal squatted, speaking low to Kirstin, keeping his balance as he unhitched the rope and secured it, dropping a long end, presumably so he could lower Kirstin down once he was on the ground. At least, she hoped. "I know ye've got n'reason t'trust me, but I'll not harm ye— I'll free ye, I promise."

She gave a conciliatory whine as Donal began climbing down the trunk of the tree. Twisting in the net, she glimpsed the Englishman standing at its base out of the corner of her eye. He spoke like an English lord, but he was dressed in travelling clothes, a pack secured to his back. He gave Donal a gloved hand down and the Scotsman gave a low whistle when an arrow thunked into the tree trunk beside his head.

Lord Eldred shouldered Donal aside as two more loosed arrows hit the tree across the way, answering the first, these from the man's captains, still hidden somewhere in the wood.

"It appears the mongrels have given a parting shot before running off into the forest." Lord Eldred frowned into the woods, where the poachers had retreated. "Shall my captains and I pursue?"

"Nay, if they're local, they'll know these woods well— and they'll be as invisible as the fey folk a'fore ye run 'em down." Donal looked at the other man, head tilted, eyes narrowing slightly. "Ye marked 'em a'fore they were even in position. And ye weren't due t'visit 'til the morrow, but ye're in the MacFalon woods. Scouting, mayhaps? The tales of yer skill in the wild haven't been overtold, Lord Eldred Lothienne."

"Nor have the tales of your courage and generosity been overtold, Donal MacFalon," the Englishman replied with a smile, clapping the other man on the back. "It would appear that King Henry was correct in his assessment. You are as forthright as your brother was treacherous. It'll be a burden lifted to carry that message back to the King. I'd wager my finest bow that you won't be threatening the peace agreed upon with the wulvers."

"Ye can wager yer *life* on that." Donal glanced up at Kirstin, still stuck in the net. She was panting lightly, waiting patiently for the men to free her, trusting Donal at his word. Not that she had much choice, given the circumstances. The Scotsman grabbed the end of the rope he'd left dangling, unhitching it with a sharp tug, and Kirstin felt the net begin to move.

Her heart raced, and the closer she got to the ground, the more the fur on the back of her neck stood up. Her instinct told her to run. Or fight. And she had to force herself to stay still in the net.

"All of these wulver traps shoulda been disarmed." Donal frowned as he slowly lowered Kirstin toward the forest floor. She tensed, seeing the Englishman fully for the first time. He was an older man—a good ten, maybe fifteen, years older than Donal, at least—with a thick, dark beard shot with streaks of gray and salt and pepper hair. His dark eyes missed nothing, and his gaze settled on her and stayed there, making her hackles rise further. "I do'na know if they missed this one, or mayhaps someone's re-arming them. 'T'will be quite a job for ye and yer captains t'undertake, I'm afeared."

"King Henry has entrusted it to me, and it will be done." Lord Eldred squatted near the net, not touching her, but his gaze moved over her in wolf form as if cataloging her. Kirstin shuddered, feeling a growl building in her throat.

"What's free is what's good, and what's good is what's free." Donal unsheathed his dirk and began cutting the net apart.

"You plan to just let her go?" Lord Eldred asked, craggy eyebrows rising in surprise. "In that form?"

"She'll change and come back," Donal assured him, working more of the net free. "Won't ye, lass?"

Kirstin just looked at him, feeling his hands moving in her fur, soft, tender, as he worked to free her.

"You trust a wulver?" Eldred Lothienne stood, taking a step back as Kirstin lifted her head to look at him.

"Aye. She's not a wulver warrior." Donal snorted, shaking his head, unwrapping part of the net from her hind leg. "She's a female, here to see to her wounded kin."

Kirstin blinked at him in surprise, at how much the man had deduced when she hadn't yet said a word to him.

"Ye go make yerself decent, lass," Donal told her softly, freeing her from the last of the net. Her body shook with the effort it took her to stay still. "And I'll take ye back wit' me to Castle MacFalon t'see yer kin. Ye ken?"

She gave a low whine, but her gaze was on the Englishman, not the Scot. It was the former she didn't trust, although she had no idea why not.

"I'll take ye to Darrow," Donal said softly, his hand moving through her fur, scratching her affectionately behind the ear. She was still stunned by his lack of fear.

Kirsten glanced down at the dirk in his other hand, the one he'd used to open the net, shredding hours of someone's handiwork. He hadn't thought twice about destroying it. Kirstin let out a growl, head low, getting quickly to her feet. She heard them before she glimpsed them, two men appearing out of the woods on foot.

"Just my captains," Lord Eldred announced, waving them over, but Kirsten had already escaped deeper into the woods, in the opposite direction.

"Come back, ye ken?" Donal called after her as she disappeared into the brush.

Kirstin crouched there for a moment, panting lightly, feeling the adrenaline course through her body as she listened to the men talking, trying to decide what to do. If it had just been the man, Donal, she wouldn't have hesitated, but the other three men gave her pause. The two that had gotten away—where were they? She was sure they had been traveling together, but the man, Lord Eldred, had called them poachers.

Mayhaps she'd been mistaken, her senses changed from hanging so high up in the tree...

She glimpsed Donal pulling an arrow from that same tree she'd been hanging in—the arrow that had nearly hit him.

"Well-made. A local arrow?" Lord Eldred asked, looking at it over Donal's shoulder.

"Aye, 'tis an honest hunter's arrow, not unmarked, fer a poacher's purpose." Donal frowned at it, turning it over in his hands. Then he slid it into his own quiver, looking at the Englishman. "Thank ye fer yer assistance wit' the marksman. I did'na wanna make two more widows t'curse t'MacFalon name if I did'na hafta."

"I understand." Lord Eldred nodded, glancing toward the woods in her direction, and Donal did, too. They would be wondering about her, if she would return—a question she was pondering herself. She had options.

She could turn tail and run home. That was one option. But had she come all this way, just to turn around again? It had taken her nearly a week to convince the wulver warriors of her need to tend to Darrow. Her need to see him, to make sure he was all right—to help heal him and make her pack whole—overwhelmed her. It had been the force that had compelled her on this journey in the first place, and she was determined to see it through.

The man, Donal, could take her to Darrow. She sensed he was honorable, and knew from the wulver warriors who had returned, that he could be trusted. She didn't know about the other men, but something in her said that Donal would protect her, if need be. Besides, she thought with a smile as she crouched fully behind a tall, thick oak tree, she could change into wulver form and snap all their necks before the first one could draw his blade, if she so chose.

She walked, barefoot, out of the brush, into the clearing where they stood talking. They didn't sense or see her until she was almost on top of them, even though she was in human form now.

"Ah, there she is." Lord Eldred spotted her first, his dark, glittering gaze sweeping her up and down.

Kirsten had changed back, pulling her plaid around her to cover as much as she could. It was a versatile garment, yards of fabric that could cover her from head to toe if needed, now gathered into the semblance of a skirt, crossing in front and pinned in place to cover her breasts. Although, if the Englishmen's gazes were any indication, she was showing far more skin than they were used to seeing.

Donal turned toward her, smiling as she approached, his words fading away mid-sentence. She had smoothed her long, dark hair out over her shoulders, picking out the leaves and twigs as best she could, making herself as presentable as possible without the benefit of a looking glass or even a stream or pond.

She saw the apple in Donal's throat move up and down as he swallowed, his gaze sweeping over her, too, from her bare feet and knees peeking out from under her make-shift skirt, to the V her plaid made between her breasts, then up to her face, their eyes meeting and locking. She had that same sense again, the one she'd experienced when she stopped in the clearing where he'd knelt, head bent in prayer. She didn't understand it, but it gave her a sudden rush of feeling, and her cheeks flushed with it.

Kirstin didn't even register the other three men—they were staring, too, although she only sensed this peripherally. It was as if the whole forest had narrowed suddenly into one, shining, sun-dappled path, and it led straight to Donal MacFalon. Kirstin's knees felt wobbly as she continued her careful approach, running a nervous hand through her hair again, seeing Donal's gaze distracted by the motion. He traced the dark waterfall her hair made over her creamy, bare shoulders, skipping to her cleavage, then up again, to her eyes—and then, finally, settling on her mouth.

She opened it to say something, but she couldn't find the words. She could only stand there, a few feet from the man, trembling like she had been while trapped in the net. Her heart galloped in her chest, and something pumped through her veins that was hotter than her own blood, something foreign and uncontrollable.

A low whistle came from one of the Englishmen, who leaned in to say to the other, "Imagine her in an English gown."

The second man shifted against the tree where he was leaning and remarked, "I'm imagining her out of one."

That statement made Donal's eyes flash and he turned his attention to the two young men. Lord Eldred caught the look and got between them, raising a gloved hand.

"Gentlemen, remember yourselves," the bearded Englishman snapped. He turned to her then, bowing slightly, and asked, "What's your name, m'lady?"

M'lady? She smiled and wrinkled her nose at that, looking back at Donal. He stared at her still, bemused.

"Kirstin," she said simply, her eyes locking again with the man standing transfixed beside her. She was glad there was a tree nearby—still stuck with two arrows—for her to lean back against. "And you're Donal MacFalon? Laird of Clan MacFalon?"

"Aye." He gave a slow nod. "That I am, lass—and I'm vera glad t'meet ye, now that yer not stuck yonder in a tree."

She laughed at that, glancing up at the branch where she'd been dangling not too long ago.

"Thank ye fer savin' me, kind sir." She held out a hand to him, and he took it, bending slightly at the waist as any gentleman would. She expected him to kiss the back of her hand like she'd heard from Sibyl was the English custom— since they were in the presence of an English lord—but instead, he turned her hand over, palm up, and pressed his lips to the inside of her wrist.

Kirstin's breath caught in her throat, and she melted. His mouth was soft and he had two days' stubble on his cheeks that prickled the sensitive skin of her wrist. Somehow, that one, small kiss, sent a thousand pulses of light through her body, bringing senses alive she'd never known before, even as a wulver. She looked at him in wonder, staring into those slate-blue eyes. They were focused solely on her like she was the only thing left in the world to look at.

"Pleasure to meet you, m'lady." Lord Eldred interrupted their interlude, holding his gloved hand out for hers, but Kirstin held the edged of her wrapped plaid and dropped into a brief curtsy instead. Sibyl had taught it to her and some of the other wulvers, and she used it to keep from having to touch him. For some reason, the thought was anathema to her. The older man nodded, lips pursing for a moment before he smiled and turned to introduce his men. "I'm Lord Eldred Lothienne, and these are my captains— William and Geoffrey Blackmoore of Blythe."

"Sirs." She curtsied for them, too, seeing Donal still watching her out of the corner of her eye. She wasn't looking at him anymore, but she was very aware of his presence. It seemed to fill the whole forest.

Lord Eldred chuckled at that. "As lord of the royal hunt, neither I, nor my men, are knights. The royal huntsmen are required to get their hands dirty doing work knights would likely feel unfit for them."

Kirstin gave a nod, acknowledging that, wondering just what kind of dirty work the man in front of her and his captains had been up to in the forest before they came along, but she didn't say anything.

"I am quite accustomed to living in the wild," Lord Eldred assured her, his dark eyes glittering, even in the dim light of the forest. "As I know you are, m'dear."

"She's a wild one, I'll give him that," one of the captains—Geoffrey—said softly to the other. She didn't think Donal heard it, but she did—and so did Eldred Lothienne. He gave them both a warning look, but his eyes raked over her when he turned back again.

"Would you like to come back to our camp for the night, m'lady?" The other captain, William, dared to ask. "Mayhaps the outdoors, sleeping out under the stars, would be more to your liking than the creature comforts of Castle MacFalon?"

She opened her mouth to say something, but Donal beat her to it.

"Nay, the lass's coming wit' me." Donal took a step nearer to her, frowning at the men on horseback. "She's anxious t'meet up wit' the rest of 'er pack."

"You have wulvers at the castle still, then?" Lord Eldred asked.

"Aye." Donal gave a short nod. "One of 'em was wounded."

"Darrow." Kirstin spoke his name, feeling her heart breaking at the thought of one of her pack—the brother of their pack leader, no less—helpless and in need of tending.

"We've four wulvers stayin' at Castle MacFalon," Donal informed the Englishman. "Raife's their pack leader. Darrow, the wounded wulver, is his brother. The other two are their mates."

"Mates." Geoffrey snickered at that, but the look Lord Eldred gave him made him cover his mouth with a hand and straighten his posture.

"They've all been given welcome refuge wit' us 'til Darrow's healed," Donal said, glancing at Kirstin as he spoke. Then he turned to Lord Eldred. "I'm sure you'll be interested t'meet them at t'castle tomorrow—when ye officially 'arrive'?"

"Indeed." The Englishman nodded, reaching out and shaking Donal's outstretched hand. "We'll continue with our reconnaissance until then, and see you after sunrise tomorrow. If we find any more traps, we'll disarm them."

"Thank ye. I'll make official welcome t'ye tomorrow as laird of Clan MacFalon," Donal replied, squeezing the man's gloved hand with his big, bare ones. Kirsten couldn't help noticing how rough and calloused they were. Donal

MacFalon was clearly not afraid of hard work. "But I hafta say, I'm grateful we've had a chance t'meet informally, man t'man."

"Indeed."

"I jus' find all that infernal pageantry hides more than it reveals 'bout men, d'ye ken?"

"I do 'ken'. We shall see you in the morning, MacFalon." The older man dropped him a wink, grinning, and turned to go. They had no horses and she wondered where they were.

That made Kirsten wonder where Donal's horse was— and how they were going to get back to Castle MacFalon without it. When she turned back to look, Eldred and his men had already melted into the woods.

"Something's amiss wit' that man..." she whispered to herself, rubbing her bare arms. She'd broken out in gooseflesh.

"Lord Eldred?" Donal asked, looking in the direction the men had ridden off in.

"Aye..." She nodded, meeting his concerned gaze.

"He acted honorably." Donal frowned, tilting his head at her. "Less stuffy than I expected of a king's lord."

"Mayhaps." She swallowed, knowing she couldn't tell him about the warning signals that had gone off inside her upon meeting Lord Eldred Lothienne—Donal wasn't a wulver, he couldn't understand.

"He's 'ere t'make sure we keep t'wolf pact," Donal explained, kicking at the shredded net still lying on the ground that had ensnared her. "To see that all such traps are dismantled and disposed of. 'Tis a noble purpose, ye ken?"

"Mayhaps," she said again and sighed. "I hafta say, I'm glad I never had t'play politics. It seems dishonest."

"I s'pose it might seem that way," Donal mused. "But it's really nuh different than posturing a'fore a battle or sword fight. Each side wants t'win the day wit'out the death or loss of self, friends or countrymen, ye ken?"

"Ye make a good politician." She smiled up at him with both mouth and eyes, and he smiled back, just as brightly. She felt a little foolish, standing there in the middle of the woods, smiling at a strange man, but there was no helping it. Just looking at the man made her face break into a smile.

"S'tell me, how's me kin?" She took a step toward him, pressing a hand to his forearm. He glanced down at where she touched him—his forearms alone were thick as tree branches, she noted. Strong, solid. "How's Darrow?"

"He's not gettin' any worse, and likely gettin' better," he soothed, putting a big, calloused hand over hers. A slow heat filled her at his touch, the way his voice dipped, seeming to caress her with sound alone. "But I'm sure yer healin' hands'll be of great use t'him—and a glad reprieve fer Sibyl and Laina. They've been splittin' nursin' duties and are sorely taxed."

"How did ye know?" she asked him, his fingertips moving over hers, not letting go.

"That ye're a healer?" he guessed.

"Aye."

"Who else'd c'mon t'MacFalon land, seekin' their injured kin?" He smiled. "Besides, ye've a kindness in yer eyes that belies ye—e'en when yer a wulver."

"Aye?" She blinked up at him in surprise.

She didn't think, in her entire existence, that anyone had ever said anything like that to her before. She'd been a healer since she could remember, a midwife, taking care of the wulver children when the other wulver women went into estrus and changed, but it was something that went unacknowledged, for the most part. They all had their individual skills and talents, and everyone understood that they would use them for the good of the pack.

She'd never realized how much the pack took each other for granted, until that moment.

And, looking up into Donal's eyes, she didn't think she'd ever been quite so fully *seen* before that moment. It made her feel far more naked and vulnerable than she'd ever experienced, even after she'd changed from wulver to woman with no plaid at the ready.

"There's such love and loyalty among ye wulvers." He patted her hand, looking down at her fondly. "It's been a rare gift t'bear witness to it. I do'na understand why men would make enemies of ye. 'Tis absurd."

"Thankfully, t'English king agrees wit' ye. 'Tis why t'wolf pact exists," she reminded him, throwing in a bit of honesty for good measure. "Although King Henry created it t'use t'wulver warriors fer 'is own benefit."

"I've seen t'wulver warriors," Donal said, shaking his head. "I would'na wanna fight on t'opposite side."

"Yer a wise man." She smiled at him, glancing around, wondering again where his horse was. Still in the clearing? She wanted to get to Castle MacFalon, to see Darrow for herself, to talk to Laina and Sibyl, to see her pack leader, Raife. That alone would quell her jittery insides.

"And a devoted one," Kirstin noted, remembering how she'd seen him, head bent, at the burial cairn. "I did'na mean t'interrupt yer prayer vigil. Is that ancestral land? Yer burial ground?"

"Aye." He nodded. "I admit, I was surprised t'see ye. But truth be told, y'have e'ery right t'be on that spot, as well, lass—mayhaps e'en more'n I do."

"Me?" She gave him a puzzled smile. "Why?"

"My family's burial ground's built on t'ancient den of yer kin—da wulvers," he explained.

"I did'na know that." Her eyes widened in surprise. "It's our sire and his warriors who share and pass down wulver history. As a healer, I know it's important t'learn and pass on ancestral knowledge of t'healing arts. I imagine the same's true of leaders—whether they be wulvers or men."

"Aye, 'tis true of t'good ones," he agreed. His fingers brushed hers again, this time turning her hand over. She watched, transfixed, as he brought it to his mouth, his lips caressing the inside of her wrist once more, making her knees feel like jelly underneath her plaid. "Yer pack's blessed t'have such a devoted healer in their midst."

"Thank ye." She swallowed, trying to find her voice. It was caught in her throat, breathy. "I'm truly anxious to see my kin, if—"

Donal dropped her hand, turning to give a whistle that startled her. Thankfully, the tree was still there behind her, giving her legs more strength than she felt they actually had in the moment.

"That's t'call of a kestrel," she observed, admiring his ability to mimic the bird.

"Aye, 'tis," he agreed, turning toward her again.

In the distance, Kirstin heard a horse's hooves.

She swallowed as Donal leaned toward her, hand above her head, against the tree. He was a big tree of a man himself, his body thick and muscled. She swore she could feel every one of them tensing in front of her, every last sinew stretch and bulge of his veins. He was only inches from her and she wondered, briefly, if he might be about to more than just chastely kiss the inside of her pulsing wrist.

Then she glanced up and saw he had hold of the two arrows in the tree above her head. He was slowly working them out of the trunk, his breath coming a little faster with the effort, his bare knee grazing hers.

"The kestrel's a sound heard both in city and forest," he explained, giving the whistle again, even though she could hear his horse coming to the call.

She couldn't help noticing the way his dark hair brushed the plaid over his shoulders. He likely kept it long, like most Scots, to remind them of their wildness—their closeness to nature, and the animals that lived there. Animals that, perhaps, man himself had once been.

"So it won't alert t'enemy?" she guessed, thinking of his bird call as she heard the horse whinny nearby, pawing at the forest floor, announcing his presence.

"Aye, wise woman." Donal showed straight, white teeth as he smiled down at her, yanking the arrows finally free with a sudden jerk. She gasped at the motion and bit her lip as the big man turned to his horse. "Here's Kestrel now."

"Yer horse is named Kestrel?" She laughed, looking at the big, spirited, fearless black beauty as Donal grabbed the reins and tugged the war horse nearer to her.

"Ye were naughty, Kestrel, givin' away me position," she scolded as the animal drew near.

It wasn't too afraid of her, now that she was human again, but all animals could sense the difference between wulver and human. It took Donal's comfort to get the big, black nose lowered in surrender, nuzzling her shoulder.

"I forgive ye." She smiled, petting the soft velvet of his snout. "He did'na like me much when I was a wulver."

"He did'na know ye." Donal smiled, watching her rub her cheek against the horse's nose.

"He's beautiful," she confessed, smiling up at Donal.

"Kestrel thinks t'same of ye, lass." Donal put his boot in the stirrup and pulled himself into the saddle. Mounted, he seemed like a giant, his smile brighter than the sun that shone through the trees behind his head as he held a hand out for her.

She didn't hesitate. She grabbed the arm he offered and slid onto the horse, settling into the saddle behind him. She sat astride, like any good Scotswoman would, although she wore nothing under her plaid.

"Do ye ride?" he asked over his shoulder.

"Aye." She nodded against his broad back, her arms going naturally around his waist. Her fingers could feel the hard muscle of his abdomen, even through his plaid.

"Good." He smiled—she couldn't see it, but she could hear it in his voice. "Then I won't hafta tell ye t'hold on."

Kestrel took off like a shot and Kirsten gasped, holding tight to Donal MacFalon while clenching horse flesh between her quivering thighs. She pressed her cheek against his back, clinging to him, feeling the steady rhythm of the animal beneath them both as they headed back toward the castle.

But that was nothing compared to the animal Kirsten felt coming alive within her since she'd seen this man and caught his scent across the clearing.

She felt Donal's thighs flexing against her own as he guided the horse on a path through the woods, and the scent of the man, even though she was currently a woman and not a wulver, made her salivate. Her whole body seemed to want to melt against his on the saddle, as if the motion of the horse could drive them together and make them one.

He didn't have to tell her to hang on—but she did. She hung onto him as if he was her second skin, as if she could crawl inside him. She clung to him, trembling, not understanding her own feelings at this closeness, at the way they moved together on the saddle.

Kirstin thought she felt him chuckle at the way her fingers locked feverishly around his waist, at the way she clutched him between her legs, and wondered if he knew she was bare and exposed beneath her plaid.

Because Donal MacFalon seemed determined to give her the ride of her life.

Chapter Two

"Kirstin!" Sibyl's eyes widened, at first in shock, then in happy surprise.

Kirstin slipped into Darrow's room, afraid of what she might find. Donal came in behind her—he'd shown her to Darrow's room himself—and stood just inside the half-open door, watching as Kirsten crossed over to a bed so big it made the giant, wulver man in the center of it appear small.

"Sibyl." Kirstin cupped the Englishwoman's sweet, freckled face, brushing her auburn hair away and kissing her cheek, so very glad to see her whole and unharmed, after her sacrificial ride from the wulver's den to Castle MacFalon. Donal had assured her Sibyl was fine, but it was good to see it for herself. "How is he?"

"He'll live." Sibyl sat back down in the chair beside the man's bed, continuing to tear sheets to make dressings. Sibyl frowned at the wulver tossing and turning on the mattress. He gave a low growl in his sleep, shaking his head, and for a brief moment he hovered between human and wulver form—a sight Kirstin was used to, but one that gave both Sibyl and Donal pause. Sibyl met Kirstin's gaze and she saw tears in the redhead's eyes. "No thanks to the cowardice of Alistair MacFalon."

Kirstin swallowed hard at the name, seeing a dark cloud pass over the Englishwoman's face. Sibyl had been promised to Alistair—Donal's older brother, who had been laird of Clan MacFalon until his recent demise—and had been willing to sacrifice herself in marriage to a cruel man she didn't love in order to save the wulver pack.

Sibyl couldn't have known—and Kirstin certainly hadn't realized, when she put the Englishwoman on a horse and sent her away from the wulver den, heading back toward Castle MacFalon—that Alistair was setting a trap for the wulver warriors, using his betrothed as bait. He'd also kidnapped Darrow's mate, Laina, just in case the wulvers decided not to pursue the Englishwoman who had been living in their midst.

But it had been Alistair's intention all along to lure the wulver army out of their mountain den and destroy them. Kirstin had heard the story, told by the wulver warriors, of Alistair's cowardice and treachery. She'd heard them talk of the way Darrow had demanded single combat blood rite—a fight to the death between two men. It was a codicil in the wolf pact intended to avoid all-out war between the Scots and the wulvers.

Alistair had refused to fight or to honor the wolf pact, which his own father had signed in blood, until the crowd shamed him into it. Kirstin knew the coward had called for a stand-in, but not even his own brother, Donal, would step up for him. The wulver warriors told the story of Alistair MacFalon's cowardice, how he'd cried like a little girl when Darrow began to best him, begging for the fight to be called off, because Laina was, in fact, not dead after all, as the Scotsman had boasted.

And when Alistair had her brought out as proof, bound and bloody but very much alive, he'd used the distraction when Darrow's back was turned to run the wulver through. What Alistair hadn't counted on was a wulver's strength, determination, and incredible resilience. Darrow had managed to turn and lop off the coward's head before collapsing at his mate's feet.

Kirstin had heard the story told a dozen times before she left the den, but she didn't really understand its reality until she saw it in Sibyl's red-rimmed eyes. She couldn't imagine what the poor woman had been through and she put her arms around her in comfort before turning her attention to the wulver recovering from his wounds in bed.

"I'd like t'take the opportunity once again to apologize fer me brother's heinous actions." Donal spoke from the doorway, looking between the two women. "I can'na say't enough. And I hope, in some way, I can make up fer—"

"You can stop with the apologies, Laird MacFalon."
Sibyl looked at him fondly, her eyes softening as she saw
him standing guard near the door. Kirstin saw the way the
woman looked at Donal, with such great affection, and
instantly, her body reacted in a way that had never happened
before. Kirstin's spine stiffened, her hands clenching into
fists, and deep in her chest, she felt a growl rising, even
though she was in human, not wulver, form. She swallowed
it down, confused by her own response, hearing Sibyl's
voice praising the laird of the MacFalon Clan. "You've been
more than generous with your time and your resources,
Donal."

Donal. Sibyl called the laird by his Christian name?
Kirstin met Sibyl's eyes and saw the tears there—real tears.
The woman had been through hell and back, that much was
clear. Donal MacFalon was a man with a big heart and a
strong sense of integrity—she'd kenned that much already.
Of course, he would offer Sibyl a kind hand, a big, strong
shoulder to cry on.

Why should that bother her? Kirstin wondered. And yet,
the tiny hairs on the back of her neck were standing up, and
her blood felt as if it was boiling in her veins when Sibyl
spoke of the laird.

"He's been such a comfort to me," Sibyl told her,
reaching out a hand for Kirstin's. She allowed Sibyl to take
it, to press it to her damp cheek, even though her hand
trembled slightly in anger. What in the world did she have to
be angry about? She reasoned with herself, trying to shake
off the feeling. If she could control her wulver side, she
could certainly control this—whatever this sudden feeling
was.

Except, she couldn't. She didn't understand it, but she
couldn't control the feeling at all.

"I can't thank him enough for everything he's done,"
Sibyl went on. Each word grated on Kirstin's ears, raked
like a wulver's claws on slate. She gritted her teeth, listening
to Sibyl's praise of the man, wondering why she had a

sudden urge to throw the redhead from the nearest high window.

She had come to love Sibyl like a sister! What in the world was wrong with her?

Kirstin's eyes fled Sibyl's, returning to the doorway, where Donal stood, hand on the hilt of his sword, at the ready. His cheeks reddened slightly while Sibyl sung the man's praises as if he were the second coming of the human's worshipful Christ, and Kirstin tried to fight her desire to separate the woman's yapping head from her little body.

"It's been me pleasure, Sibyl," Donal muttered, clearing in his throat. "The least I could do fer ye..."

"Well, he rescued me from a trap." Kirstin's voice was much more strident than she meant it to be, and she stood there, crossing her arms over her chest, feeling her face growing red. "I mean, he... I..."

"Oh, Kirstin, no..." Sibyl gasped at the thought. "The same one Laina was trapped in?"

"Nay, t'was a net." Donal frowned. Kirstin knew Laina had been trapped in a cage, a message left in her blood for the wulvers to find after she'd been taken to Castle MacFalon. "Should've been disarmed. But we'll have help with that in the morning. King Henry's sent his royal huntsman to ensure all the wulver traps are taken out of the MacFalon woods."

"Oh, that's wonderful news." Sibyl perked up at that, eyes bright. "Does that mean... King Henry intends to honor the wolf pact then?"

"Aye." Donal gave a satisfied nod. "I expect the wulver messenger Raife dispatched will return with similar news. But Kirstin and I—we met Lord Eldred Lothienne and his captains in the woods. They were already working on disarming the traps."

"I ran into an armed one," Kirstin said wryly.

"Are you all right?" Sibyl asked.

"Donal saved me," Kirstin reminded her, taking far too much pleasure in saying it, and enjoying the way Donal smiled in response. Kirstin approached the bed, putting the back of her hand to Darrow's forehead. No fever—that was a good sign. "Where's Laina? I would've thought she wouldn't leave 'is side."

"I sent her to fetch some bread and soup for our wounded warrior." Sibyl sighed. "Every time he sees her, he wants to get up, and he's going to pull out all the stitching I did."

"So ye did stitch 'im up then?" Kirstin lifted the dressing to look. Sibyl was a fine healer, for a human, and had done a good job with needle and thread. The wulver in him had done a great deal of healing already, Kirstin noted—although she was shocked by how bloody the wound still was. It must have been very serious, quite deep. Wulvers healed from the inside out. Superficial wounds could heal within hours, sometimes minutes.

"Yes, I think we have him well in hand," Sibyl agreed, watching Kirstin's hands moving over Darrow's body, checking him for other injuries. She didn't feel anything broken or out of place. "It's just keeping his pain controlled—and keeping him in bed—that we have to deal with until he's well enough to come home."

"Home..." Kirstin smiled at Sibyl's choice of words.

The Englishwoman had run away from this castle, away from the cruel Alistair MacFalon, her betrothed, and had ended up in the wulver's den. Sibyl had spent months falling deeply, madly in love with Raife, the wulver pack leader. Kirstin had watched it happen, had been heart-glad of it. Raife sorely needed a mate, and while many of the wulver women had hoped to be marked by him, he'd never taken to any of them.

Until Sibyl came along. Not a wulver—not even a Scot! An Englishwoman. A *shasennach*. But Raife loved her, and she loved him. Sibyl had been so changed. She no longer wore English gowns—even her English accent had begun to fade. And she now thought of a wulver den as her home!

"It'll be good t'have t'pack together again." Kirstin agreed, seeing Donal's brow knit at her words. It was a phrase that should have instantly filled her with peace and calm, but she, too, felt a strange new tug at her heart she didn't quite understand at her own words.

"Kirstin... you should know..." Sibyl glanced at Donal, biting her lip, and Kirstin felt that strange zing of feeling again, like a lightning strike. Then it was as if someone had suddenly dropped a weight on her chest. It was hard to breathe. What was it that Sibyl wanted her to know, and what did it have to do with Donal MacFalon?

And why in the world did it matter to her, all of a sudden?

"Raife is... angry with me," Sibyl confessed. Donal snorted from the doorway at that, and Sibyl's cheeks filled with color to match her hair. "To put it mildly. And he's likely to be angry with you, too."

"Is that all?" Kirstin asked, filled with relief. Sibyl blinked at her, looking so hurt Kirstin couldn't help but go and put her arms around her. "I ju't mean—a'course he is. He's a wulver. I knew he would be. Ye had t'know he'd be angry..."

"Well... yes." Sibyl sighed, wringing the cloth in her hands as Kirstin knelt by her chair. "Of course, I expected he'd be angry with me for leaving. But I did it to save him, Kirstin!"

"Aye." She patted the Englishwoman's worried hands. "Ye should've seen him when I told 'im ye'd gone."

Kirstin paled at the memory alone. She'd never seen Raife in such a state. Sibyl searched her eyes, and Kirstin knew what she was looking for. She wanted proof that Raife loved her, that he wanted her, that he had truly meant it when he said that Sibyl was his one true mate.

"I thought he was goin' to take me head right offa me shoulders," Kirstin confessed, swallowing hard. "He was crazed. He could'na b'lieve ye'd gone."

"I couldn't believe it either." Sibyl lowered her head at the memory. "I really thought, if I came back here, and told Alistair I'd marry him, that the wulvers would be safe..."

"Aye." Kirstin nodded. "I know Raife'll be angry when he discovers I've come 'ere. But Sibyl, I could'na stay 'way. Not when I knew Darrow was hurt—and 'tis all my fault. If I hadna put ye on that horse..."

"But we couldn't have known," Sibyl whispered. "We both thought we were doing the right thing."

"Och, what a fine mess this is," Donal said softly from the doorway, and when Kirstin met his eyes, she saw the sympathy in them.

Kirstin opened her mouth to speak, to explain, but a voice interrupted her.

"Kirstin! What in the da world're ye doin 'ere?" Laina exclaimed from the doorway, carrying a tray. She was so startled, she nearly dropped it—Donal's quick reaction kept that from happening. He carried the tray over to the bedside table while the women gathered together.

"I came t'bring all'ye home, safe'n'sound." Kirstin put her arms around her. Laina's thick, white-blonde hair was pulled into a long plait down her back. She was dressed in her plaid, just like Sibyl. "How's Darrow?"

"Cranky." Laina smiled at him and Darrow moaned in his sleep, like he'd heard her. "But I s'pose that's understandable, given he was run-through with a broad sword."

"And how're ye?" Kirstin asked, touching the other woman's bruised and battered face. Laina was a stunning beauty, and Kirstin could tell the marks had already begun to heal. Wulver women didn't mend quite as quickly as the warriors, but they still had a significant ability to mend themselves. "They hurt you?"

"Alistair's men—a few of them." Laina shook her head, glancing over at Donal, who looked like he wanted to make yet another apology for his brother's conduct. "But I'm no worse fer t'wear."

"How's me bairn?" Laina grasped her shoulders, searching Kirstin's face with the hungry eyes of a mother who had been without her babe overlong. "Garaith's well?"

"Aye, he misses ye," Kirstin replied, smiling at the memory of Laina and Darrow's dark-haired little boy. "But Beitris is taking good care of him in your absence."

"I miss 'im so." Laina sighed. "I need t'return soon a'fore me milk disappears altogether."

"He'll be well enough t'travel soon." Kirstin assured her, glancing at Darrow, thrashing on the bed now. He was clearly waking up.

"I'm well enough now," Darrow muttered. Kirstin smiled. It was good to hear his voice. "If ye'd stop givin' me that witch's brew, I'd be on me horse and... Laina?"

Darrow went up on an elbow, the sheet falling down his chest to his waist, revealing the bandage that wrapped around his middle. He rubbed his eyes, blinking.

"Where's Laina?"

"She's here," Sibyl assured him, pressing Laina closer to the bed so he could peer at his mate. "You're feeling no pain because of that witches brew, Darrow. But if you keep pushing yourself, you're going to pull those stitches and bleed out."

"He's a wulver, not a man." Laina pushed him back on the bed in spite of her words, covering him again with the sheet as she pressed a gentle kiss to the top of his head. "He'll heal much faster than ye're used to."

"I understand that, but he's a very lucky wulver, given his wounds," Sibyl reminded her softly.

"Raife." Darrow blinked up at the ceiling. "We need t'go. Where's Raife? And what's that MacFalon doin' in m'room?"

He tried to get up again, but Laina succeeded in keeping him down with another kiss, this one pressed to his lips.

"The tonic I give him for pain makes him wake confused," Sibyl explained softly to Kirstin. Then she spoke loudly to Darrow. "Donal is the laird of Clan MacFalon now, Darrow. He is honoring the wolf pact. We're safe here. I don't want you riding a horse just yet."

"Where's Raife?" Darrow asked the ceiling, then looked at his mate, frowning. "Where's m'brother? Raife! Raife!"

He yelled Raife's name so loudly Kirstin thought he might tear his stitches just from the force of the word. It seemed to echo throughout the whole castle.

"Donal, do you know where Raife is?" Sibyl asked, standing and pressing a hand to Darrow's chest, helping Laina keep him in bed.

Donal gave her a pained look. "He will'na come, if'n yer in 'ere, Sibyl..."

"Why?" Darrow pushed Laina aside, glaring at Donal.

"He won't be in the same room with me," Sibyl confessed, tears coming to her eyes.

"He b'lieves ye left 'im fer Alistair." Darrow's gaze narrowed at her. "Did ye? Why did ye come 'ere, Sibyl?"

"She was tryin' t'save yer hide," Kirstin snapped, wagging her finger at him. Then she looked around the room, putting a hand on Sibyl's quivering shoulder. "All of ye. She was goin' t'exchange herself for Laina, t'keep t'wulver pack safe."

"Alistair would never've let t'wulver woman go," Donal said softly. He was speaking to Kirstin—she had the feeling that the rest of the people in the room had heard this already. "His intention was t'kill all t'wulvers."

"Why?" Kirstin asked, giving him a long, puzzled look. "The MacFalons've honored t'wolf pact fer years."

"He claimed t'was an order from King Henry, but given that Henry's sent 'is huntsman t'help us dismantle the wulver traps, I do'na b'lieve it." Donal glanced around the room, from person to person, and Kirstin felt the weight of his words as he spoke. "I think m'brother felt threatened by t'wulvers. Especially after they kidnapped 'is bride."

"I wasn't kidnapped," Sibyl protested with a snarl that any wulver would have been proud of. "I ran away."

"Aye," Donal agreed. "But Alistair did'na wanna b'lieve that, ye ken?"

"But why defy t'English King's wishes and break t'wolf pact?" Kirstin asked him. "I do'na understand..."

"He was m'kin, but I will'na make excuses fer 'im." Donal told her with a sad shake of his head. "He was a cruel and duplicitous man."

"It's been awful." Sibyl's voice shook and she cleared her throat, blinking back her tears. "But Darrow's healing nicely and the wulvers are safe. That's the important thing."

"Aye," Donal agreed. "Thanks to ye, Lady Sibyl."

"And if we can keep Darrow in bed," Sibyl said, giving him a long, quelling look. "Mayhaps he'll be ready to travel within the month."

"The month?" Darrow exploded, struggling against Laina's hold—she was a woman, but she was a wulver, after all. "I'll be ready t'go in two days! Less, if ye stop makin' me drink that godawful—"

"Laina, keep your mate in bed, please." Sibyl crossed her arms and glared at him.

"Mayhaps I should show Kirstin to a room?" Donal suggested, smiling as Kirstin glanced over at him. "I thought I'd have Moira find 'er a more suitable wardrobe?"

"She's a wulver and a Scot, MacFalon." Darrow glared at him, eyes narrowed. "D'ye expect 'er t'wear more'n 'er plaid?"

"I notice yer wearin' a plaid, Lady Sibyl," Donal noted with a smile, ignoring Darrow's obvious hostility. "In spite of the closet full of English clothes me brother had made fer ye."

"Sibyl might have been born English, but she's been chosen by our pack leader as his mate," Kirstin reminded him—reminded all of them. "She is *banrighinn* now."

"*Banrighinn?*" Sibyl stumbled over the Gaelic word.

"Queen." Donal translated quietly, looking at Sibyl with soft eyes.

"Aye," Laina agreed. "*Banrighinn.*"

"I'm no one's *b-banrighinn*," Sibyl muttered, flushing. "Besides, Raife won't even talk to me, let alone mark me."

Kirstin saw Sibyl look longingly at the intricate tattoo that decorated Darrow's shoulder. A matching one was inked on Laina's hip and thigh, marking them as one another's.

"Raife's a stubborn fool," Kirstin snapped, putting an arm around Sibyl's shoulders.

"Kirstin!" Raife's voice boomed as he appeared in the doorway, his big frame filling it completely. His face was a thundercloud, his brow low and drawn. There were new worry lines on his face, and his eyes were as dark as a night sky. "What're ye doin'ere?"

"I came t'tend the wounded," Kirstin said simply, feeling Sibyl shrink against her side at the sight of Raife.

"There's only one wounded, and from t'sound of 'im yellin' fer me, he's jus' fine," Raife snapped, pointing at his half-naked brother. "I want m'pack back in the den. Darrow, are ye well enough t'travel?"

"Aye, brother." Darrow's voice sounded strong as he pushed the covers back, sitting up and swinging his bare legs over the side obediently. He clearly thought he was ready to follow his leader, but bright red blood bloomed on the sheet Sibyl had tied as a bandage and he winced.

"No, Darrow," Laina soothed softly, trying to press him back onto the bed.

"Raife, he's not well enough to travel!" Sibyl cried, fleeing to Darrow's side in order to look at his wound. Kirstin could see, when she slid the bandage aside, that some of the stitches had been pulled by his motion. "Please, don't move him! I beg you."

"He's a wulver," Raife growled, glowering at his brother. He wouldn't even look at Sibyl, even if he was speaking counter to her words. "If he's awake, he can travel now."

"He was run-through with a sword, you man-beast!" Sibyl hissed with anger.

Kirstin saw rage flicker in Raife's eyes. The whole room sizzled with the heat of their argument—and it was clearly not the first time they'd had it. Donal was already stepping in, trying to make peace.

"Ye can all stay as long as ye need." Donal put a hand on Raife's arm. "We've plenty of room."

"I'm grateful fer yer honorable treatment and hospitality." Raife straightened, frowning, glancing down at Donal—Raife was a head taller, and Donal was a big man. "But we need t'get home."

"Don't be in such a hurry ye lose one of yer own," Donal said softly, watching as Laina and Sibyl worked to re-bandage Darrow's now openly-bleeding wound.

"In other words, don't be a bull-headed fool," Kirstin translated, glaring at Raife, arms crossed over her chest.

"Kirstin..." Raife snarled in her direction, eyes narrowing, a warning. Then he spoke to Donal. "Can ye make room for one more of m'charges, Donal? I hate t'ask, but she's clearly taken it upon herself t'impose."

"'Tis no imposition at all," Donal soothed. Kirstin caught his eye and saw something in his that made her smile. He was amused by this whole scene—Darrow's stubborn posturing, Raife's even more stubborn resolve. Then his words, the warmth in them, made her melt. "She's more'n welcome. Ye'll are."

"Good. Then it's settled." Laina brushed her mate's hair away from his face, looking concerned again. "Darrow stays put until he's ready t'travel."

"You're not going any farther than your chamber pot," Sibyl insisted, shaking a finger at the wulver in her care. "Not until I'm convinced your outsides are ready to keep your insides *in*."

"If yer goin' t'be 'ere, then ye can keep me posted on Darrow's progress." Raife pulled Kirstin aside, speaking quietly. His gaze softened as he glanced at his brother, growling at the two women who fussed over his wound. "I'm sure Laina can use t'help."

"I imagine, so can Sibyl," she said pointedly, waiting for his response. There was one, but it was deep, buried in the bright blue, gold-flecked recessed of his eyes. It was so brief, a human might not have even noticed, but Kirstin did. Raife was in pain. A lot of pain. And none of it was physical.

"Donal, may I speak wit' ye?" Raife turned away from Kirstin to talk to the MacFalon.

"Aye," Donal agreed amiably.

"Darrow, mayhaps ye could come wit' us?" Raife asked, and Darrow actually started to get out of bed again.

"No!" All three women shouted at once.

"Raife, are you deaf?" Sibyl cried. "I've told you over and over—I am not letting him out of this room."

Raife folded his arms over his chest and glared at her, but he didn't say a word.

"I think she knows what she's speakin' of," Kirstin reminded her pack leader, poking his shoulder. "She's been carin' for him since he almost got himself killed."

"T'was her doin'," Raife snarled, speaking lowly, for Kirstin's ears, not Sibyl's.

Sibyl had gone back to tending to Darrow, urging Laina to try to get him to eat something, although she did glance up at them, a look of such hurt in her eyes it broke Kirstin's heart to see it.

"No, Raife, t'was mine," Kirstin confessed. She swallowed hard, seeing the way Raife's gaze turned to her, his eyes blazing. "I was t'one told her that Laina'd been taken. I was t'one who put 'er on a horse. If ye want t'blame someone, blame me."

Kirstin waited, breath held. She waited for him to rage at her, to accuse her. She saw Donal's eyes flash, saw his hand move to the hilt of the sword at his side, but that was all. He was waiting, too, watching Raife for a reaction.

Raife's jaw worked, and his gaze skipped over Kirstin to focus on Sibyl. She stood beside the bed, facing him, cheeks pale, pleading at him with her eyes. Kirstin saw the love Sibyl had for him—she felt it. There was a deep, unspoken apology in the way she looked at him that moved Kirstin, and she expected it to move Raife, too. Even Donal was affected by it—there was a great deal of sympathy in him for Sibyl.

Then Raife's eyes hardened and he turned back to Kirstin, directing his words at her, although his intended target was the petite redhead across the room, and he verbally hit his mark—hard.

"I'm sure ye did'na 'ave t'do much convincin' t'get 'er t'run back t'marry 'er betrothed."

Sibyl gasped as if someone had just punched her in the gut. Laina's arm went around her shoulders, and she drew the redhead close to her, steering her around the bed.

"Why don't the three of us go down t'get somethin' t'eat," Laina suggested softly, guiding a trembling, stricken Sibyl around Raife, toward the door. "Kirsten, let's go."

"Ye—" Kirstin pointed at Darrow. "Stay in bed.

"Aye, jus' hand me t'food then." Darrow nodded at the tray beside him.

Kirstin slid the tray onto the bed, watching him move to his elbow to tear bread and dunk it into the stew. He was getting his appetite back. That was good.

"And ye." Kirstin turned back to Raife, who pulled a chair up beside his brother's bedside and straddled it. Her voice shook as she addressed their pack leader. He was a formidable man on a good day, and a downright frightening one when he was angry and glowering, like he was now. "Did ye get knocked on t'head out there on the battlefield? Do ye need me t'examine ye?'

"Nuh." Raife grunted, waving her away. "Leave us."

"Are ye sure?" Kirstin leaned in and opened one of his eyes wider with her fingers, peering in. "Given t'way yer actin', I'm not so sure. Might you've left most of yer mind out there somewhere on t'field? Should I go look fer it?"

Darrow snorted a laugh from the bed and Raife gave him a cool look.

"Kirstin..." Raife shifted his attention to her, catching on to her not-so-gentle hints at his behavior.

"That woman's t'best thing that's e'er happened t'ye." Kirstin pointed to the door where Sibyl had been led out, so hurt by Raife's words she could hardly walk. "Yer mad t'let 'er go."

"She made 'er choice." Raife's lip curled in disgust when he spoke. "Leave us, Kirstin."

"How can ye say that?" Kirstin wasn't ready to give up—not yet. She imagined Laina had been too distracted by Darrow and his wounds to really take Raife to task, and he wasn't going to hear it from Sibyl. He clearly wasn't listening to her at all. Maybe Kirstin could get through that thick skull of his. "How can ye sit here and not understand why she came? What she sacrificed fer ye?"

Raife's brow lowered as he scowled. "I did'na ask her to."

"Nuh, you did'na. And she did it anyway," Kirstin reminded him. "Because she loves ye. God only knows why, ye stubborn, foolish, pig-headed—"

Raife stood, his hand going to the hilt of his sword. Darrow continued to shove stew-soaked bread into his mouth, glancing between the two of them, chuckling to himself.

"A'righ', a'righ'!" Donal stepped between the two of them, Kirstin barely coming up to Donal's shoulder, and Raife a head taller than that. She just glared between the two men. "Mayhaps it's time fer ye t'join t'women in t'kitchen and let us menfolk—"

"Oh, don't ye start, Donal MacFalon!" Kirstin turned on him, eyes blazing. "The menfolk're t'ones who made this mess in t'firs' place! We weren't t'ones goin'round forcin' people into marriage or kidnappin'em and holdin'em against their will! Last time I looked, we women were jus' tryin' t'clean up after ye 'menfolk'!"

She poked her finger into the middle of Donal's chest, punctuating her words, hearing Darrow sputter a laugh behind her, which just made her madder.

"How did I get in t'middle o'this?" Donal held his hands up in surrender. "'Twas Alistair who trapped Laina, not I. And Sibyl's marriage t'Alistair was arranged by King Henry, not I. I've gone outta me way t'honor t'wolf pact, I've taken in wulvers into me castle, which, I might add, has most of me men and all of t'women afeared, in spite of my assurance of their safety. I fail t'see how anythin' I've done could possibly be construed as... "

"Oh,what could ye possibly know about it?" Kirstin snapped, crossing her arms over her chest and uttering an exasperated sigh. "D'ye know what it's like to be afeared the one ye love's gonna die, and ye might be t'cause? Because that's the weight that woman carried on 'er lil shoulders, and *that's* the reason she came 'ere to *yer* castle. T'satisfy *yer* brother's demands."

Donal's spine stiffened and he frowned down at her. "I fail t'see how me brother's actions have anythin' to—"

"Give it up, man," Darrow called, his mouth half-full with stew-soaked bread. "No use arguin' wit' a woman— especially not a *wulver* woman."

"What would ye like me t'say?" Donal asked, giving Kirstin a truly puzzled look. "That yer right?"

"That would do well, fer a start," she agreed, realizing she'd been directing her anger at the wrong man—Donal wasn't even a wulver, or part of her pack. He was their host, and had clearly been generous and kind. She'd overreacted, and she knew it, but she wasn't quite sure how to fix that, especially with Darrow snickering and Raife growling.

"If King Henry's gonna send ye another English bride, ye might as well get used to sayin' that phrase," Darrow remarked, licking his fingers clean and grinning over at them.

Even Raife had to chuckle at that.

"What're ye babblin' about?" It was Kirstin's turn to scowl, raising a quizzical eyebrow at Donal.

"Well, Sibyl was s'posed t'marry t'eldest son, Alistair," Darrow explained, his eyes glittering with amusement. "Now he's dead and Donal's The MacFalon. I imagine King Henry'll jus' decide t'give 'er to *this* brother instead..."

"Enough, Darrow." Raife snarled at his brother, moving to draw the sword at his side. "Unless ye want another hole in yer belly."

"What would ye care?" Kirstin snapped. "Ye don't want Sibyl anymore—do ye?"

"Kirstin..." Raife said her name through gritted teeth, looking at the chuckling Darrow, not at her. "Do'na make me cut off that sharp tongue of yers."

"Enough." Donal spoke, his voice clear and definitive. He turned to Kirstin, taking her by the elbow, putting his hand at the small of her back, and steering her toward the door. "Come wit' me."

As soon as they were in the hallway and Donal had closed the door behind them, Kirstin hissed at him, "That man's insufferable! How can ye sit by and watch 'im treat 'er that way? He's actin' like—"

"Aye, he is." Donal put a finger to her lips to keep them from moving anymore, and the motion startled Kirstin. Her breath stopped, and for a moment, so did her heart. Those slate-blue eyes of his pinned her in place and she stilled, listening to him. "But he's in pain. He feels betrayed, and e'en if he realizes she did'na love m'brother—and I can attest to the fact that she mos' definitely did'na—his pride's hurt. Give 'im time. He'll come 'round."

She nodded, not saying anything, feeling the press of his finger against her mouth, suddenly aware of how close they were standing in the hallway with no one around. There were distant sounds of people, and the low rumble of

Darrow and Raife talking behind the closed door, but she swore the beating of her own heart was much louder than any of that.

Donal didn't say anything either, but his gaze moved down from her eyes to focus on her lips, where his finger was tracing their outline, so lightly she felt as if a butterfly was kissing her. She shivered, feeling something thick and hot pumping through her veins, forcing blood into places that throbbed in sweet, swollen torture.

She heard him draw a sharp breath in when her tongue peeked nervously between her lips for a moment, and then Donal took a step back, his hand moving to the door knob.

"I'm sorry," she murmured, and she was, but not because of what she'd said. She was sorry that he'd moved away, instead of toward her. She was sorry she hadn't bridged the distance herself.

He cleared his throat. "Ye mus' be hungry."

You have no idea.

"Aye." She nodded, agreeing, although it wasn't her stomach that was growling.

"The kitchens're downstairs, through t'great hall," he told her, pointing to the staircase he'd brought her up. "Moira'll be feedin' Sibyl and Laina. She'll be happy t'feed ye, too."

"Smooth as silk," Kirstin murmured, giving him a bemused smile. "Ye're a true politician, aren't ye?"

Donal chuckled, shaking his head.

"Open yer mouth," he directed, putting a thumb against her chin to try to get her to comply.

"What?" She smiled, waving him away. "Why?"

"I jus' wanted t'see fer m'self if that tongue's as sharp as it feels."

"Oh fer heaven's sake..." She couldn't help laughing, but she also couldn't help feeling a little bad about what she'd said. "I did'na mean—"

"Och, lass, I understand." He smiled, too, and that good-natured warmth had returned to his eyes "Ye show a great deal of love fer yer pack, and e'en more spirit in defendin' it. Tis a fine and lovely thing. As are ye."

"Smooth as silk..." she said again, feeling the warmth of his words filling her all the way to her toes.

"Trust me when I tell ye, I've been doin' e'erythin' I can t'help pave t'way fer a reunion a'tween Sibyl and Raife." He rolled his eyes at the closed door. "I intend t'see't happen a'fore the wulvers leave."

"Ye mean—ye don't wanna marry 'er yerself?" The words escaped her mouth before she could even think and she felt her cheeks redden when he looked at her, nonplussed.

"Marry Sibyl?" He blinked in surprise at the thought, then he chuckled. "And risk me head being divided from me shoulders by that half-beast in there?"

"Oh, so that's all that's stopping ye?" Kirstin asked, arms crossed, eyes narrowing, as she turned to go.

"Och! No, lass." Donal caught her around the waist, whirling her toward him, and she found herself pressed fully against his big, solid frame. The hilt of his sword dug into the soft flesh of her belly and his hands pressed against her lower back, keeping her close. "Mayhaps, yesterday, if King Henry'd offered the woman t'me, and she hadn't already been claimed by the insufferable wulver in there, I would've accepted..."

"Would ye?" she challenged, feeling a slow fire heating her chest at the thought. For some reason, thinking about any other woman with this man filled her with such a rage it made her tremble. She didn't understand it, and she wondered if her own confusion showed on her face, because Donal looked at her with such warmth and sympathy, it made her legs weak.

"Mayhaps yesterday," Donal said softly. "But not today."

Kirstin swallowed. "What changed between yesterday and today?"

"I met a beautiful wulver woman wit' a big heart an'a sharp tongue."

"Oh..." Kirstin felt like she couldn't breathe.

"I want ye t'get some food in yer belly," he told her. "And I'll have Moira find ye s'more clothes—a good pair'a boots fer walkin' and ridin'."

"I'll be fine," she assured him, but his arms tightened around her in protest.

"I'd like t'take ye ridin' on the morrow, Kirstin," he said. "I'd like to show ye somethin', if'n ye let me."

"Oh..." She hesitated. She barely knew him—and this was a man, not a wulver. She knew well enough from Sibyl that it wasn't proper for a Scotswoman or Englishwoman to be alone with any man—but she remembered the ride in from the forest on the back of his horse, and couldn't resist.

"I'll understand if ye wanna stay 'ere and nurse the ailin' Darrow, but..." His gaze moved to the closed door, then back to her.

"Nuh." She shook her head, seeing the disappointment in his eyes, feeling it in her gut, and she was quick to dispel it. "I mean, aye. Aye, I'll go wit' ye."

"Good." A smile lit up his features. "And we'll talk more about what we can do, t'bring those two together. Because somethin' needs doin'."

"Aye, that it does," she agreed, scowling at Raife as if she could see him through the door.

"I'm glad ye came." Donal turned her chin back to look at him, and the look in his eyes, so full of emotion, turned her knees to jelly. But he had her, held against him. She wasn't going anywhere. His gaze moved down to her mouth, and his head inclined, and for one breathless moment, she thought for sure he was going to press his lips to hers.

"Sir, I came fer the dishes." Behind them, the voice was small and unsure and Donal let Kirstin go, whirling around. "Moira sent me."

Kirstin looked at the little kitchen maid who had somehow snuck up behind Donal. She was a small blonde with big, round blue eyes and a gap between her teeth. She stood, looking between the two of them, curious.

"Go 'head." Donal waved her into the room so she could retrieve Darrow's supper dishes.

"Ye were sayin'?" Kirstin prompted him, but the moment was gone. Kirstin could still feel the steel heat of his body against hers, even though they now stood a doorway apart. "Somethin' about bein' glad I was 'ere...?"

"Aye." He cleared his throat as the maid hurried out with the dishes on a tray. "I know ye'll be a great help t'Sibyl and Laina."

"Gayle." He smiled down at the maid as she scuttled by him. "Will ye take Lady Kirstin down to the kitchens so she may join 'er kin?"

"I'm not a lady," Kirstin protested before Gayle's eyes even fell to study Kirstin's plaid—and lack of footwear. Or any other adornment.

"Her kin?" Gayle's eyes widened then and she took a step back. "She's a wulver, then?"

"Aye, but I promise, she will'na bite ye," Donal assured the maid, giving Kirstin a pointed look.

The blonde, Gayle, didn't look so confident.

"I'll see ye on the morrow," Donal called after her and Kirstin smiled back at him as she followed the maid down the hall. He watched them head down the stairs before going back into Darrow's room.

As Donal had promised, Sibyl and Laina were in the kitchen, being fussed over by a stout old woman who kept bringing more food to the table. Gayle deposited the dishes and was quickly off again, giving them all a long, fearful, sidelong glance as she slipped through the door.

"Ye look pale," Kirstin observed, putting a cool hand against Sibyl's cheek. "How long's it been since she's eaten anything?"

The question was directed at Laina, who shook her head.

"I'm not hungry." Sibyl pushed the bowl of stew away from her. Kirstin caught the delicious scent and her stomach growled.

"Ye still need t'eat, *banrighinn*." Kirstin pushed the bowl closer,

"Don't call me that." Sibyl's eyes filled with tears.

"But ye're, *banrighinn*," Laina agreed, smiling as Moira put a newly baked loaf of bread on the table. It was warm and Kirstin couldn't resist tearing off the end, dipping it into the bowl.

"Here, you eat it." Sibyl pushed it toward her. "You must be starving."

"I ate a rabbit on the way," Kirstin confessed, her mouth full of warm bread. "But this is delicious."

"There's more where that came from, lass," Moira assured her with a pat of her hand on Kirstin's. "I'll get ye a bowl. Ye see if ye can get this one t'eat."

"Thank ye." Kirstin washed the bread down with a swallow of mead from the cup Moira set in front of her.

"Moira, this is Kirstin," Laina said, making the introductions. "She's a midwife in our den—and a healer. She came t'help wit' Darrow."

"Och, well he's a handful," Moira agreed with a laugh, putting a bowl of stew down in front of Kirstin, who dug in, her stomach making grateful, growling sounds. "We can certainly always use an extra set of hands 'round 'ere."

She glanced at the door where the maid had disappeared.

"They're afeared of us," Laina explained to Kirstin, speaking of the maid who'd left soon after bringing Darrow's dishes down. "Wulvers. *Demons.*"

"They're young and foolish." Moira brought out a knife and began slicing the bread. "Do'na pay attention to 'em. Lady Sibyl, please will ye eat some bread? I'll butter it fer ye. Mayhaps some jam?"

Moira brightened at this, rushing off to get some.

"Och, I need me bairn." Laina gave a little groan, sitting back in her seat and pressing her breasts with both hands, her face pained. "He's not ready t'wean."

"Ye can express yer milk," Moira suggested. "Since yer bairn's away and yer husband's not yet up to the task."

The old woman chuckled at the way Kirstin gasped, looking at the younger woman's shocked face.

"She's not married, this one?" Moira observed with a toothy grin.

Kirstin flushed, eating stew faster.

"Kirstin?" Laina laughed. "Nay, she's not found 'er mate, nor had 'er first estrus."

"Isn't she a little old?" Moira blinked in surprise.

"Oh, she's had 'er first moonblood," Laina told her, explaining to the confused Scotswoman. "Wulver woman have their first moonblood sometime during our thirteenth summer. That's when we can start changin'. Into wulvers, ye ken?"

"Hm." Moira's face didn't smooth out—she still looked puzzled.

"After our first moonblood, we're ready to be mated," Laina explained.

Laina's words even had Sibyl interested, Kirstin noticed. Sibyl was listening, spreading the brambleberry jam Moira had brought over onto a piece of buttered bread.

"But we do'na have our first estrus—when we go into heat—until we find our mate."

"So ye only bleed once?" Moira asked in awe. "And then not again until you mate?"

"Aye." Kirstin agreed, dunking her bread into her stew. It was venison, thick, fatty and rich. And utterly delicious.

"Och, I wish I was a wulver then!" Moira exclaimed with a laugh, taking a seat at the low table with them. "I'd stay a maiden forever."

"Well, there's something to that." Laina smiled, glancing over at Kirstin. "A wulver woman who's never mated always has control over her change."

Kirstin nodded in agreement. She still had full control over when she changed from woman to wulver and back again. There were very few wulver women who went their whole lives without finding their true mate, although Kirstin often thought she might end up like the old midwife, Beitrus, who had trained her and taught her all her healing skills. Mayhaps that was her calling after all, she mused, taking another swig of mead.

"But it isn't matin' that brings on estrus," Kirstin interjected. "It's *findin'* yer mate."

Moira gave them a puzzled shake of her head, looking between the two wulver women as if trying to figure something out. Then, slowly, realization dawned on her, even before Kirstin explained.

"A wulver woman doesn't hafta remain chaste," she told Moira, knowing how shocking that sounded to the Scotswoman. It had been even more shocking to the Englishwoman who was now their *banrighinn*—their queen. Maidenhood was highly prized in the human world, she'd discovered. "After our thirteenth year, we reach maturity. We can be wit' whomever we choose after that. But we can'na become wit' child 'til we meet our true mate."

"Yer true mate?" Moira mused, mulling this over.

"Aye. Wulvers have one true mate." Laina smiled, glancing toward the ceiling. Darrow was upstairs, recovering—her one true mate, the father of her bairn. "Fer life."

"How d'ye know ye've found 'im?" Moira asked. "Yer one true mate?"

"Oh, believe me, ye know." Laina's smile widened, her eyes dancing. "Besides, a month later, ye change into a wulver during yer estrus, and ye can'na change back 'til it's through."

"Ye can'na control it?" Moira asked, eyes growing big. "And I thought bein' a Scotswoman was bad!"

Sibyl snorted, saying through a mouthful of bread and jam, "Try being an Englishwoman."

"Sibyl's been workin' on our cure." Laina put her arm around the redhead's shoulder. Sibyl almost smiled, which made Kirstin's heart feel a little bit lighter.

"A cure for the curse?" Moira laughed. "Oh what a happy day that would be!"

"Well, the *wulver's* curse," Laina countered. "It wasn't broken soon enough for my mother, but maybe it can be for our daughters."

"Raife and Darrow think it's a fool's errand." Sibyl picked the crust off her bread. "They keep telling me I'm wasting my time. But too many wulver women have paid the price for not having control over their cycles."

"Men, they never understand the woman's plight." Moira sighed. "No matter their species, do they?"

"They're stubborn animals, regardless." Laina squeezed her arm around Sibyl, who rested her head on the blonde's shoulder.

"Especially wulvers." Sibyl wrinkled her freckled nose and sighed.

"He loves ye," Kirstin assured her. She knew it was true—she'd seen it in his eyes. Sibyl was his one true mate, and always would be. "He'll come 'round. He's jus'..."

"Raife." Sibyl said his name with such longing it made Kirstin's heart break for her.

"Aye." Laina rolled her bright, blue eyes—all wulvers had blue eyes—and groaned.

"I want to give Darrow time to heal," Sibyl said. "But the truth is—he's probably already well enough to travel. I'm still shocked that wound didn't kill him instantly."

"I told ye, wulvers heal vera fast."

"That's an understatement." Sibyl laughed, and Kirstin thought how good it was to hear her laugh again.

"D'ye want more t'eat, Lady Kirstin?" Moira asked, nodding at Kirstin's empty stew bowl.

"It's jus' Kirstin—and yes, actually, I'll take another bowl." Her appetite was incredible all of a sudden. Moira got up to get her more food and Kirstin noticed Sibyl was finally eating a little of her own stew.

"The truth is," Sibyl said. "I'm afraid, if I tell Raife that Darrow could travel now—he'll go... and leave me behind."

"Nuh, he would'na do that," Moira exclaimed, putting a new, steaming bowl of stew in front of Kirstin, who dug right in. "Would he?"

"He's stubborn." Kirstin made a face. Talk about understatements.

"Well, then we'll have to keep Darrow recoverin' in bed." Laina's eyes brightened. "Ye ken?"

"Aye." Kirstin's smile widened as she caught on to Laina's plan. "Until Raife starts comin' round."

"Oh, aye!" Even Moira brightened "And there are plenty'o'ways ye can bring a man back to ye, lass. They're simple creatures, in t'end."

"How?" Sibyl looked around the table, frowning. "He won't talk to me, he won't even *look* at me! He leaves a room if I come into it."

"Trust us." Kirstin's heart felt a lot lighter, knowing that both Laina and Moira were in on this new plan to get Sibyl and Raife together again.

"Ye leave it to us, lassie." Moira chuckled, patting Sibyl's hand. "He won't know what hit 'im."

Chapter Three

"That man is more stubborn than a corpse." Sibyl slid off her horse, tying it to a tree.

"Aye," Kirstin agreed, doing the same, tethering her horse as well.

Moira had made them all a delicious breakfast. The women had gathered around the kitchen table, laughing at Donal's jokes—the man's eyes lit up from the inside every time he made Kirstin laugh—when Raife came in. He saw Sibyl and froze.

"Come in, eat!" Moira called, waving him into the room. She even bravely put herself between Raife and the exit, but it was no use.

"I'll meet ye at the catacombs," Raife said stiffly to Donal, giving him a nod and turning to go. He actually had to dance his way around Moira, who moved from side to side, insisting he stay and have something to eat, but in the end, he'd escaped.

The men—Raife and Donal—were already there. Their horses were tethered across the field. Kirstin couldn't help remembering seeing Donal across the clearing, head bent, praying at this burial cairn and the memory filled her with a warmth she was coming to both understand and expect.

They'd tried to talk Laina into coming with them to explore the first den catacombs, but she didn't want to leave Darrow, even if Moira said she'd look after him. Not that Darrow really needed that much looking after—his wound was healing nicely and it had taken all three women finally telling him their plan to keep him in bed, at least until Raife came around, to finally subdue him and keep him from jumping on a horse and heading to the catacombs himself to take part in the wolf pact reaffirmation.

Laina confessed privately to Sibyl and Kirstin that she was going to take Moira's suggestion and see if Darrow could alleviate some of the pressure she was experiencing because she was without her nursling. Before they left the castle, Sibyl had warned the pair not to do anything too strenuous, but Kirstin had heard the moans coming from their room before the two women had even reached the end of the hallway.

"Raife migh' be stubborn, *banrighinn*, but he's our leader fer a reason," Kirstin reminded her. "He's both smart and wise. I've never known a man wit' a heart any greater, and he's as far from a coward as a wulver gets. If he knows the righ'thing t'do, he'll do it."

"I just miss him." Sibyl stood at the entrance to the catacombs, taking Kirstin's hand in hers with a sigh. "The stupid oaf."

"Well—he *is* still a man." Kirstin squeezed her hand. "Which means, he needs to be pushed—or dragged—in the righ' direction sometimes."

They looked at each other, grinning.

"Let's hope this herbal silvermoon does what Moira claims." Sibyl looked doubtful as the women linked hands. Sibyl's head came up at the sound of a distant gun shot. "What was that?"

"Poachers?" Kirstin wondered aloud.

They were on MacFalon land, but reavers—thieves that preyed along the borderlands, always poised to steal a laird's cattle—were prevalent. Middle March was like a lost world of misfits, where everything rode along a knife edge. The English and Scots clashed constantly up and down the border of their two countries. It was one of the reasons Sibyl was in their midst in the first place. It had been the English king's idea to "marry the border"—giving English brides to Scottish lairds all throughout Middle March.

"So near the castle?" Sibyl shivered, stepping a little closer to Kirstin. It wasn't easy being a human woman, Kirstin thought to herself. They were fairly defenseless. Wulver women, on the other hand, could take care of themselves if need be, whether they were human or wulver.

"Could be. We ran into some yesterday." Kirstin frowned at the memory and her eyes narrowed in the direction of those woods and the trap where she had been ensnared. Had poachers re-armed the trap? It was possible, she supposed—but for some reason, Sibyl's remark stayed with her. *So close to the castle?* They weren't that far from the keep. They likely could have walked their way back within half an hour. It was hardly any time crossed on a horse. Poaching on a laird's land was punishable by death. Would a poacher risk his life so close to Castle MacFalon? She didn't know. Maybe a hungry one, as Donal had said.

"Did I tell ye, t'was the king's own huntsman who came along and chased off t'poachers?" Kirstin asked, scanning the edge of the woods for movement. Her wulver's eyes would be better, but even in human form, she saw more than any person could, even in the dark.

"King Henry's huntsman?" Sibyl perked up at that. She was English, after all. Sometimes Kirstin forgot. "Mayhaps he has news about the wolf pact?"

"Donal says he'll defend t'wolf pact, e'en if King Henry does'na," Kirstin reminded her. She didn't see or smell anything—her sense of smell as a human was seriously impaired, compared to her wulver one—and decided there was no immediate danger.

"But that would mean war." Sibyl shivered again, although Kirstin couldn't tell if it was at the thought or because they were stepping down into the depths of the catacombs. "Between the Scots and the English. Between the wulvers and... everyone. No one wants that."

"Nuh." Kirstin's blood ran cold at the thought of the wulver warriors going to war. They'd armed themselves and had ridden out of the mountain den to save Sibyl and Laina. The memory of hundreds of horses thundering though the mountain, their usually barred, secret entrance thrown wide, still gave her gooseflesh.

She really had believed, if Sibyl went back and offered herself to Alistair MacFalon, that the man would return

Laina unharmed and war could be avoided. She hadn't imagined the depth of Raife's rage at Sibyl's self-sacrifice or how he might interpret the act. Jealousy was a strange emotion, she decided, as they reached the bottom of the catacombs.

It had been a very long descent. They were deep underground and it was dark, dank, and cold.

"Did the huntsman bring any word from the king?" Sibyl asked, reaching up to take an oil-soaked torch down off the wall.

"Lord Eldred said he was disarming traps." Kirstin slipped a flint out of her pocket and used it to light the torch. "Although t'tell the truth—I do'na trust 'im any further than I could toss 'im."

"When you're a wulver, I think you could toss him a fair distance." Sibyl grinned in the sudden, orange-glowing light of the torch.

Kirstin laughed at that.

"Moira said the MacFalon tombs were to the left, that way." Sibyl pointed and, with her keen ears, Kirstin though she heard the sound of Donal's voice. He and Raife were supposed to be performing the yearly wolf pact reaffirmation. It was a quiet ceremony, done once every year between the laird of Clan MacFalon and the leader of the wulver pack. Scotsmen were a superstitious lot, and while there was peace between them and the wulvers, it was a wary one. It wasn't easy for humans to trust things they didn't understand, and they didn't understand the wulvers.

"So t'old den mus' be down that way?" Kirstin pointed to the right. It was hard to believe that she hadn't known this part of her own pack's history until Moira had told them the night before, while Kirstin finished the rest of what was left of the woman's delicious stew—much to Moira's delight.

"Yes, she said the silvermoon was supposed to grow by a spring. Are there springs down here?" Sibyl frowned at the high, wide, rock walls. To Kirstin, they were like coming home. Familiar markings and drawings painted the way. She would have liked to spend hours looking at them, transferring them onto paper, but there was no time. They were on a mission to find the silvermoon.

"There're springs in our mountain den," Kirstin reminded her.

"Oh, yes..." Sibyl looked sad at that and Kirstin knew she was thinking about the hotspring in Raife's mountain room. The pack leader had access to that spring to bathe and relax in. "So your ancestors once lived down here? I wonder how long ago?"

"Generations." Kirstin followed Sibyl down passageway. The ceilings were vaulted, high. She wondered at the construction of the place. It was a marvel. Had they carved these out of rock under the ground, or had they built them up? "Me mother's mother lived in our mountain den. I did'na e'en know this place existed 'til Moira mentioned it."

Well, that wasn't completely true. Donal had said something about it yesterday, hadn't he? When she'd mentioning stopping and seeing him praying. But he hadn't told her its history, not like Moira had.

"It reminds me of home." Sibyl gave a little half-smile and she peeked into one of the rooms. "Your home, I mean."

"'Tis yer home, as well, *banrighinn*." Kirstin squeezed her hand, peering into the room and seeing it had once been a woman's room. Dried herbs, old, hung on lines. There was an old table in the center of the room with a few old, cracked mortars and pestles. But the room smelled of healing, a familiar, welcome scent.

"This was a healer's room," Sibyl remarked, sniffing the air. Even she could smell it. "I wonder if there is any dried silvermoon in here?"

"Whatever they left here will'na be of any use anymore." Kirstin looked around. "'Tis all cleared out. They planned their move."

"It's not as big as the mountain," Sibyl observed

"Not as safe, either." Kirstin imagined the possibilities.

The entire pack could get trapped in a den like this. In their mountain, they were safe within, and they had a valley where they had a running stream and sunlight and they could raise their sheep for wool and meat. In a den like this, they'd have to go up top to hunt. No wonder the MacFalons were wary of the wulvers, she thought. They'd once been much closer neighbors—and she imagined her ancestors had made a meal of a few of Donal's. The wulvers hadn't hunted and killed humans for meat in generations, but they had, once.

"You always have such giant kitchens," Sibyl exclaimed as they reached the end of the passageway that opened into a wide space. A large fireplace took up almost all of one wall, and a long table where all the wulvers had once sat to sup together spanned the big room.

"Wulvers like t'gather in one place." Kirstin smiled and could almost picture her wulver ancestors tussling and laughing and playing and eating here. Many of the wulvers slept in the kitchens together in a big wolf pile by the fire at night, especially before they were paired off. Kirstin had spent many a night in a big, warm, fuzzy pile of wulvers. There was nothing else like it.

"Moira said the spring was near the kitchen."

"Aye, 'tis likely," Kirstin started across the open space. "Water's life. There's always a spring in a wulver den."

"Through here, do you think?" Sibyl edged around the corner of a rock wall and they both heard the sound of running water. The passageway got lighter as they went through it, making the torch unnecessary.

"Beautiful!" Sibyl put the torch into a notch on the wall as they entered the grotto, looking around in wonder. "I wondered how anything could possibly grow down here."

"Someone carved that into t'rock t'let the light in." Kirstin looked at the running body of water where a slant of sunlight lit its clear surface. It came from high above, an opening in the deep rock. She wondered at the construction of it. Where did it come out, she wondered, on MacFalon land? Had anyone accidentally discovered it before? But there was a grate—metal bars—over the opening.

"Moira gave me a picture of silvermoon." Sibyl dug into a pocket in her plaid, searching for it, but there was no need.

"It's righ' there." Kirstin pointed to the plant growing up between the rocky crags at the edge of the spring.

"Why do they call it silvermoon?" Sibyl wondered, squatting to gather it.

"'Tis silver in t'moonlight." Kirstin glanced up at the skylight above. "The leaves're reflective. You can see't clearly at night if the moon's full."

"Really?" Sibyl rubbed the leaf of one of the plants between her fingers. "I've never seen it before."

"'Tis an ancient wulver plant," Kirstin told her "I've only e'er seen pictures of it. Like the huluppa ye found growing on the borderlands."

The huluppa was the other plant, mentioned in what was considered the "wulver bible," that Sibyl was using to try to develop some sort of cure for the wulver woman's curse.

"It wouldn't surprise me if it only grew here." Sibyl frowned at the plant. "I can't get that damnable huluppa to grow anywhere else. I tried growing it in the wulver valley, but it will not take root. And I can't find the cure for a wulver curse without it. Your wulver plants behave oddly."

"Like wulvers." Kirstin laughed.

"They use this in the wolf pact reaffirmation ceremony then?" Sibyl asked.

"Moira says so." She nodded. "But the men do'na know where t'harvest it. Beitrus is our oldest healer and t'wulver who always came wit' Raife to t'wolf pact reaffirmation e'ery year, and wit' his father, Garaith, a'fore him, t'bring the silvermoon to the ceremony."

"What does it do?" Sibyl brought it to her nose, smelling its sweetness.

"Our book describes it as a mender." Kirsten took some too, feeling its slippery surface. She could smell it already, light and almost minty sweet. "'Tis what Moira said t'was for. It's largely symbolic in t'ceremony, a'course. As a binder, it brings things together. Helps hold them in place."

"It would be useful for Darrow's wound, then." Sibyl brightened. Then her face fell. "Although, the faster I heal him..."

"Well, mayhaps it'll bind more than just physical wounds this day."

Sibyl looked up. "What do you mean?"

"We'll take it to the men, like me ancestors a'fore us," Kirstin explained. "They'll use it t'help bind t'wolf pact. But mayhaps it'll also work t'help mend things a'tween ye and Raife. Heals broken bones—and broken oaths."

"Mayhaps." Sibyl looked so hopeful, and Kirstin truly was.

A binder like this was a powerful herb, especially in raw form. Besides, she reasoned, Raife couldn't possibly hold out much longer. His resolve was already weakening. She'd seen it in his eyes the night before, and again this morning, when he'd come into the kitchen, seeing Sibyl laughing.

It was when he realized it was one of Donal's remarks she was laughing at, that he'd turned around and stalked away. She was learning a great deal about that emotion, jealousy, from these two. It was a powerful thing. Made it hard to keep your wits about you. It made you see things that weren't there, that a rational person would just shrug off. Raife couldn't, for a moment, think Sibyl and Donal were a match, could he?

Of course, thinking of it herself, put her own feelings in a jumble. Donal was free to marry whomever he liked—or, at least, whomever the king liked, and since he'd already sent Sibyl to the MacFalons, she was obviously a good choice. And technically, Sibyl was free to marry whomever she liked as well. She hadn't been marked, even if she and Raife had consummated their love.

But thinking of a match between Sibyl and Donal was ridiculous, because... well, just because. Besides, Sibyl loved Raife. And Raife loved her too, if he would just stop seeing through green, jealous eyes instead of his clear, bright blue ones. Kirstin hoped the silvermoon truly would do what they all hoped. If it did not, they were going to have to resort to more drastic measures.

"Shall we take this to Donal and Raife?" Sibyl suggested, a small smile playing on her lips.

"Aye." Kirstin picked her way over the rocks in her soft boots, careful not to fall into the spring. The water would be cold, not like the hot springs back at the mountain den.

Sibyl took the torch from the wall and led the way. She was in a hurry now, no longer looking into rooms and exploring. Kirstin would have liked to spend more time down here—and mayhaps she would in the next week or so, if they stayed long enough—but Sibyl was a woman on a mission.

They passed the entrance to the catacombs, the light practically a pinpoint far above the long stairway, but they didn't stop. Sibyl pushed on, heading in the other direction, where the MacFalon ancestors were entombed. It seemed fitting that the wolf pact reaffirmation took place where so much history had taken place between the two—the wulvers and the MacFalons.

Kirstin heard the men talking, just their voices, a low rumble, not the words. They rounded a corner in the passage and the cavern opened up into a wide space. An altar stood at one end, unadorned, a slab of rock. That's where Donal and Raife were talking. Surrounding them were the catacombs, hundreds of slotted tombs, sealed off with the remains of the MacFalon's ancestors.

"Raife." Sibyl put her torch on the wall—the men had lit several around the room, making it far brighter than the passageway they'd traversed. "I brought you something you need."

Kirstin hung back, letting Sibyl move forward toward the men. She saw Donal glance over at her, his face breaking into a smile, those grey-blue eyes lighting up in delight. She knew the feeling—it felt as if a bird had just taken flight in her chest, soaring, leaving her breathless at the sight of him.

She remembered the way he'd pulled her aside that morning, telling her about his meeting with Raife at the catacombs, the planned reaffirmation of the wolf pact.

"I'd like ye to come t'me there after the ceremony," he told her softly. She was very aware of everyone's eyes on them. "There's somethin' I'd like t'show ye."

She'd agreed. It was when she told Moira, Laina and Sibyl about her intention to go out to the catacombs to meet Donal that Moira had expressed her concern about the lack of silvermoon at the ceremony. That's when this plan had been hatched. Sibyl and Kirstin had quickly made preparations to follow the men to the catacombs, while Laina stayed behind to tend to her husband's needs—and he, to hers, Kirstin thought with a smile.

Now that they were here, silvermoon in hand. Kirstin wondered if it had been such a good plan. Raife scowled at the interruption, which wasn't an unusual expression for him lately, but it was a dark scowl. His mood had shifted suddenly from somber to wary as Sibyl approached. Kirstin felt as if she was watching some priceless vase toppling back and forth, waiting to see if it would fall or right itself again, unable to do anything but observe.

"You, too, Donal." Sibyl smiled at the laird, remembering him only when he greeted her warmly, and Kirstin saw instantly that this was a mistake. Raife's scowl deepened as he glanced between the two of them, and she saw the green of jealousy move into his eyes.

Sibyl went on, not realizing, holding out the plant leaves as a peace offering.

"It's silvermoon," Sibyl announced happily. "Moira said it's always been used at the wolf pact ceremony, to bind things, and I thought—"

"Ye thought what?" Raife's lip curled in anger. "Ye'd come down 'ere on sacred ground and violate t'wulver's ancient first den t'bring me some leaves?"

"Well, I..." Sibyl hesitated, glancing back at Kirstin. "I was told... a wulver woman usually brings them..."

"Ye're nuh a wulver," Raife reminded her coldly, straightening and crossing his big arms over his chest. "And ye do'na have business 'ere."

"Raife," Kirstin protested, seeing the crestfallen look on Sibyl's face.

"'Twas a kind thought, Sibyl." Donal reached out and touched the Englishwoman's arm. "Thank ye. Leave it on t'altar."

"I brought the new spring mead instead," Raife told Sibyl as she brushed by him to put the leaves on the altar next to two cups and an uncorked bottle. "We do'na need the silvermoon."

Sibyl didn't answer him. She walked by, head held high, moving toward Kirstin, who was the only one who saw the tears she was blinking back. She also saw the look of pain flash over Raife's face as he looked at his mate's retreating form. Kirstin thought, for a moment, that he might say something to bridge the gap between them.

He did call out, but it wasn't what Kirstin expected.

"Why don't ye put the silvermoon on Alistair's tomb?" Raife reached out and grabbed the leaves in his big fist that Sibyl had so carefully pulled, stalking over to where Sibyl stood next to Kirsten. "Or mayhaps ye'd like t'give't to the other MacFalon brother?"

Raife whirled to glare at Donal. Kirstin had heard them talking, even chuckling together, before the two women had come in. Now Raife looked at him like he wanted to tear his limbs off.

"Here, Donal, mayhaps this'll bind 'er to ye better than I could cleave 'er to'me." Raife tossed the leaves up in the air toward Donal and they floated down toward the dirt.

"Raife!" Sibyl called as he brushed past her, staring, aghast, as he stalked around the corner, headed toward the exit. She turned to Donal, her cheeks almost as red as her hair. "I'm so sorry. He's... just..."

"Raife." Kirstin sighed, shaking her head and looking after him.

"Do'na concern yerself, Sibyl." Donal shook his head too, sighing. "The man's more stubborn than most. And most men're stubborn."

"Should ye go after 'im?" Kirstin wondered aloud.

"I've tried." Sibyl shook her head. "He won't talk to me."

"*Banrighinn*, I'm so sorry." Kirstin put a soothing hand on her shoulder.

"I should go back and tend Darrow." Sibyl stooped to carefully retrieve the silvermoon Raife had cast aside, her head bent. Kirstin's gaze met Donal's and they exchanged a knowing, sympathetic look. Sibyl stood, putting the leaves into a pocket in her plaid, turning to look at them with a sniff, blinking quickly to clear her eyes. "Mayhaps Moira will have some idea how the silvermoon might help his wound."

"Mayhaps," Kirstin agreed as Sibyl went by her.

Donal was still looking at Kirstin, and his gaze made her feel warm all over.

"Are you coming, Kirstin?" Sibyl called, reaching for the torch she'd brought in.

"Oh... aye." Kirstin sighed, turning to follow her, but Donal's hand on her arm stopped her.

"I beg yer pardon, *banrighinn*," Donal called to Sibyl, his gaze never leaving Kirstin's face.

"Why do people keep calling me that?" Sibyl sighed, rolling her eyes as she turned back toward them. "Can't you see that he doesn't want me to be his... whatever it is..."

Sibyl looked at them, her gaze moving from Kirstin's face to Donal's and back again, then flitting down to see the way Donal was holding onto Kirstin's arm.

"I'd asked Lady Kirstin t'come to the catacombs so that I might show 'er somethin'..." Donal's hand tightened on Kirstin's arm, a slow, steady squeeze. She felt the blood rushing through her, suddenly hotter than she remembered.

"Might ye find yer way back t'Castle MacFalon on yer own?"

"Unaccompanied?" Kirstin shook her head in protest. "But—"

"Absolutely!" A slow, secret smile started at the corners of the redhead's mouth. The way she looked at them made Kirstin blush. "Don't you even think of coming with me, Kirstin. I'm heading straight back to the castle with this silvermoon. I know the way—and so does the horse. You two don't worry about me."

"Thank ye." Donal winked. "We'll be back to the castle in time fer dinner."

"Oh, you both take your time!" Sibyl backed toward the passageway. Her smile was almost a grin, now, her eyes sparkling with a life Kirstin hadn't seen in them since she'd arrived at the castle. "All the time in the world! I'll tell them not to expect you any time soon."

"Sibyl!" Kirstin protested, her cheeks flaming now, and she was glad for the darkness of the environment. "Please."

"I won't say a word." Sibyl mimicked locking her lips with a key. "I'm good at making excuses. You two... just... enjoy yourselves!"

"Oh fer heaven's sake," Kirstin muttered as Sibyl gave them a wave and ducked down the passage where Raife had recently disappeared. She glanced up at Donal, seeing the laughter in his eyes, and couldn't help breaking into a smile. "What did she think we were goin' t'do, make a fire and strip naked t'dance 'round it?"

"I would'na be averse to either of those things." Donal laughed when she punched him in the upper arm. He rubbed it like she'd actually hurt him. "What man would say no to a pretty woman offerin' t'strip and dance naked in front of the fire fer 'im?"

"'Twasn't an offer." She nudged him with her shoulder.

"Och, that's a shame." He grinned.

She felt the heat in her face and decided to change the subject. "So—what is it ye wanted t'show me?"

"This." He waved his hand around at the MacFalon tomb. "And the ruins of t'first den, a'course—but it seems Sibyl beat me to it?"

"Aye, we went to the spring to get the silvermoon," Kirstin admitted. "But we had to be quick. I'd love to really explore."

"Good." He smiled, hands behind his back, rocking onto his heels. "I thought ye might."

"So this is where ye buried yer brother?" she mused, moving forward toward the newest tomb.

"Aye." Donal sighed.

"I'm so sorry." Kirstin put her hand against the cool stone. "'Tis not easy t'lose a sibling, e'en if—"

She couldn't finish, wouldn't hurt him with the words.

"Ye can say it, lass." Donal moved in behind her, his voice close to her ear. "I hold no delusions 'bout me brother."

"I'm sure ye had a lot of good times, when ye were young." She gently stroked the stone, wondering what Donal had been like, when he was a wee lad. She could imagine him, bright-eyed, mischievous, always laughing. Not so different from now, mayhaps.

"Aye, some. He changed when I was... vera young." Donal pressed his hand to the front of the tomb, his fingers overlapping hers. "But after our mother passed—she died of a fever, soon after she weaned me, and the healers could'na cure her—Alistair became an angry child. Bitter. Cruel."

Kirstin sighed. "It's so hard t'lose a mother."

"Me father said Alistair was born with a black streak in his heart only our mother could lessen. Alistair was her shinin' star. They loved each other overmuch." Donal gave another sigh, dropping his hand from the tomb's cold surface. "Me father said Alistair was always proud to show off t'her—whether t'was his skill wit' sword or bow, or jus' a boast about 'is ridin' and wrestlin'. She indulged 'im."

"She sounds like a lovely woman," Kirstin murmured, turning to face him.

They were very close in the dimness. She saw the way his gaze moved over her face in the light of a torch.

"All I remember of her is golden hair fallin' into me face, a rosy-cheeked smile, and the warmth of fallin' asleep against her breast." Donal's gaze moved over these parts of Kirstin as he spoke, from the cascade of dark hair over her shoulders to her definitely flushed cheeks, and then down, to her bosom, exposed at the V of the white shirt Moira had brought her to wear under her plaid.

"Alistair had far more of me mother than I ever did," Donal confessed. "And when she died, me father said... Alistair's heart caved in."

"Nothin' can e'er replace a mother's love," Kirstin agreed softly.

"So what about yer parents, Kirstin?" he inquired as they turned together and started walking slowly through the catacombs.

"Oh, me mother was a healer and a midwife," she told him. "Me father—he was the warmaster fer Raife's father, Garaith."

"But I thought Raife's father... was...?" Donal hesitated, looking at her, as if wondering, but she put his mind at ease.

"King Henry?" Kirstin smiled, nodding. "'Tis not a secret in the pack. In fact, 'tis the stuff of legend. But Raife never even met King Henry. Garaith raised him, and Raife always thought of him as his father. And Garaith treated him as such, passin' on leadership of the pack to him, even though Darrow was his blood, not Raife."

Donal sighed. "I wish me father'd been s'wise."

"Ye mean, by makin' ye laird instead of Alistair?"

"Aye. He could've," Donal told her. "Scots do'na hold to the 'first-born' standards of t'English. But I think he felt he owed m'mother. And he hoped it'd change Alistair, givin' him that kind of responsibility."

"But it did'na."

"Nuh. It only made things worse," he said sadly. Then he brightened, looking sidelong at her. "So yer father was Alaric, the Gray Ghost, then?"

"Aye." Kirstin laughed, surprised he knew her pack's history. "But t'me, he was jus' me father. Not grim at all. He loved t'tell stories and laugh—at least, he did, until me mother didn't return from her fall medicinal gathering one year."

"Och." Donal's face fell. "Wha'happened, lass?"

"He rode out t'find me mother," she said, frowning at the memory. "T'was t'last night I saw 'im."

"They searched?"

"A'course." she nodded. "But they found no sign of either of 'em."

"I'm sorry."

"Well, I was a mature wulver by then, not a child, like ye were when ye lost yer mother," she said. "I think t'was e'en harder for me adopted sister, Laina."

"Laina's yer sister?" He looked at her in surprise.

"Not by birth," she explained. "But when 'er mother was killed by The MacFalon, me mother had just pupped me, and she adopted Laina and suckled 'er as 'er own. T'was hard on Laina t'lose not jus' one but two mothers."

"The MacFalon killed Laina's mother?" Donal's voice shook with anger. He stopped walking, leaning against the stone of the tombs to look at her.

"Yer grandfather." Kirstin nodded, facing him. "Before t'wolf pact."

"*She* was the one..." Donal breathed, realization dawning.

So he did know the history then.

"Aye. She-wulvers can'na change when they're in estrus or givin' birth," she explained. "Both Laina's mother and Raife's were caught in one of The MacFalon's traps. Laina's mother gave birth to Laina in that cage. The pup was small enough and escaped. But The MacFalon shot an arrow through Laina's mother's heart."

Donal closed his eyes as if in pain, whispering hoarsely, "I'm so sorry."

"Raife's mother..." Kirstin went on. "Her estrus'd jus' ended, and she changed back t'human form. I hear tell that The MacFalon put the naked woman over his saddle and brought 'er home as a gift to t'visiting King Henry, and dragged t'body of t'wolf behind 'is horse..."

"I've heard t'same," he replied, opening his eyes and shaking his head in disgust. "So that's how Raife was conceived then?"

"Aye." She nodded in agreement. "And how t'wolf pact came into bein'. King Henry told t'wulvers he'd deliver the kidnapped Avril—that was Raife's mother's name—and swear eternal peace between the MacFalons and the wulvers, if only the wulver warriors would fight for 'im t'gain the throne."

"Because he was'na King Henry yet, then, was he?"

"Not yet," she told him. "He gained the throne because he had the full force of the wulver warriors behind 'im."

"'Tis a horrible tragedy, Kirstin." He reached out and took her hand, pressing it between both of his. "So many wulver lives lost. Ye know, there was a time when yer number was very great."

"Aye," Kirstin agreed with a little shiver. "'Tis the reason the Scottish king started demanding hunters kill the wolves twice a year."

"Yer pack outgrew this den."

"Our new den's far more secret than this one and I'm glad of it, even though we have the protection of t'wolf pact," she confessed. "Still, wulvers've gone missin'. Like me parents. Not as many as a'fore, though. A'fore..."

She gave another shiver, remembering the stories she'd been told about the days before the wolf pact.

"I've heard 'em, too." Donal nodded. "Men would, as you say, drag their corpses behind 'em on their horses."

"Must've been a surprise when they got back t'the castle and discovered they were draggin' a man or woman instead." Kirstin gave a little, strangled laugh at that. "That's when they knew they'd killed a wulver, not a wolf. The ol' timers say we lost more'n half our wulver population a'fore t'wolf pact was signed."

"I'm glad there's no longer a feud a'tween us." Donal squeezed her hand in his. "I meant it when I said I'd defend t'wolf pact wit' me life, Kirstin."

She met his eyes, seeing the hardness there, behind the softness, knowing he meant it.

"Thank ye."

"Ye know, I saw yer father trainin' in the yard at t'castle when t'wulvers came. I was jus' a boy," he told her, not letting go of her hand as they started walking again.

"Did ye?" She smiled up at him as they headed toward the passageway leading between the MacFalon tombs and the first den.

"He bested e'ery wulver or man that faced him in trainin'," Donal remembered. "All the boys gathered whisperin' how like a ghost he really was. I've ne'er seen a man or wulver move like that. No one laid a blade on him."

"He was a fine warrior," she agreed as they moved into the tunnel.

Donal held Kirstin's hand tight in his own. "I'm glad the Gray Ghost's daughter isn't so evasive—I would'na wanna lose 'er in the dark."

"If ye think me father was fast, ye shoulda seen me mother." Kirstin laughed, swinging his hand as they walked. "If she had'na been faster than the Gray Ghost, I would've had two dozen brothers and sisters!"

Donal chuckled at that.

"Besides, don't ye know that wulvers can see in the dark?" she asked, glancing over at him.

"Yes, I did know." Donal squeezed her hand, smiling.

"C'mon." Kirstin was excited to explore as she pulled Donal deeper into the tunnels, following the recent prints she and Sibyl had left in the long accumulated dust.

Chapter Four

They made their way down the passage, side by side. Donal carried the torch to light the way. If the den had been inhabited, there would be torches lit along the walls, she knew, both for light and warmth. She didn't mind the damp or the cold——Scots were a hardy people, and wulvers even moreso.

Besides, with Donal beside her, she couldn't possibly be cold. Her body radiated like a furnace when he was around. They'd known each other barely a day, but already she responded whenever he entered a room, or even when she heard his voice. Laina had spoken his name that morning, as they went down to breakfast, and Kirstin's whole body had flushed with heat as if a flame had been ignited inside her belly.

And Laina had noticed.

Mayhaps Kirstin had been successful at keeping it from everyone else, even at breakfast when her gaze kept skipping over to Donal——every time she looked at him, he was looking at her, too——but Laina was her sister. They'd nursed together, hunted together, had their first moonblood within weeks of one another. Laina knew her like no one else.

Stopping and pulling Kirstin into an alcove, Laina had cupped her face in her soft hands, searching her eyes. Then Laina had broken into a grin, laughing at the way Kirstin blushed and pushed her away, but she knew. Kirstin's protests had fallen on deaf ears, her insistence that it was nothing met with peals of delighted laughter.

"He's yer one true mate," Laina exclaimed, grabbing both of Kirstin's hands in hers when she whirled to go. "Do'na spend another minute denyin' it or runnin' from it. There's no sense. He's t'one, Kirstin. Yer body knows it. I can see't jus' by lookin' at ye."

"Ye can'na..." Kirstin swallowed, afraid she really could. She'd spent the night on a bed so soft it was like sleeping tucked under the wing of a goose. After the forest floor or the kitchen of the wulver den, it should have been like heaven, but she'd tossed and turned, fitful and restless. Laina was right. Her body had responded almost instantly to Donal, from the moment she'd met him in the forest, and it was only getting worse.

"Aye, 'tis true." Laina's blue eyes danced.

"But he's..." Kirstin had struggled with it all night long, vacillating back and forth, unable to come to terms with it. "He's a human!"

"Aye." Laina agreed, shrugging. "But at least he's a Scot. Our own *banrighinn* is a *shasennach*. What difference does it make? Look how long Raife tried to fight against it, and fer what? She belongs t'him, and he t'her. Donal's yers, Kirstin. Oh, I'm so happy fer ye!"

Laina had thrown her arms around Kirstin and pulled her into a giant wulver hug that, if the sisters had been transformed, would have ended up in a tussle on the floor. And might have, still, if they hadn't been in the hallway of the MacFalon castle.

So Laina knew. And in spite of the arguments she kept making to herself, Kirstin knew, too. And now, Sibyl knew, or at least, suspected. The question was—did Donal know?

And if he did—if he felt the same as she—what in the name of all that was holy were they going to do about it?

"Ye've been down 'ere a'fore?" Kirstin asked as they walked together. Donal kept hold of her hand under the pretense of making sure she didn't stumble in the darkness. Even if he knew wulvers could see in the dark.

"Aye. We liked t'play 'cloak'n'find' down 'ere," he told her. "If our da knew, he would've tanned our hides, but what boy could resist such a find?"

"There're certainly plenty'o'places t'hide," Kirstin agreed, smiling at the thought of them running through the tunnels. She stopped at one of the rooms and pushed open the door, letting go of his hand to enter. "I think this was t'healin' room."

"I always liked t'way this room smelled," Donal observed, sniffing, as he followed her inside. "I liked hidin' under this table."

Kirstin examined the abandoned mortar and pestles. "My grandmother's mother probably stood right 'ere, mixin' herbs."

The thought was both strange and comforting to her.

"Ye come from a long line of healers and midwives," he said admiringly. "Wise women."

"Aye." She ran a finger through the dust on the table, wondering how long it had been since one of her ancestors had stood here, preparing poultices or mixing remedies. "Longer than I e'en realized. S'much history 'ere—fer both our families."

"This place's been a part'o'me since I was wee," he told her, glancing around the room, his eyes filled with memory. "I used t'wonder what it was like, when t'wulvers lived 'ere, when it was full'o'life..."

"A wulver den's always busy." Kirstin smiled as they stepped out into the hallway. She took time to peer into more of the rooms, most of them small individual dens for wulver families. "These tunnels would've been full'o'wulvers, comin'n'goin'. I wonder where they kept their livestock?"

"Up top." Donal pointed at the high ceilings. "There's an old barn not too far from 'ere—I think they kept horses and sheep there. It's on MacFalon land, but I wonder if it might've been wulver land long before it belonged to me family..."

"Mayhaps." Kirstin smiled in the darkness when his hand found hers again, keeping her close when she wanted to wander ahead. She didn't mind.

"I'm still amazed that a horse doesn't spook when a wulver rider gets on," he remarked.

"Ye can break a horse to a wulver rider, jus' like ye can a human one," she scoffed. "They get used to it. I imagine horses don't much like human riders either, to begin wit'."

"Aye." Donal chuckled. "I've near broken me tailbone enough t'know that's t'truth."

"This would've been t'pack leader's quarters." Kirstin opened a door larger than the rest, revealing a room three times the size of the others. There was a large bed in the center of it, raised high, its base built of stone. It had clearly been built inside the room and was too large for anyone to move. Kirstin stopped, frowning as she looked at the mattress and coverlet still on the bed. "'Tis strange..."

"Hm?" Donal inquired, stepping closer.

"E'erythin's covered in dust... but this beddin' looks freshly laundered." In fact, the whole room looked cleaner than the rest of the den. There was an animal skin in front of the big fireplace that looked quite new.

"Oh... aye." Donal cleared his throat, rocking back on the heels of his boots when she looked at him. "I confess, we did'na jus' play down 'ere as children. When we were older, we found other uses fer this place..."

"Did ye bring lasses down 'ere, then?" She crossed her arms at the thought, staring at the bed.

She could picture a younger Donal, fumbling under the plaid of some kitchen wench he'd invited down here.

I want t'show ye somethin'...

I just bet he had!

"A few." He cleared his throat. "T'was away from t'pryin' eyes of m'father—and Moira. That woman misses nothin'. Eyes like a hawk. One time..."

But Kirstin was striding across the room, away from him.

"Where ye goin', lass?" Donal puzzled, seeing her moving along the back of the room near the big fireplace, her hands tracing over the stone.

"I'd wager ye did'na show yer lassies this secret..." Sure enough, her guess was correct. There was a section of the wall that, when pressed, revealed a narrow stone passage. She could hear the running water of the spring.

"What's this?" Donal asked, following Kirstin through the dark passage, toward the light at the end. The sun was higher now and the room glowed as if lit from the inside, the slant of light coming in from above, making the water of the spring look cool and inviting.

"There's a way in from the kitchen," Kirstin pointed to the other exit, where she and Sibyl had come in.

"That's how Alistair did it!" Donal's eyes widened, and then he chuckled, shaking his head as he notched his torch into the wall. "He'd disappear down the tunnel, and I'd go lookin' fer him—and he'd end up in the kitchen somehow."

"Now ye know how." She laughed.

"He always was a sneaky little buggar," Donal mused. "But how did ye know about it?"

"'Tis the same in our den," she explained, picking her way over the wet rocks in her boots. "The pack leader's room has access to the spring. Did ye not know it was 'ere?"

"Oh, aye," Donal agreed, catching her arm before she could slip. She smiled back at him gratefully. "I jus; did'na know about t'secret entrance. This is one of m'favorite places in the world. So calm and peaceful. Ye've a spring in yer den now?"

"Aye, there's always a spring in e'ery den," she told him as they reached flatter ground. The rock here was dry, warmed by the slant of the sun, and Kirstin drew up her plaid to sit down, pulling off her soft boots. "Water's life. 'Tis said t'very first wulver was born in a spring like this one, to his wulver mother, Ardis."

"Born in the water?" Donal marveled, sitting beside her on the rock as Kirstin scooted forward to slide her feet into the cool water.

"Aye," she told him as Donal tossed his boots aside, too, dangling his feet in next to hers. "I've seen it done."

"Doesn't the bairn drown?"

"Nuh, the bairn's a'ready livin' in water." She wrinkled her nose at the question, which seemed so silly to a midwife.

"How do they breathe?"

"No need 'til they're birthed."

He splashed her bare calves with his foot, making her laugh and nudge him with her hip. They sat very close, thigh to thigh, separated only by their plaids. Kirstin felt the press of his belt against her waist.

"Tell me more 'bout t'first wulver," he said, moving more comfortably against her, his arm sliding behind her. His palm was flat against the stone, but he still framed her with his body, making a little niche for her to settle into.

"Well, some say we're descendants of Lilith," she told him, wondering just how many lasses Donal had brought down here. Did he do this with all the women he fancied? She didn't like thinking about that, but she couldn't help it. "In yer bible, she was the first woman, but she was cast out of Eden, doomed to give birth to demons."

Donal grunted, disapproving. "And wulvers're the demons?"

"Aye." Kirstin glanced up at him, but he was looking down into the water. It was a deep spring, fresh water, crystal clear. He didn't seem to mind how close they were, so Kirstin fit her head against his shoulder. "Men's history is so oft different from a woman's, ye ken?"

"Aye, lass." He nodded. "But what'd Lilith hafta do wit' t'first wulver?"

"Likely naught." She snorted a little laugh. "Seems the masculine view of the feminine has twisted all women into demons these days. Mythology becomes history becomes reality. But the older legends... they ring truer to me. Me mother told me this, and her mother a'fore her. 'Tis the story of Ardis and Asher."

"Who were they?" Donal's hand moved from the stone to her hip. Kirstin didn't shy from his touch. Instead, she snuggled closer. Her heart was racing as fast as if she was on a hunt.

"Ardis was a wolf who could change into a woman, but only durin' t'full moon. She fell in love with a huntsman named Asher, who saved her from a trap near the spring."

"Hmm." Donal mused. His fingers traced lightly up her arm toward her shoulder. "Why does this sound familiar?"

Kirstin smiled at that. He had saved her from a trap, just like Asher had saved Ardis. The similarities didn't end there, though. She looked up to see his gaze on her now. His eyes were clear blue today, no clouds, his brow smooth. A smile hovered on his lips, which were full and slightly parted and she had an incredible urge to press hers there.

"He took one look into her eyes and knew she was meant to be his," she whispered, feeling his hand moving over her shoulder.

"Mm hmm..." He nodded, as if he understood this, too.

"And Ardis took one look at him..." She bit her lip, knowing this was her confession, not just the story of Ardis and her found one. "And knew he was her true mate."

"Her true mate?"

She nodded. "Wulvers only have one, their whole lives."

"Good." His meaning was clear and she felt her body tremble slightly as his hand moved through her hair.

"They would meet at night at the spring to make love in the moonlight e'ery full moon," she said, swallowing as she felt his fingertips brush the back of her neck, the tiny hairs there already raised and sensitive. "Me mother told me that the moonspring shone a silver light for them so they could see each other, but no one else could see them or their secret meetin' place."

"And this is where the silvermoon grows," he said. "I've ne'er seen it anywhere else."

"It only grows at a wulver spring," she replied. "They say it's because Asher wept into their secret spring when Ardis was murdered by the witch, Morag."

"Ardis was murdered?" Donal blinked at that, but his fingers didn't stop moving, stroking, petting her.

"Aye, but their child was t'first wulver," she told him. It wasn't easy to continue with the story, considering how distracted she was by his body—and her own. "A lil boy with red hair and red eyes. He's our first descendent. Asher raised 'im alone but they say Asher visited the spring e'ery full moon, and wept fer 'is lost love."

She was glad the story was over, because she couldn't possibly think anymore. Something inside her was growing, taking control. It felt a little like the tension she experienced just before she changed from human to wulver form. Except this was more intense. Every nerve ending felt alive, her senses keen. The smell of the man beside her, even to her human nose, was intoxicating. She wanted to devour him.

"'Tis a sad story." Donal's whole hand, not just his fingers this time, slipped behind her head, cradling it against his shoulder.

"Aye," she whispered, but she wasn't thinking about the story, or Asher and his lost Ardis, even if the feelings coursing through her were so similar, bred into her, generations of matings just like the first.

"I ken Asher's tears," Donal said softly, the briefest of creases appearing on his brow. "You can'na find fault wit' a man who weeps when all he loves is taken from 'im."

"'Tis always a risk t'love."

Oh, what a risk it was. Kirstin had heard it said her whole life, had listened to wulver women lament their inescapable love for their mate, had seen Sibyl's pain at the thought of losing Raife, and still, she had never fully understood, not until this moment.

To love this man would mean risking losing him. And that would mean losing everything.

"Aye, 'tis a risk." Donal nodded slowly, "But when a man finds what he wants more than anything; else, there's nothin' can quiet the fire inside him."

Kirstin saw that fire in his eyes, felt it in her own loins, in the heat of his body as he leaned in toward her, so close she was dizzy with him.

"Not e'en the spring water of Asher and Ardis," he murmured, before pressing his lips to hers.

His kiss was everything she had dreamed it would be.

Her mouth opened under his, letting him guide her head, slanting his so he could press his tongue deeper, probing the soft recesses of her mouth. She let out a soft moan when his hand moved to the small of her back and he pressed himself fully to her, the hard, ridged planes of his torso against the yielding softness of her breasts.

Her body responded instantly to his touch, as if a fire had been lit inside of her. Kirstin wasn't inexperienced—her kind didn't have any qualms about doing what came naturally. But the act, to her, had always been one of comfort and warmth, nothing more than a closeness that felt, well, pleasant. And that was all. The male wulvers she'd been with—just two, in her pack, who she had a particular affection for—had seemed to enjoy it far more than she ever had.

"Kirstin, yer so beautiful," Donal whispered as they parted, his gaze moving from her eyes down to her mouth, as if he wanted to capture it again. "So vera sweet. I'm afeared we should'na be 'ere, doin' this... but I can'na help meself when I'm 'round ye."

"Aye." She touched his cheek, feeling a day's stubble there, the roughness of it thrilling her. "I feel the same."

"I've been dreamin' of kissing ye since I met ye in the woods yesterday." He slowly traced the outline of her lips with one finger. "I'm surprised I held meself back this long."

"Is that all ye wanna do?" The disappointment in her voice was obvious, maybe too obvious. "Jus' kiss me?"

"Nuh." He chuckled, moving his hand down to her shoulder, running one finger over her collarbone, spreading gooseflesh over her skin. "But I'm afeared I can'na do everything I want. Not unless ye wanna come wit' me now to the vicar t'say yer vows. And I thought, mayhaps, you'd like a lil longer courtship than one day."

"Why?" Kirstin shook her head, smiling, bemused. "I'm a wulver, Donal. I know me own nature better than most men e'er will. I know who ye're t'me. I knew it the moment we met."

His eyebrows went up, a smile playing on those full, oh-so-kissable lips. "Who'm I?"

"Yer Donal MacFalon," she said simply, as if it explained everything. And to her, it did. He had eclipsed everyone and everything until she could see naught else. "Yer the man I've been waitin' a lifetime fer. Yer me one true mate."

"Aye," he breathed, kissing her again, this time with a soft assurance that spread through her like warmed honey, filling all the cracks and crevices in her soul. It was like coming home, like breathing after coming up from being underwater, lungs bursting, and finally breathing the air your body craved.

"I've ne'er experienced anythin' like this a'fore," he confessed, kissing the corner of her mouth, then licking it. "I do'na understand it."

"Ye do'na need t'understand it," she murmured, tilting her head back for the press of his lips on her long, slender throat. "Ye jus' need t'feel it."

"I feel as if I'm fallin' in a dream, and I'm afeared to wake up. Kirstin, I want ye," he growled into the hollow of her throat, his teeth raking her flesh, sending needlepoint pricks of sensation all the way to her fingertips. "I *need* ye."

"I'm yers," she admitted fully, to him and to herself. She didn't care if he was a man and she was a wulver, if it was unconventional, or even impossible. Laina had said it would come like a lightning strike, that you couldn't mistake the feeling for naught else, and she had been correct, even if Kirstin hadn't really believed it. Until now. "I've been yers since the day I was born."

"Och, lass, the things I wanna do t'ye..." he groaned, wrapping his arms around her, encircling her completely so she was lost in them.

"Stop talkin' and do 'em," she moaned, turning toward him fully and sliding a thigh over his, hooking her wet foot around his ankle.

He let out a low growl as he claimed her mouth again, He wasn't gentle anymore. There was no holding back. Kirstin encouraged him, wrapping her arms around his neck, opening her mouth to his deep, probing kiss, feeling his hands moving over the soft curves of her body through her plaid. But it wasn't enough for her. Not nearly enough.

Donal let out a strangled groan when Kirstin's hand moved under his plaid. The MacFalon was a true Scot, so there was no barrier between her fingers and the heat of his erection. She wrapped him in her fist, claiming the MacFalon sword as her own in one easy stroke, making the man's arms tighten around her until she thought he might break her spine.

"I can'na hold sway wit' what ye do t'me, lass," he panted in her ear as she pumped him slowly in her hand. "I can'na stop where this is goin'."

"I'll die if ye stop." She nibbled his lower lip. The man's honor was too ingrained. He was far too used to maidens who teased and tempted, who withdrew to protect their precious virginity. "I do'na want ye to e'er stop. Make love to me. Make me yers."

Her eyes met his in the slant of sunshine coming from the window high above and she saw the lust in them, knowing it was reflected in her own. There was no holding back from this for either of them. It was a force out of their control, compelling them forward, drawing their bodies together. She could no more ignore the urge to mate with this man than any woman could deny the force that brought wee bairns into the world from their full-moon bellies.

"Och, lass, please." Donal's voice was hoarse as she rubbed her thumb over the mushroom-head of his cock, feeling sticky wetness. And still, he tried to do the honorable thing. "I can'na..."

"Aye, ye can." Kirstin took his hand and guided it between her legs, to the center of the universe. He cupped her, moist and swollen, just one thin piece of cloth separating him from the Promised Land. "'Tis yers. Now and always. Fer the takin'."

His mouth moved against hers as he moved her body underneath his on the rock. He was careful not to put too much of his weight on her, but Kirstin wanted it. She wanted all of him. They rolled together on the flat rock, Kirstin caught between the earth's unforgiving stone and Donal's hardness. Their plaids were easy garments to remove and made a buffer between their skin and the rock beneath them when Donal spread the material out.

"Come t'me, lass." Donal stretched out in his shirtsleeves, holding his arms out to her.

Kirstin pulled her shirt, its long tail hanging down to mid-thigh, over her head, and Donal groaned when he saw her bared to him. Then she did as he bid her, stretching out beside him on their plaids, letting him touch her everywhere, the sensation so sweet, so beyond words, it was sublime.

Kirstin expected him to mount her, take her, claim her. This was the wulver way, and she rolled to her belly in anticipation, but Donal was not eager to force himself on her, not right away. Instead, he kissed the wings of her shoulder blades, the dimples at the small of her back, his tongue moving down the split of her behind, making her flush with heat. He drove her mad, with his tongue, his hands, his words.

By the time he flipped her over and pushed her knees back, she was so ready for him, she was sopping. And still, he didn't take her. His big, calloused hands moved over the soft velvet of her thighs, parting them so he could get his broad shoulders between them. She moaned when she felt his breath, hot against her throbbing sex, and cried out when he began to feather kisses on her mound.

Nothing had ever felt so good.

His tongue was magic, and he seemed determined to devour her from the inside out, to drink her up completely as if he wanted to drown in her juices. Her hands moved through the mass of his hair, trying to pull him to her, but he wouldn't be budged. The sweet torture went on and on until she thought she couldn't stand it another minute.

That's when he finally—*finally*—knelt between her trembling thighs, his cock rising up like a sword between his. The man still had his shirt on and she tugged at it, wanting all of him. Donal peeled it off over his head and she gasped at the sight of him, broad chest and ridged abdomen from years of training. His arms were heavily muscled from wrist to shoulder and she grasped his upper arms in both hands as he propped himself over her, gazing into her eyes.

"Are ye ready, lass?"

"Aye," she agreed, too breathless to say much else. "Please, do'na make me wait another moment."

He didn't. He parted her flesh easily, with perfect aim, sinking in swiftly, all the way to the hilt. Kirstin howled, digging her nails into his upper arms, arching beneath him at the sensation of being filled, being taken. She'd never been face-to-face with a man this way, at this moment. Donal claimed her, not just with his body, but with his eyes, pinning her beneath him.

He waited, watching her face, arms tense, thighs bulging against the supple softness of hers, his cock throbbing inside of her, so big it almost hurt. It felt as if he had penetrated her all the way to her womb, piercing her insides and making them spill forth more of her wetness. Kirstin licked her lips and then bit down on her bottom one as he began to move.

"Och, lass, ye feel s'good," he murmured, his eyes fluttering closed for just a moment as he withdrew almost all the way and sank back in again. She whimpered, arching up, wanting more. He opened his eyes to look at her, eyes searching. "Are ye'll right?"

"Please, do'na tease me," she pleaded, using every muscle she owned between her legs to clamp down on him.

Donal let out a low moan, hissing air between his teeth on his next intake of breath. "I'm n'delicate. I will'na break, I promise ye."

His eyes lit up at her words and he leaned in to claim her mouth once more. Kirstin let him have that, too. She let him take it all. She was his, meant for this man—for this moment. Her body writhed under his as he began to thrust, his tongue and cock making the same, delicious motion, a hot, velvet friction that built up and up. Any experience she'd had before of quick, awkward fumblings in the dark and a fast, rough hump that left her aching and somehow wanting more, were completely taken over by this singular experience.

This man knew exactly what he was doing, every movement, every whispered word, every touch. He knew just where to touch her, and when, and how. Donal drew her bottom lip between his teeth and sucked it, his thrusts coming deeper, harder. When she thought she couldn't take another moment of sensation, of that breathless, aching need, his mouth moved lower to her swaying breasts, capturing a dark-tipped nipple between his lips and sucking that instead.

"Och, Donal!" she cried, looking at him in awe, wondering if there was some pleasure-string connected between her breast and her sex, because it felt as if his mouth was on them both at once.

"That's it, lass," he panted, hips grinding into hers, making little moon-like circles, his steel heat buried so far up inside her she could have sworn she tasted him in the back of her throat. "I want ye. I want ye t'give yourself t'me. All of yerself."

"Oh aye, aye," she gasped, but she didn't understand him, because she was. This was everything she had to give him, her whole body, her mind, her soul, it was all of her, splayed for him. All for him.

"Look a'me, lass," he whispered, his blue eyes gone grey with lust. "Look a'me. I want ye t'give it to me. All of it. I want all of ye."

"Oh Donal," she cried, feeling something blooming low in her belly, opening like a flower, as he moved faster, grinding his pelvis into hers. "Oh what... what... I... ohhhhh!"

"Do'na close yer eyes," he insisted, his voice low, throaty, commanding her. "Look a'me when ye give yerself t'me. Ohhh Kirstin, yer so beautiful, so..."

She shuddered underneath him like an earthquake, her body taking over in a way she'd only ever experienced during her change. And this was something else altogether, something uncontrollable. She'd never been more in or out of her body at the same time, even when she was transforming from human to wolf. Delicious waves of pleasure rocked her body, her sex pulsing around his shaft, sluicing juice all down the length.

Donal watched her, his face lost in an expression of awe and wonder, and then he grabbed her shoulders, driving himself into her with three good, long, hard thrusts, burying his cock into her depths and his face into her neck. His seed spilled, hot as a geyser and just as forceful, deep into her womb.

This was the moment they'd both been searching for, and they found heaven and home all at once in each other's embrace. As he began to withdraw, Kirstin caught him between her thighs, crying out at the loss.

"Do'na leave me," she begged hoarsely, clinging to him, even as she still quivered with her climax.

"Nuh, lass," he whispered. "I'll ne'er leave ye. Not as long as m'body draws breath. Yer mine, Kirstin MacFalon, and ye'll be mine e'ermore."

"What did ye call me?" she whispered, lifting the curtain of hair away from his stubbly face as he leaned in to kiss hers, brushing his lips over her forehead and cheeks and chin, soft presses of love.

"Kirstin MacFalon," he said again, going up to his elbow to look down at her. "Me wife. If ye'll 'ave me. I know 'tis fast, but ye said ye felt the same way I did..."

"Oh, aye," she breathed, arms snaking around his neck, her face moving to the soft, damp skin of his throat. "I'd settle for nothin' less, Donal MacFalon."

"Do I need t'ask Raife fer yer hand?" He cocked his head, quizzical. "What do wulvers do?"

"Ye do'na e'en need t'ask me, Donal." She traced the strong, square line of his jaw with her fingertip. "Wit' wulvers, there is naught any askin'—only claimin', and ye've a'ready done that."

"Isn't there some sort of markin'?" he asked.

"Aye," she agreed, nodding. "But if I'm t'be t'wife of The MacFalon, I should hold t'yer traditions."

"We should do both." He caught her hand and turned it, face up, so he could kiss her palm. "King Henry wanted me t'mend the rift at t'border by marryin' an Englishwoman, but instead I'll marry t'border b'tween t'wulvers and t'Scots."

"Seal t'wolf pact wit' a kiss?" she teased, sliding a thigh over his. Their feet were still wet from the water, but the slant of sun was warming and drying them.

"I'll seal it wit' more'n that." He kissed her, mouth open, tongue meshing with hers, tracing slowly over her teeth, exploring every inch of her.

"Oh Donal," she whispered when they parted, dizzy with wanting him. "I want ye so much... when can we do't again?"

"Och, I'm a man, not a wulver," he groaned as she reached her hand down to squeeze his length. To her surprise—and apparently to his as well, given the way his eyebrows went up—he began to stiffen in her fist. "Ye bring out the beast in me, lass."

"Good."

She pushed the man to his back, tracing her tongue over around the mounds of hard muscle on his chest, pausing to flick each nipple, making the cock in her hand swell. The hair on his chest curled around her fingers as she explored every glorious plane and angle, a hand raking over his belly, a delicious, ridged mountain range of flesh. Her tongue traced the dark line of hair that traveled from navel to nest, his snake now rising up, staring at her with its one good eye.

"Och, lass, yer mouth—"

She sucked the head between her lips, tasting his musk, her juices, taking as much of him inside her as she possibly could, all the way to the back of her throat, and still she couldn't take him all. The man was more claymore than broad sword, a giant mass of swinging steel meant to take what was rightfully his. And she wanted to be taken.

Her fingernails raked the soft seed sacks hanging underneath his cock, and Donal hissed, shifting his hips, pushing himself deeper into her throat so she gagged a little on his length. But she didn't mind. His hand moved through her hair, guiding her, a hot, steady rhythm they both lost themselves in. She could have gone on forever, worshipping his staff, kneeling at the altar between her mate's thighs, but he pulled her off, looking down at her with half-closed eyes.

"Yer mine," he whispered hoarsely, his eyes filled with it, both the longing and the knowledge at once. "I will'na let ye go, Kirstin, not e'er."

"Ye talk overmuch," she teased, rubbing the head of him against her swollen, red lips. "How 'bout ye show me instead of tellin' me, Donal MacFalon?"

"Oh, aye." His eyes darkened at her words. "I'll show ye."

"If ye can catch me." She grinned and was off like a shot before he could move, laughing as she heard him swear behind her, struggling to catch up.

She made it into the pack leader's chambers, almost all the way to the bed before he caught her from behind, grabbing her around the waist and pulling her into his big arms. She giggled and squirmed, loving the way he roughly turned her to face him, hands moving down to squeeze her bottom.

"Caught ye," he growled in her ear, his erection rising up to nudge her belly, trapped between them. "Now I get t'claim ye."

"Aye." She nodded, wrapping her arms around his neck as he lifted her easily in his arms. Kirstin's legs went around him, heels digging into the small of his back as he lifted and aimed her, sliding his thick length in, deep and hard, as if he were running her through. Kirstin cried out at the sensation, thinking she would never, ever stop wanting this, craving him, needing him.

Donal moved toward the bed but Kirstin shook her head.

"Like this," she whispered hoarsely, beginning to move her hips in little circles. "Standin', jus' like this."

He moaned and turned toward the fireplace. The room was full dark, the only light coming from the torch at the end of the passageway. They could barely see each other, but it didn't matter. Kirstin felt every big, beautiful inch of him as he pressed her to the rock wall beside the big fireplace, driving up inside her with fierce, harsh thrusts that threatened to break her spine against the stone.

Not that she cared.

She was crazed with heat, her nails raking his back like claws, her teeth sinking into the hard, muscled skin of his shoulder. Donal grunted at that, but he didn't stop pounding into her, the slap of their flesh a hot, rhythmic beat. Kirstin's sex squeezed and massaged him, and she rocked in his arms, meeting him thrust for thrust.

"Yer lil cunny is so tight, lass," he panted in her ear. Words during mating were new to Kirstin, but she liked them. She liked the way he panted them, hot breath against her ear. "I could ride ye from dusk 'til dawn and still want more."

"Aye," she gasped, her walls quivering at his words, the dam threatening to flood. "Oh Donal, do'na stop. Do'na e'er stop."

"Nuh," he agreed, but he did stop, just for a moment.

To slide out of her, whirl her around, and bend her almost in half as he took her again, fingers probing between her legs, finding her crevice, and sliding back into the hot cavern of her sex. Kirstin's hands raked the stone, looking for something to hold onto, bracing herself against the rough thrust of his hips, the sweet torture of his cock up against her womb like a battering ram seeking entrance to something deeper inside her.

"Och, lass, I can'na hold out much longer," he cried, fingers gripping the curve of her hips, hard enough to leave bruises.

"Give it t'me," she urged, remembering his words to her. "I want all of ye. Please. Fill me wit' yer seed. Please, please, please, pl—"

Her sex was already spasming around his shaft, that unbelievable, quivering wave of pleasure pulsing through her, milking him. Kirstin howled, reaching back as he thrust forward, feeling the hard muscles of his behind working as he buried himself in to the base, shoving her flat against the wall, legs spread, feet completely off the ground, crushing her with his shuddering weight.

He didn't say anything then. He just picked her up in his arms like a bit of fluff and carried her to the bed. He pulled her on top of him, wrapping them up in the coverlet. It was soft and freshly laundered and they floated on a cloud together in the darkness. She might have slept—must have, because when she woke, there was a fire lit in the fireplace and her mate was no longer in bed.

"Donal?" She lifted her dark head from the pillow, hand searching the mattress for his big frame, but finding only empty space.

"Here, m'love," he called.

She saw him sitting on a deerskin by the fire, something in his hands.

Kirstin wrapped the coverlet around her and went to him, putting her arms around him from behind, kissing the broad, hard planes of his back, resting her cheek there as she knelt on the deerskin. She had woken, afraid she'd been dreaming, only to find him still here. Questions loomed in her mind, threatening the flood of happiness rushing through her veins, and she pushed them away.

They'd deal with reality later. This, here, now—was all that mattered, all that ever would.

"I found somethin'." Donal put a hand over hers at his middle, caressing. "Come see."

"Is it food?" she asked, crawling around to sit beside him. "Because I'm starvin'."

"I'll rustle us up some game." He chuckled, meeting her gaze in the firelight. "Och, Kirstin, yer so beautiful ye make me chest hurt."

She smiled at him, bemused. This man said the most extraordinary things.

"Is that a book?" She blinked in surprise at the leather-bound tome in his hands.

"Aye." He nodded, flipping through the pages. "I got up t'build a fire, and one of the stones at the bottom had come loose from our... uh... acrobatics. When I went to seat it, I found this..."

"Mmmm." She snuggled closer at the memory, her sex pulsing already, wanting him. How was it possible to want someone so much? "Is that... that's a wulver!"

The drawing was unmistakable. She recognized the half-wolf, half-human form, and more than that, the drawing itself had been done by a wulver hand. Wulvers were all amazing artists and could draw nearly anything. Their style was definitive.

"Aye." He flipped to another page and Kirstin squinted at it in the firelight, seeing a drawing of a birthing wulver and her pup.

"'Tis a midwife's text!" she exclaimed, taking it from his hands and pulling it into her lap. "Look, there are drawings of plants—it's full of them!"

"Yer pleased?" He smiled as she turned more pages, wishing she could read the text.

"Oh, aye," she breathed, looking up at him with bright eyes. "Sibyl and Laina'll be pleased, too."

"I do'na care 'bout pleasin' Sibyl and Laina." He pulled her into his lap, settling her there, and she felt his erection begin anew against her bottom. "I care 'bout pleasin' ye, Kirstin MacFalon."

"Ye do please me." She turned her face to his to be kissed. She would never get enough of this man's kisses, until the day she died. "Ye please me greatly, Donal MacFalon. I can'na wait to call ye husband as well as mate."

"And I can'na wait to mate wit' ye as yer husband." He used her hair to pull her head back, exposing her throat to his hot, hungry mouth.

"Aye," she agreed happily, lost in the fantasy of being his, even if the reality of being The MacFalon's wife meant something else altogether.

"No, I meant it, I can'na wait," he breathed, taking the book out of her hands and pushing her back onto the deerskin. "I want ye now."

She opened her arms and surrendered herself to him.

Chapter Five

Kirstin's hackles rose before she even knew the man was in the room. She turned to see Lord Eldred standing near the back of the gathering hall. He was dressed as an English lord today, not like the huntsman she'd met him as, but there was no mistaking those keen eyes. They surveyed the room quickly and she straightened when she saw his gaze hesitate as he came to her. A small smile flitted over his features and he gave her a brief nod before turning to someone at his side who wanted his attention.

"Kirstin?" Laina slid into the chair beside her, breathless from her race down the stairs and into the gathering room. "Did ye hear?"

"Hear what?" Kirstin's attention moved from Lord Eldred—she still didn't understand why he raised her hackles the way he did—to Laina, although her gaze stopped at Donal, sitting like a king in full dress plaid at the front of the room. The ceremonies were getting close to starting—the hall was filling up with people—and while Donal smiled and nodded to the man who was bending his ear, Kirstin could tell he was impatient.

"Lorien's back." Laina told her.

"Aye, I saw 'im." Kirstin smiled at the memory of the big wulver she'd greeted when he came into the castle. Donal had frowned at the way Kirstin hugged him, the way he swung her up in his arms and kissed her cheek in greeting. "He brought word from t'king."

"Aye, so y'know 'tis good news?" Laina asked.

Kirstin nodded. Lorien had been happy to give her the news, even before he told Donal, which had irritated Donal even more. But Lorien had been like a brother to her since she was small. They'd grown up together, played together, and yes, so they'd been together, when they were adolescents. For a while, Kirstin thought Lorien might be her true mate, but once she'd seen Laina with Darrow, and now Sibyl with Raife, she knew it wasn't meant to be. He was a friend, sometimes lover, but not her one true mate. She'd never gone into estrus around Lorien. Her body knew what it wanted.

And it wanted Donal

Lorien had returned safe and well, though, and that made her happy. And he had confirmed what Lord Eldred had told them in the forest. King Henry was honoring the wolf pact. It should have been a relief, but for some reason, Kirstin's hackles remained raised.

"Does Raife know? What 'bout Sibyl?" Kirstin looked around for both of them.

"I think they know. I'm jus' so relieved." Laina gave a happy sigh. "Our bairns'll be safe from war and strife."

Kirstin nodded in agreement, the mention of bairns sending a sharp stab of pain through her heart. She shook it off, glancing back to where Lord Eldred was shaking hands. Her mistrust of him had been based on her fear that he was lying about the wolf pact, that King Henry had actually been behind Alistair's plan all along. But mayhaps she was being too cautious. If Lorien had returned with word—she still marveled at his travel time, but wulvers could travel very fast, over long distances, without wearying—then she had to trust it.

Didn't she?

"How did ye hear?" Kirstin asked her pack-sister, frowning. "Did Donal tell ye?"

"No, I saw Lorien jus' a few moments ago," she replied. "He came up t'see Darrow. I had to practically tie that man to his bedposts to keep 'im in it, in spite of t'sleep-stuff Sibyl had 'im drink."

"And how's Darrow healin'?" Kirstin asked. She'd come to nurse her fellow pack mate and she'd spent all her time so far with Donal. She felt a little guilty about that— but when her gaze found Donal's and he pinned her with those glittering, steel-blue eyes, she didn't feel too horribly bad about the way she was spending her time at Castle MacFalon.

"He's well." Laina smiled. "Truth told, he's ready to travel, and itchin' to get home. We hafta get Raife and Sibyl reunited, and soon, or Darrow's goin' t'ruin everythin'."

"Tell 'im he has to keep up the ruse," she insisted. Donal's gaze hadn't left her, although someone had bent to tell him something. The way he looked at her made her feel as if he was stripping her bare with his eyes alone.

"I promise, I'm doin' m'best t'distract 'im." Laina sighed, tossing her long white-blonde hair over her shoulder, turning more to face Kirstin. "And *ye've* been distracted yerself these past few days."

"Aye." Kirstin flushed, when Donal dropped her a wink and she felt her blush deepen, hearing Laina laugh beside her. Were they so obvious? She wondered.

They'd met for the past three nights at the spring. Donal told her they could spend the night in his room and no one would care—he was the laird, after all—but Kirstin didn't want everyone in the castle talking, any more than they already were. Besides, their reenactment of Ardis and Asher beside the spring in the wulver den felt right to her. She was at home in the first den—and in Donal's arms.

"Yer so in love wit' him." Laina nudged her with her hip, laughing softly, delighted.

"Aye, I am." Kirstin admitted. If she couldn't admit it to her sister, who could she admit it to? She was completely besot. There was no getting around it, no more denying it. She had fallen like all wulvers do—hard, fast and without warning. It was like waking up finding you'd fallen asleep on a charging horse with no saddle and no reins, and you could do nothing but hold on for dear life and enjoy the wild, albeit slightly terrifying, ride.

"Have ye told 'im?" Laina lowered her voice, so the people filling the chairs around them wouldn't hear. Kirstin was saving the seat beside her for Sibyl. "About... how't works, for wulvers? Or does he know?"

"I... I do'na know what he knows. We haven't really talked overmuch..."

Laina chuckled knowingly at that.

The truth was, she was afraid to tell him. More than that—she was afraid of the truth herself. Her body was changing. She could feel it, in every cell. It wouldn't be long—another week, maybe two—and she would change. And she wouldn't be able to do anything about it.

If Donal had been a wulver warrior, they would run off under the full light of the moon when her estrus-time came and mate like the animals they were. But Donal wasn't a wulver, he was a man.

A very powerful, handsome, and virile man, to be sure. Their lovemaking had been wild, raw and abandoned. Kirstin had surrendered herself to him completely, and he had claimed her as his own. She couldn't have wanted any more from a wulver lover. In fact, the words he spoke into her ear while he was inside her, the things his hands did to her woman's body, far surpassed the animal act wulvers performed under a full moon. To Kirstin, their lovemaking left nothing to be desired—just thinking about it made her feel warm all the way to her toes—except for one thing.

Unless they made love while Kirstin was in wulver form, she could never bear his children. She-wulvers only experienced estrus as wulvers. The weight of this fact was like a thousand stones pressing on her heart. The MacFalons were Scots, so they weren't quite as particular about producing heirs as the English, but Donal was a man, and men wanted sons to carry on their lineage. They wanted daughters they could marry off to their neighbors to create alliances. And she wanted to give him sons and daughters.

She was a midwife—she'd been bringing pups into the world since she was a child herself, attending Beitrus—and the thought of not being able to bear children of her own left her feeling cold and alone. Looking at Laina, she thought of her wee bairn, the sweet, big-eyed, dark-haired Garaith, holding his chubby fists out to be picked up. She remembered the way Darrow had looked when his son was born, how proud he'd been. If she couldn't give that to Donal, she didn't know how she could possibly stand it.

And how could she tell him? How could she look him in those beautiful, kind, blue eyes and tell him that, loving her meant he would never have an heir? She wondered, sometimes, after their lovemaking, when he was stroking her hair or just watching her in the light of the fire, if he had put all the pieces together and figured it out for himself. Mayhaps he already knew the wulver ways, as Laina had intimated? But somehow, she didn't think so.

Because if he knew, she had a feeling he would end things between them as quickly as they'd begun.

And that's what she was really afraid of. Now that she had given in to herself—mind, body and soul—given into him, she couldn't imagine losing him.

So she had managed, every time he hinted about moving forward with marriage plans, to distract him, to keep things secret, just a little longer. She had been using Sibyl and Raife as a good excuse—not until things were settled between her pack leader and his mate, she said. Then they could share the news with everyone.

"Ye haven't talked 'bout it at all?" Laina asked, frowning, bringing Kirstin out of her reverie. "What'll ye do? Where'll ye live? How'll ye—?"

"Shh, 'ere comes Sibyl." Kirstin stood, welcoming Sibyl into their row of chairs with a hug.

Kirstin noted that Raife was watching his mate closely, although only from the corner of his eye, trying to appear as if he wasn't. Their latest plan to throw the two together had involved going riding under the pretense of looking for wulver traps—Lord Eldred had been keen to show them the various places where he and his men had begun disarming them—with Sibyl and Kirstin riding behind Donal and Raife.

Donal and Kirsten had planned to ride off and leave the two together alone in the woods, but Kirsten's horse had spooked at something—Laina claimed it was because she was so close to her estrus, but she didn't know for sure—and had taken off at a gallop. Donal and Raife gave chase, and by the time they caught her, Raife was so angry he threatened to pull Kirstin over his saddle and wallop her like a pup. Was it her fault the horse had spooked? Then, to top it off, it had begun to rain, and Lord Eldred begged off to go somewhere with his men, while the four of them rode back to Castle MacFalon in silence.

So much for plan B.

They'd moved on to plan C, which they would implement some time later in the week. It had to be soon, though, because while they were still bandaging Darrow's wound, he had nearly healed, and if Raife came out of the glowering mood he was in and started paying closer attention, he would know they were trying to deceive him. The only thing that kept Darrow in bed was the prospect of helping to alleviate his wife's discomfort because of her lacking nursling. He was clearly enjoying that part of the ruse.

Sibyl sat beside Kirstin with a smile, but there was no time for small talk. The room was full to capacity with all of the MacFalon armsmen as well as local villagers and several of the guests who had stayed on, after being invited to the wedding of Sibyl Blackthorne and Alistair MacFalon—which had never taken place.

The castle was still full of them, and Moira was busier than ever trying to feed everyone. Kirstin imagined the woman would be glad when they were all gone, which would likely be soon. Right about the time the wulvers left for home. Raife said the guests were staying on only to see if they'd turned themselves into wolves—like they were a curiosity or a freak show—and Donal had reluctantly confirmed as much.

Now, though, they were all crammed into the common room to watch the pomp and circumstance of their new laird being affirmed. He would also name his new guard captain and hunt master this day. After the ceremony would be a great party—poor Moira had been cooking for days and had brought in several extra sets of hands from the village to help her—and Kirstin was looking forward to it.

Beside her, Sibyl fidgeted, pulling at a stray thread at the edge of her plaid. Her nails were ragged, as if she'd been biting them, and she looked even more pale than usual. Her gaze kept skipping to Raife, who sat on the other side of the hall, as far away from her as he could get, while still being able to keep an eye on her.

Kirstin tried to listen and pay attention, but she kept getting distracted by Donal in his dress plaid. Her mind kept wandering to what he looked like out of it, and that made her feel as fidgety as Sibyl. It wasn't until Donal introduced Lord Eldred Lothienne to his clan that she really started listening. Up until then, the master of ceremonies had droned on about MacFalon lands and tracts and sections, as if he had to tell them every bit of dirt and rock the new laird of Clan MacFalon owned. Kirstin didn't know—mayhaps, according to some law, that's exactly what he had to do, but why subject them all to it?

Lord Eldred shook hands with the laird and Kirstin heard whispers around her about who he was and speculation about what he might be doing there, but no one had to wait long. The man was happy to steal the spotlight, stepping in front of Donal, literally upstaging him as he spoke to the crowd.

"I've come to deliver a message from King Henry VII of England," he proclaimed. His voice boomed through the hall, carrying all the way to the back, bouncing off the wall. "In my hand, I hold a royal decree, sealed by the king himself. This is a proclamation written in his own hand, reaffirming the crown's support of and enforcement for the original wolf pact decree as it was written."

This news was met with sighs of relief and general applause.

The people who lived on the MacFalon lands had long known about the wulvers, even if those from far-away did not quite believe the tales of the half-men, half-wolf warriors who lived in the borderlands.

And they had all heard the stories of what life was like before the wolf pact, when wulvers ran free and hunted men. No one wanted those days to return.

Many of the MacFalons strained their necks to look over at Raife, and Kirstin felt dozens of eyes turn her way as well. Laina clapped along with the rest of the crowd, nudging Kirstin to do the same. Kirstin nudged Sibyl, urging her applause, and she complied, although not with much enthusiasm.

This worried Kirstin, because Sibyl had been quite concerned about King Henry's response. They'd all hoped Alistair's claims that King Henry was behind his plan to eliminate the wulvers were just lies, and now they had proof, from the England's high royal huntsman himself. She would have thought Sibyl would be thrilled.

Lord Eldred handed the sealed proclamation to Donal. He actually had to turn around to do it, and Donal accepted it graciously. Lord Eldred handed him another piece of paper, also sealed, leaning in to say something to the laird no one else could hear. Donal gave a nod, his brow knitting for a moment, before setting both scrolls aside.

"King Henry VII of England will condemn any act against the wolf pact," Lord Eldred went on, bragging about his position as royal huntsman, and how the king had put him in charge of enforcing his wishes. Lord Eldred also made the announcement that, due to the recent death of King Henry's eldest son, Arthur, the crown was in mourning, otherwise King Henry himself would have made the trip.

Lord Eldred strutted like a peacock, completely commanding the room, and just watching him made Kirstin's blood boil. This was Donal's day, his affirmation of laird, and this pontificating fool was literally standing in front of him in order to address the crowd. No one seemed to care much, though. They were all taken in by his swagger, which made Kirstin's lip curl in a sneer she actually had to cover with her hand.

"Oh no." Laina whispered, craning her neck to look behind them. "Oh no, no, no."

"What is it?" Sibyl asked, turning to look.

Kirstin whirled in her chair and saw him.

Darrow was up, dressed, and making his way into the hall.

"Oh nooooo!" Kirstin echoed Laina's sentiment with a howling whisper. "Go! Fetch 'im a'fore Raife sees!"

But Sibyl was already up, heading toward the back of the room to corral her charge.

Laina followed and Kirstin sat there for a moment, watching as the master of ceremonies attempted to take control again—it was time for Donal to name Aiden and Angus MacFalon as his guard captain and hunt master, respectively. They were Donal's cousins, a lively pair of brothers with long, dark hair and bushy brown beards who liked nothing more than to drink and eat, as far as Kirstin could tell, but they were amiable enough. And, she supposed, it was good that they were big men, thick and barrel chested. People moved out of the way when they came into a room. Even Lord Eldred stepped aside as the brothers approached their laird to take the knee and pledge their fealty. She watched this happen out of the corner of her eye, but her attention was focused on Laina and Sibyl, who were now trying, as quietly as they possibly could, to drag Darrow back to bed before Raife saw him.

When Darrow opened his mouth to speak—likely to tell his wife to leave him the bloody hell alone, and not quietly either—Laina put a hand over his mouth. That's when Kirstin got up and made her way through the crowd standing in the aisles—there weren't nearly enough chairs for them all—to see if she could help get Darrow sorted before Raife caught wind. She saw Donal look her direction and she smiled at him, hoping he'd understand. He would, of course, once she'd told him why she'd slipped away.

Kirstin found Laina and Sibyl pushing a frustrated Darrow back through the crowd, but given the number of people, and Darrow's resistance, they weren't getting far.

"Darrow, please," Laina pleaded. "Don't do this. If Raife sees ye..."

"I need t'be'ere," Darrow insisted, ignoring the looks people were giving him. "Lemme go, woman!"

"If he sees ye up, he'll insist on leavin'," Kirstin hissed, getting in front of Darrow—at least the three of them made some sort of barrier. It wasn't much, but it was something. "Please, Darrow, think of Sibyl. Think of yer *banrighinn*."

That did stop him, for a moment.

He frowned down at Sibyl, head tilted, considering. Kirstin could almost see his thoughts flitting over his face. He'd gone along with their plan thus far. What was a little longer? Laina said he'd been angry about not coming to the ceremony, but she said she would placate him. In the end, though, Sibyl had given him something to make him sleep, because nothing else would calm him. It appeared he'd either only pretended to take it, or he'd woken up sooner than they'd expected.

"Darrow." Sibyl looked up at him, and Kirstin saw the tears in her eyes. Sibyl took a step back, shaking her head. "Go. Go to him. He's your brother, and you're right, you should be here."

With that, Sibyl ran. Laina looked at Kirstin with wide eyes, then at her husband—who was already pushing his way through the crowd, now that he had Sibyl's blessing. Kirstin could hear Donal announcing that the time for mourning his brother, Alistair, had come to an end.

"Go to'im!" Kirstin pointed after Darrow. "I'll take care of Sibyl."

She found her just outside the doors of the great hall, the ones that opened to the outside. Sibyl was crouching at the side of the stairs and Kirstin flew down them. When she reached her, Kirstin went to her knees beside Sibyl's small, trembling form, pulling a curtain of red hair away from her damp face.

"I'm sorry," Sibyl whispered. Then her body jerked violently and she leaned forward to vomit onto the dirt.

"Oh *banrighinn*," Kirstin whispered, holding her hair back as Sibyl emptied her stomach of what little she'd had for breakfast onto the ground. When she was done, Kirstin pulled her into her arms, rocking her and stroking her hot, flushed face with cool hands. "How long've ye known?"

"Known... what?" Sibyl frowned at her, blinking in surprise.

"Ye do'na know?" Kirstin's smile widened and she hugged her closer. "Oh m'sweet, lovely *banrighinn*, ye're wit' child. Ye're carryin' Raife's bairn. Ye'll bear t'wulver heir. Don't ye know what this means? He can'na deny ye now!"

The doors of the hall flew open and Kirstin heard Donal's voice from a distance, carrying to them, thanking everyone for coming and telling them that the kegs were being tapped outside—hence the avalanche of Scotsmen and women pouring forth from the gathering place.

"I'm pregnant?" Sibyl whispered, disbelieving.

"Aye. I'm almos' certain of it." Kirstin nodded, cupping her face in her hands.

"No." Sibyl's chin quivered and she pulled away, standing up and wiping her mouth with the back of her hand. "If I tell him... that will be the only reason he takes me back. I can't. I won't..."

And with that, she turned and ran. Kirstin went to follow her, but there was such a crowd rushing down the stairs, it was impossible. Even with her bright red hair, Sibyl was soon swallowed up.

"Kirstin?" Someone grabbed her arm and she looked up to see a man with a very bushy brown beard holding onto her. She recognized him as one of the recently pledged

MacFalon brothers, either Aiden or Angus, but she couldn't remember which.

"Aye." She tried to shake him loose, but he held her, not rough, but firm.

"The MacFalon requests yer presence in 'is chambers."

Kirstin followed Angus—it was Angus, not Aiden, who came to fetch her, she remembered when she saw the jagged scar on his calf and the story he'd told about the axe that had caused it—around the side of the castle, through the crowd. There was no sense going back up the stairs against the herd coming down it. Even with Angus's bulk leading the way, it would be too much of a fight. Instead, he took her through the breezeway and into the castle, down another long hallway.

Her heart was beating too fast, wondering why Donal had requested her so formally, why he hadn't come to get her himself. Mayhaps it was just another part of the ceremony, but she had a feeling it had to do with Darrow coming into the hall, and Raife realizing that his brother was now fit to travel. She wished she'd managed to catch Sibyl before she ran, but she would deal with that later—as soon as she could talk to Laina, alone.

Angus paused to knock on the big, solid, oak door.

"Aye, enter," Donal called out. He sounded weary. Mayhaps all the pomp and circumstance had been as exhausting for him as it had for her. She smiled, thinking of the night they would spend together in the first den, just the two of them alone. She would do her best to make him forget all of it, the responsibilities of being laird, the thousand small and large things weighing him down.

Angus pushed the door open with a grunt and Kirstin marveled at how heavy the thing was. It was thicker than her wrist. She didn't think a full grown wulver warrior could break it down without quite an effort.

"Kirstin." Donal's smile only reached his mouth, which was very unusual. She glanced around, expecting to see

Darrow and Raife, perhaps even Laina, ready for the fight that surely was about to ensue, but there was only Donal, sitting behind a wide, dark desk scattered with papers and maps and other documents, including two scrolls, their seals broken.

The King's seal, she realized, as Donal asked Angus to leave them and close the door behind him.

"Is somethin' t'matter?"

He held his arms out to her, now that they were alone, and she went to him. Donal pulled her into his lap, kissing her hungrily, hands moving greedily under her plaid, seeking the velvet of her skin. His tongue made soft, swirling patterns with hers and she melted against him, moaning softly when he cupped her sex, parting her thighs to give him more access.

Had he called her here for this, then? She wondered.

But doing this here was dangerous, and they both knew it.

"Donal," she whispered, burying her face against his neck as they parted, feeling the hardness of his body against hers, the steel of his erection through his plaid. "We should'na do this—not 'ere, not now. There're hundreds of people waitin' t'see their laird..."

"Damn them all t'hell n'back," he swore, grabbing a handful of her hair and pulling her head back so he could take her throat, leaving hot, wet trails with his swirling tongue. "Yer mine, Kirstin. D'ye hear me? And I want e'eryone t'know't."

He shifted in his chair, and she gasped when his cock pressed against her behind and his hand moved to cup the fullness of her breast. She couldn't deny him—wouldn't. She was his, truly. They were destined—she was sure of that. Her body knew it far better than her mind. It wept for him, opened to him, ached for him.

"Tonight," she whispered, crying out when his hand moved once again under her plaid, cupping and rubbing her through the thin silk barrier. "At our spring. We'll be together then... but now..."

"Kirstin." Donal wrapped his arms around her waist, surrendering to her words, bending his head to her breasts and resting it there. She stroked his hair, long, silky, soft under her fingers, a lion's mane. She sensed a sadness in him, a desperation that had never been there before.

"What is it?" she murmured, cradling his head against her breasts. "Tell me..."

He lifted his face to look at her, searching her eyes, looking for something.

"Let's run away." A small smile played on his lips at the shocked look that must have appeared on her face. "I'll ask Raife t'take me into yer pack. I know it's been done before. I'll live among t'wulvers, be one of ye. We can be together, as we're meant to be. I can'na be wit'out ye. Not as long as I draw breath."

She stared at him, heart hammering in her chest. All of the scenarios she'd seen playing out in her mind, and yet, this had never been one of them. She had never dreamed that the laird of Clan MacFalon would give up everything to follow her into the wulver den.

"I can'na ask that of ye..."

"Ye do'na need t'ask, m'love." He stroked her cheek with his fingertips. "I will'na lose ye. I can'na."

"We can talk 'bout it later." She swallowed, nodding, hearing the sound of the crowd, both inside and outside the castle walls. There were hundreds of guests roaming the halls, and they would expect to see their laird sooner rather than later. "But righ' now, ye have responsibilities. People are waitin' on ye, Donal MacFalon, and I—"

She was thinking of Sibyl, of Darrow and Raife and Laina. There were more immediate fires to put out, that Donal likely did not yet even know about.

"I do'na want them." His voice was urgent, hoarse, as he turned his face up to look into her eyes. "I want ye."

"And I want ye," she assured him, wiggling in his lap to prove it. He groaned and she smiled. "But ye can 'ave both."

"No, I can'na."

Her brow wrinkled at his words. "What d'ye mean?"

The look on his face struck fear—real fear—into her heart. They'd been playing at being together, pretending they could, at some point, announce their betrothal to the world. That Donal could present her to his people as The MacFalon's new wife. It begged so many questions it made her head hurt to think of them. Her mind told her one thing, her body, heart and soul another.

She'd been ignoring her head in favor of the latter.

"This." Donal angrily grabbed one of the scrolls off the desk, depositing it into her lap. "This is what I mean."

"What?" She puzzled as she unrolled the paper. It was finely inked and signed, adorned with the English king's seal, now broken.

"Can ye not read?" he thundered, standing and practically spilling her onto the floor. Kirstin caught herself against the desk, watching Donal begin to pace the room like a caged animal, hands behind his back.

"Nuh," she confessed in a small voice, sinking into the chair he'd vacated. "I can'na... only my name, a few words..."

He gaped at her for a moment, truly shocked.

"Wulvers do'na need t'know how t'read!" she exclaimed, rolling her eyes. "What does it say?"

Donal hung his head for a moment, eyes closed. Then he lifted his gaze to meet hers.

"It says King Henry's sendin' me an English bride," he told her softly. "And he expects me t'marry her wit'in the month."

"What?" She breathed, glad she was seated, because her legs wouldn't have held her if she hadn't been.

"Aye." He started his pacing again, back and forth. "Lady Cecilia Witcombe, the Earl of Witcombe's only daughter. She's on her way t'Castle MacFalon righ' now. Will probably arrive wit'in a fortnight."

"This is..." She raised the scroll in her trembling hands. "From King Henry? Himself?"

"Aye." Donal whirled, stalking toward the tall bookcases at the other end of the room. "King Henry says I'm t'marry this stranger or forfeit m'claim to the MacFalon lands."

"How can he do that?" she cried, seeing him turn on his heel and pace back in her direction, his face nothing but scowl. "He isn't Scotland's king—he isn't yer king *or* mine."

"Alistair made an agreement wit' him as The MacFalon," Donal reminded her darkly. "And I'm duty-bound t'honor it."

Agreements. Duty-bound. Honor. Words her heart did not recognize or care about in the least. Her heart knew this man was hers, no matter what claim the English king thought he had on him. Kirstin hung her head, looking at the scroll in her hands, knowing it had all been too good to be true. They'd been dreaming of being together, when all along, they'd both known it was impossible.

"Mayhaps 'tis for the best," she whispered. Big, fat tears fell onto the parchment, blurring the words.

"What? How can ye say that?" Donal exploded, stalking over and grabbing the scroll. He crumpled it in his big fist with a sneer, tossing it aside. Then he took a knee in front of her, grasping both of her hands in his. His tone was pleading, desperate. "Kirstin, I love ye. D'hear me? I love ye more than any man has e'er loved a woman. I've naught interest in any other."

The thought of him bedding another woman, let alone marrying her, made her stomach clench in pain. She met his eyes, tears trickling down her cheeks, seeing the pained look on his face and knowing it was mirrored on her own.

"Donal... if ye refuse..." She swallowed, not liking to think of it. "You do'na know what yer sayin'. Yer not thinkin' clearly. Ye can'na give up yer lands, yer position as laird of Clan MacFalon, not for me, not for any woman."

"So I should keep it t'marry a woman a do'na love?"

"Mayhaps." Her own words pierced her heart and she saw them run him through, more painful than any sword. And she was going to have to break him further, now that they were facing these harsh realities. "Donal... there's somethin' else I hafta tell ye..."

"What is it?" He looked as if he was waiting for something to fall out of the sky and land on top of his head.

"I did'na wanna talk 'bout this 'ere, now, but..." She lowered her head, shaking it, the weight of it breaking her heart in two. "I do'na know how t'say't."

"Tell me." He lifted her chin, forcing her to look into his eyes. "Ye can tell me anythin', lass."

"Donal, e'en if we run away, as ye suggest..." She swallowed, trying to gather enough courage to say the words, to face the reality out loud. "E'en if Raife would agree t'such a thing, and we go live among me pack..."

"He damned well will agree," Donal snapped, his face a thundercloud.

"Listen t'me." Kirstin took his face in her hands, clean-shaven today, smooth. "Yer a man, and I'm a wulver. We'll ne'er be t'same."

"I do'na care 'bout that," he said with a shake of his head. "It does'na matter, Kirstin, we—"

"I'll never be able t'have yer children," she blurted out.

The words hung there between them and she saw his confusion, his bewilderment. So he didn't know, then. Didn't understand how it worked for the wulvers, the basic mechanics. It was impossible—it would always be impossible.

"What?" He shook his head again, as if to clear it.

"A she-wulver can only accept her mate's seed when she's a wolf," she confessed. "I can'na have yer bairn, because we can'na mate when I'm changed. D'ye ken?"

"Aye." He looked thoughtful, the realization slowly dawning. "But Raife... how was he conceived, then?"

She swallowed, telling him the awful truth. "King Henry took Avril when she was in heat. When she'd changed to a wulver."

"What?" he breathed.

"Some men see't as a challenge, a badge'a honor, t'take a wulver woman when she's in animal form..."

He gaped at her, clearly unaware of this part of the history between their families.

"Men like yer brother, I imagine," she murmured, hammering the point home. "Or yer grandfather."

"Och, Kirstin..." He held his arms out to her and she went to him, let him cradle and rock her. They huddled together on the floor behind his desk like children hiding from their parents. He stroked her hair, kissed her temple, whispered how much he loved and wanted her until she thought her heart would overflow with feeling for him.

"Listen t'me," he urged. "'Tis ye I want. Children would be a wonderful expression of our love together, if they were possible, but they're not necessary. Ye're the one I want."

"'Tis easy t'say that now." She sniffed, fitting her head under his chin. "Mayhaps 'tis time t'face some hard truths. We've been livin' the dream of Ardis and Asher, but mayhaps that dream's over now... and it's time t'wake up to the reality of who we really are."

"I know who I am." Donal's arms tightened around her. "I'm The MacFalon, and ye're mine. I will'na let ye go. That's the truth."

"The truth..." She gave a long, shuddering sigh. "The truth is, ye would'na be happy wit' the wulvers. And I..."

"Oh Kirstin, ye've been happy 'ere," he countered, whispering against her hair. "I know ye have."

"Aye," she confessed, holding back a sob. "I love ye, and Moira, and yer family, and the castle... I do. But..."

"Then stay," he urged, wrapping her up completely in his arms as if that alone could keep her. "I'll send word t'the king that I will'na marry this Englishwoman, and—"

"And start a war?" she cried. "Bring King Henry and 'is army down on yer head, so soon after reaffirming t'wolf pact? Put me pack and yer family in danger? At the vera least, lose everythin' ye own?"

"I do'na care 'bout that..." he told her hoarsely.

"But I do," she replied softly. "And we both know, e'en if... e'en if Lady Cecilia Witcombe wasn't on 'er way t'marry ye... no one would accept the laird of Clan MacFalon marryin' a wulver."

"'Tis not true..." He denied it, but she heard the hesitation in his voice.

"Aye, 'tis," she insisted. "I've heard what they say 'bout us. They all talk, when ye're not 'round to silence 'em. They say things like 'I'd love to lie wit'er, but I'd be afeared t'get fleas'."

"Who said it?" he growled. "I'll 'ave their heads."

"You can'na quell hundreds of years of prejudice and superstition with yer sword, m'love." She smiled. She didn't want to tell him about the Alistair loyalists, the ones who continued to hate the wulvers. There was one man in particular, Gregor, who had said very rude, crude things, but she'd done her best to ignore him. "Ye'd hafta chop off e'ery head in the land t'were that yer solution."

"There's a way..." he insisted. "There mus' be."

"If'n there is, I do'na know't." She sighed, closing her eyes against the truth, not wanting to face it.

"Leave't t'me." He lifted her chin and kissed her lips, soft and sweet. "I should'na've burdened ye wit'this. But I wanted ye t'hear't from me, a'fore..."

"A'fore?" She raised her eyebrows.

He sighed, a pained look crossing his face. "A'fore ye heard it from someone else. Like Lord Eldred."

She shuddered at the mention of that man's name. Of course he would make it a point to make that sort of announcement at his leisure. He liked to take the spotlight, and he would likely see it as a good opportunity to do so.

"What're we gonna do, m'love?" she lamented, searching his eyes for an answer.

"Right now?" He brushed hair away from her face. "We're goin't'go out there, put on smiles, an'dance."

"I can'na dance wit' ye," she protested with a shake of her head. "Not now..."

"I can'na dance *wit'out* ye." He pressed his mouth full to hers and she tasted the salt of her tears slipping between their lips.

She would do as he asked, although, the thought of joining the gathering after this news made her stomach turn. And then she remembered Sibyl's morning sickness.

"Oh, Donal, there's somethin' else," she said.

He sighed. "I do'na think I can stand another thing..."

"It's Sibyl... she's wit' child."

He blinked in surprise. "Well, this is good news, isn't it? It solves our problem of tryin' t'get those two together, doesn't it?"

"No." Kirstin laughed, shaking her head. "Sibyl refuses t'tell him. She says she will'na use it t'get him back."

"Och." He smacked his forehead with his hand, rolling his eyes. "Women!"

"We're the bain of man's existence, aren't we?" She giggled.

"Aye," he agreed, grinning. "And the boon."

"I love ye, Donal MacFalon," she said suddenly. "No matter wha'appens, I'll always love ye."

"And I love ye, Kirstin MacFalon." He pressed his forehead to hers, looking deeply into her eyes.

"I do like the sound of that." She sighed.

"Good, because I'm goin' t'marry ye. Some way, somehow, I'll make ye mine. I promise ye that."

Kirstin nodded, kissing him back when he touched his lips to hers again, not protesting in the least—because she wanted so very much to believe him.

Chapter Six

"Raife, I can'na go back wit' ye." Kirstin wrung her hands, meeting her pack leader's concerned gaze with her own pleading one. "He's me one true mate."

Raife scowled at her over the breakfast table, although she wasn't surprised. He wore a scowl most of the time now. They were leaving on the morrow, and still, his face hadn't cracked a smile. She couldn't believe he was still holding out, keeping his mate at arm's length. This was their last-ditch effort to bring the two of them together, and it had better work, because they'd run out of other options.

Unless they locked them in a room together that neither could escape, she couldn't fathom any other plan but this one.

"He's not a wulver," Raife protested, glancing over at his brother, Darrow, who snorted at this from behind his mug of mead. Laina just looked into her bowl of meal, scraping the bottom brown bits, ignoring Raife's cool look in their direction.

Kirstin had to point out the obvious. "Neither's Sibyl"

"We're talkin' about ye, nuh me." Raife's scowl deepened. And here she thought that wasn't even possible.

"I love 'im." Kirstin confessed, glancing up as Moira brought a bowl of hard-boiled eggs to the table. It was dangerous, telling Raife this in front of Moira and the servant girls who hurried around bringing food out to the gathering hall and the people there. The wulvers ate in the kitchen with the servants, not because they were forced to, but to avoid the stares and whispers of most of the MacFalons.

Raife frowned, but for the first time, he looked like he was taking her seriously. "You've given yerself t'him?"

She nodded, glancing at her sister. "Laina says I'll go into estrus soon."

"But ye can'na 'ave bairns wit' this man," Raife reminded her, his voice soft, more concerned than angry now.

"Aye." She swallowed, nodding again.

"And he knows that?"

"Aye."

"Kirstin, he's the laird of Clan MacFalon." Raife reached across the table to take her hand in his. "How well d'ye think those people out there're goin' to accept ye? They do'na e'en like havin' us eatin' at t'same table beside 'em."

What he said was true and made her eyes fill with tears. Raife frowned at that and sighed, watching her tears fall into her lap as she lowered her head, letting a dark curtain of hair hide her face.

"Kirstin, I'm not sayin' it t'be cruel," he murmured. She knew he wasn't, and his kindness and sympathy hurt more than anything else. Raife had been chosen their pack leader for a reason. He was both intelligent and shrewd, and he almost always knew the right thing to do—unless it involved his own love life, apparently. "Besides, I do'na b'lieve King Henry'll e'er allow the match."

"But he upheld t'wolf pact." She lifted her tear-filled gaze to meet his.

"There's a difference a'tween livin' peacefully alongside wulvers and marryin' them, ye ken?" He squeezed her small hands in his giant ones. "But if it's what ye really want, I'll n'stop ye."

"Thank ye." Kirstin's lower lip trembled. She wasn't even acting—she didn't have to. "I'm afeared ye may be right 'bout King Henry. He's... he's sent a royal decree."

"What decree?" Raife glanced up at Darrow and Laina to see if they knew about such a decree but they both kept quiet, busying themselves with their breakfast.

"King Henry's promised Donal another bride. An English one." She wasn't lying. She comforted herself with that as Raife's eyebrows went up in surprise.

"I was afeared of that." He shook his dark head, frowning.

"He sent a sealed scroll wit' his royal huntsman. King Henry's ordered 'im t'marry S—" She stopped herself mid-sentence, biting her lip. Mayhaps now she was putting on a bit of an act for his benefit. But it worked. His eyes widened when she wouldn't finish the sibilant word and simply said, "An Englishwoman."

"An Englishwoman," Raife murmured. He was an intelligent wulver and could put a puzzle together. She was counting on it. His gaze skipped to Laina and Darrow, who avoided it. Even Moira rushed off to busy herself with something at the other end of the kitchen. "What Englishwoman?"

Kirsten lowered her head, feeling his hands tightening over hers in a vise-like grip. She nearly yelped, but used it to elicit a sob of pain from her throat.

"Kirstin!" he growled, letting go of her hands—he'd realized he was hurting her—and grabbed her little shoulders, shaking her. His eyes were wild. She saw the fear in them—and knew his pain. It wasn't Raife who would have to fight to keep his mate from marrying someone else. Sibyl was no longer promised to anyone but him. And mayhaps, after this little ruse, he'd finally realize that it was only Raife she'd ever loved.

"What Englishwoman?" Raife thundered, standing and knocking the chair out from under him.

She shook her head, remaining mute, pretending she couldn't talk because she was sobbing so hard—and it wasn't hard to do. Because the tears were real. There was an Englishwoman who would soon be at the MacFalon doorstep who expected to marry Donal and bear his children on orders from her king. It brought up pain so great for Kirstin, she could barely breathe, let alone talk, and she just sobbed into her hands, unable to answer Raife's questions.

"Sibyl...?" Raife's big fingers dug into her shoulders. *"Is it Sibyl?"*

"Enough, Raife!" Darrow snapped, glaring at his brother.

"Look at 'er!" Laina clucked, shaking her head. "She's so upset, she can'na e'en speak..."

"D'ye know?" Raife pointed a finger at Darrow, then Laina. "Who's this Englishwoman?"

"I—" Laina looked at Darrow, blinking innocently. "I... uh..."

"Well..." Darrow cleared his throat, leaning back in his seat. "Uh..."

"Ne'ermind!" Raife kicked the toppled chair out of his way as he stormed toward the exit. He nearly knocked over the little blonde maid, the one with the gap between her teeth called Gayle, as she came in. She shrank away from him, pressing herself flat against the wall, clearly afraid of the wulver warrior.

"I'll speak to The MacFalon meself and wring it out of his scrawny neck..." Raife growled, sweeping past the maid without even seeing her.

"He's in the chancery!" Moira called helpfully after him, chuckling when the door swung closed.

"Did it work?" Kirstin lifted her tear-filled cheeks, lowering her hands completely. She'd been peeking out of them between her fingers until that moment.

"Aye. That was quite a performance." Darrow scowled, tearing roast chicken off the carcass in front of him. His appetite had come back threefold, his body requiring more protein to heal faster, and Moira had been happy to roast a chicken or two a day for him. "I hope so. Now it's up to The MacFalon."

Kirstin wasn't about to tell them how little she'd had to pretend.

"The MacFalon plans t'keep Sibyl in the chancery 'til Raife arrives?" Moira asked, pouring more mead into Darrow's empty glass.

"Aye." Kirstin sniffed, cooling her red cheeks with the wave of her hands. "Angus'll signal 'im when Raife's almost there, so Donal knows just when he should propose to Sibyl."

That thought brought more tears to Kirstin's eyes, even though she knew it was all a ruse. She didn't like the thought of Donal proposing to anyone—except her. And he'd done that, several times already, in the past couple weeks. If only she could accept him...

"Nothin' like jealousy and possessiveness t'motivate a wulver t'action." Laina smiled coyly, nudging her husband with her elbow.

"Since t'dawn of man, when Eve took that first bite of apple." Darrow sighed, reaching to the middle of the table to grab one out of a bowl of fruit, taking a large chunk of apple flesh out with his teeth and chewing noisily. "Ye women've been so vera cruel."

Kirstin wiped her face with the edge of her plaid, and both Darrow's words and the bulge beneath it reminded her.

"Speakin' of the dawn of time..." Kirstin produced the book from where she'd hidden it in the folds of her Scots garment. "I've somethin' I wanna show ye."

"What's this?" Laina frowned at the leather-bound tome as Kirstin put it up on the table.

"I found it in t'first den," she confessed, flushing when Laina gave her a knowing smile. Did everyone know that she and Donal had been sneaking off to meet there? "Hidden in t'pack leader's room."

"Is that what I think 'tis?" Moira saw the book, her craggy gray eyebrows going up in surprise.

"Is it a witches book?" Gayle, the blonde maid, peered over Moira's shoulder at it, her eyes wide. "It looks like witchcraft t'me."

"It's the Book of the Moon Wives." Moira scoffed at the girl's assumption, retrieving the chair Raife had kicked and sitting upon it so she could look through the book in question. "I thought t'was jus' the stuff of legend..."

"I've ne'er heard of such a thing." Laina stood to go look over Moira's shoulder as well, watching the woman turn pages.

"I'd heard such a book existed," Moira told her. "But I thought t'was jus' a tale, or mayhaps that it'd once existed but it'd been lost long ago."

"T'was well concealed," Kirstin said, blushing at the memory of how they'd discovered the book, but no one noticed. They were all too interested in its contents—everyone except Darrow, who continued to pick meat off the chicken carcass with his fingers.

"What kinda book is't?" Gayle inquired, curious but at the same time looking as if she might bolt at any moment should the book do something untoward.

"It's said t'be a history of wulvers'n'men," Moira informed them. Then she chuckled. "Well, mayhaps a history of wulvers'n'women might be a better description. It's a sort of midwives'n'healer's guide."

Laina perked up at that. "Not many words..."

It was true, the guide was mostly pictures, although there were some words. Those words they saw were written mostly in Gaelic, and sometimes another, ancient language. The handwriting was mixed, making the assumption that the book had been written by more than one hand a good one.

"At the time, neither human women nor wulver women were allowed t'learn t'read or write," Moira said.

"Only ladies need to learn t'read." Gayle wrinkled her nose. "I can'na waste m'time learnin' nonsense."

"If we start teachin' women t'read, mankind is doomed," Darrow joked, ducking when Laina reached out to smack his head.

"I wish I'd learned." She stuck her tongue out at him.

"I can'na read the words..." Kirstin lamented with a sigh.

"Nor I..." Gayle shrugged.

"I can," Moira said, surprising them all. "But I do'na know all of the plants. Some, but n'all...

Laina and Kirstin looked at each other and they both said, "Sibyl."

"Aye," Laina nodded, her eyes shining. "She can read—*and* she knows all t'plants. Likely more than all of us combined."

"Mayhaps the cure lies within these pages..." Kirstin smiled at her sister.

"'Tis my greatest hope," Laina confessed. "For yer sake, and mine... and the sake of our daughters."

"Gayle, more mead!" Another servant girl stuck her head into the kitchen and the little blonde sighed, moving to get back to work.

Moira abandoned the book to fetch a pitcher for Gayle to take out to the guests.

Laina came over, standing beside Kirstin's chair, gently stroking her long, unbraided hair. Kirstin put her arms around her, resting her cheek against Laina's belly.

"I do'na like th' idea of ye stayin 'ere, sister." Laina sighed. "What'll we do fer a midwife? Who'll deliver the wulver heir?"

Darrow's head came up at that, distracted from his mission of debriding the chicken of all its meat. She had told Laina and Darrow, but had sworn them to secrecy.

"Shhh!" Kirstin urged her sister to be quiet, glancing around at the servants. They were all busy, but still, you never knew who was listening. "Do'na give 'way that secret a'fore our *banrighinn*'s ready t'reveal it."

"'T'would bring Raife 'round in a heartbeat," Darrow said again, for the hundredth time. He'd been quick to suggest they just outright tell their pack leader about Sibyl's condition, but the women had talked him out of the idea. He kept pushing it though, saying it was the one sure thing that would be certain to endear Sibyl to him again.

"Aye, but I ken Sibyl's hesitation," Laina told her husband. "She'd ne'er know if Raife wanted 'er—or the bairn..."

"No man'd walk away from a woman carryin' his heir." Darrow licked his fingers noisily. "That woman's more precious than gold."

She knew he wasn't talking about her, but Kirstin couldn't help the tears that welled up at his words. She saw Gayle looking at her curiously as she carried a tray toward the door and Kirstin averted her eyes, not wanting her to see. She didn't want anyone to see.

So she bolted. She heard Laina calling after her, alternately berating Darrow for his thoughtlessness, but Kirstin didn't stick around to hear the rest. She pushed past Gayle, who nearly spilled her tray, and ran down the hallway blindly, her chest tight with Darrow's words.

More precious than gold.

Would she be worth nothing, then, if she could not bear Donal an heir? Even Raife had been doubtful about that aspect of their relationship. He and Sibyl had no such restrictions, as her budding pregnancy proved.

Kirstin heard men's laughter at the end of the hall and slowed, seeing Angus and Aiden slapping each other on the back. Donal stood to the side, head cocked, listening. She wiped her tears, considering turning around and running the other way, when she heard it.

Shouting. Banging. Someone was pounding on Donal's chancery door—from the inside. Too curious to resist, Kirstin approached. Donal smiled when he saw her, slipping an arm around her waist and bending his head to her ear.

"I locked 'em in."

"What?" She startled, hearing Raife demanding to be let out. "Ye did what?"

"That stubborn fool was still gonna walk out, e'en after he'd heard me propose—and her refuse, a'course. I fully expected him t'barge in and go after me like a bat outta hell. I had Aiden and Angus waitin' to come to me aid if need be, jus' to restrain 'im. But e'en after all that, he was not gonna back down. So—I locked 'em in there together."

Kirstin heard Sibyl shouting—screaming at Raife. Weeks of pent-up anger and hurt and frustration that she was finally allowing herself to feel and say. It didn't help that she was with child. The bairn made her far more emotional than usual.

"We should start makin' wagers on how long they'll be in there," Aiden said with a chuckle, nudging his brother.

"I jus' hope he does'na bust up m'grandfather's desk and bookshelves." Donal winced.

"Wait..." Kirstin cocked her head, eyes widening in surprise. "It's quiet..."

"He did'na kill 'er, did he?" Donal whispered.

"Mayhaps *she* killed *'im*," she countered, listening for any sound.

She heard Sibyl give a cry and for a moment thought she might be hurt. Kirstin took a step toward the door, and then another sound followed the first. This one much clearer in origin.

"That's not t'sound of someone bein' murdered." Donal grinned.

"Mayhaps we should give 'em some privacy?" Kirstin waved the two big men away who had leaned in closer to the door. Angus actually had his ear pressed right up to it. "Shoo! Both of ye, go! Moira has roast chicken in t'kitchen. Go do what ye do best! Go eat!"

Aiden and Angus grumbled about it, both of them grinning ear to ear at the sound of Sibyl's moans of pleasure, but they went, as instructed.

That left Kirstin and Donal standing in the hallway, grinning at each other like fools.

"That gives me an idea." Donal jerked his thumb toward the closed, locked door, behind which Sibyl and Raife were making unholy noises, pulling Kirstin to him with his other arm around her waist.

"Tonight..." she whispered, putting her hands against his chest and pushing, but he wrapped both arms around her, not budging.

"Now," he growled in her ear, his big, muscled thigh sliding between hers as he pressed her against the tall, oak door. "I wanna make love t'ye in a bed, in a room wit' windows. I wanna see yer beautiful body in the daylight."

She couldn't resist him. Not with the clear sounds of Sibyl and Raife mating on the other side of the door and Donal's rising erection pressed hard against her hip. She wanted him like she always wanted him. Desperately, hungrily, without question or reserve.

"Aye," she whispered, tilting her head so he could have better access to her throat. His kisses were hot and greedy, his hands roaming over her even though anyone could come down the hall at any moment.

"Come wit' me," he demanded, grabbing her hand and leading her down the hall. They went upstairs, passing maidservants on the way, as well as both Aiden and Angus, who had been waylaid by two pretty girls before they reached Moira's kitchen. Angus's brows went up as Donal dragged Kirstin through the castle. She stumbled after him, blushing from the roots of her hair to the tips of her toes, realizing every single person who saw them must know where they were going, and why...

But when Donal got her into his room, slamming the door behind him and locking it, she didn't care anymore who heard them. They were on each other like animals, tearing at each other's clothing like they couldn't get skin to skin fast enough. Donal's bed was one befitting the laird of Clan MacFalon, a huge four-poster affair, so high there was a stool beside it. The thought of him sleeping there alone at night made her crazy. The thought of him sleeping there with someone else?

That was unfathomable.

"Kirstin, m'love," he whispered against her lips, pulling off the last vestige of her clothing, her shirt over her head, leaving her bare before him.

Donal went to his knees, looking at her in the bright light spilling in from the tall windows, his gaze sweeping her from head to toe and back again. Then his eyes settled between her legs, at the soft patch of fur there.

"Lemme see ye," he murmured, using his big hands to part her thighs. "Open yer cunny fer me."

She slid a hand down to do as he asked, using her fingers to spread her swollen sex, showing him everything he wanted to see. The look of lust in his eyes went from white hot to molten in an instant. Donal growled, wrapping his thickly muscled arms around her and burying his face between her thighs. Kirstin cried out, his tongue lapping at her like a dog, up and down and back again, a fast, frenzied motion that made her thrash, head going back, hips thrust forward. She grabbed a handful of his hair, grinding against his face, against the fierce, hot lash of his tongue.

The man's mouth was absolute magic.

"Donal, nuh, nuh, please," she begged him, knees beginning to buckle, unable to hold her weight under such an onslaught.

He pushed her back against the side of the bed, pulling her legs up over his powerful shoulders, and in one swift motion, he stood, vaulting her up onto the mattress. Kirstin squealed, laughing as she flew through the air, landing breathless in the middle of his bed. It was like landing on a cloud.

Donal crawled up after her, pulling his shirt off, leaving him naked and stalking her, his erection bobbing between his legs as he knelt up between hers. Kirstin thought he would slide inside her, but instead, he pushed her knees back, all the way to her ears, bending her body near in half before leaning in to fasten his mouth over her mound.

"Ohhhhhh my God!" she cried, getting a very clear view of him parting her swollen lips with his tongue, teasing the little button at the top of her cleft, then sliding down to dip into the pink hole of her sex. He drank her up, eyes locked on hers, watching the pleasure rise with the flush on her cheeks.

"Donal! Oh please! Donal!" She called for him, begging, pleading, wanting nothing more than this sweet torture to come to its final conclusion—or, mayhaps, never to end at all. But it couldn't go on forever, and she finally surrendered to him, her body giving in, as it always did, to his demands.

"Och! Ohhhhh yes, yes!" She moaned and writhed, her sex clenching and releasing with her climax, toes curling, feet braced against his shoulders. Her body twisted and vaulted on the bed, but Donal had her hips grasped in his hands, refusing to allow her to go too far.

"Aye, aye, lass, that's so good," he murmured, kissing her juicy thighs—she'd already made his covers wet. "A vera good start."

"Start?" she panted, taking a deep breath as he let her loose, allowing her legs to slide back down, past his shoulders, settling around his waist as he leaned over to kiss her.

"Taste yerself." He pushed his tongue deep into her mouth. "How good ye taste. I could eat ye fer breakfast, lunch and supper and still have ye fer dessert."

She blushed at his words, feeling her body sing with them. Nothing affected her like this man, the words he spoke to her when they were alone together. No one knew her like he did, had ever known her this way. It had happened so fast, this falling, it almost felt like flying.

"I wanna taste *ye*," she urged, reaching down to grasp his shaft.

Donal gave a little grunt of pleasure, letting her yank him closer with each stroke, until he was in her mouth, straddling her. Kirstin swallowed his length, greedy to taste him deep in her throat. She loved the way he moved, the way he gathered her hair in his hands and simply used her mouth for his pleasure. It readied her for him more quickly than anything else, feeling the soft, velvety head of his cock slipping between her lips again and again. Her hands roamed over the glorious terrain of his body, his powerful thighs tense as he stroked himself in and out of her wet, swollen mouth, his sack swaying below, caressing her throat with each thrust.

"Och, wait, wait," he cried, pulling back, sliding himself out of her mouth with a soft popping sound. His erection swayed above her head, just out of reach, a thick strand of white hot liquid dripping from the tip to fall onto her waiting tongue. She swallowed it, eager for more, but Donal rolled off, reaching for and taking her with him.

"Ride me," he commanded, stretching out on his back and grabbing his cock in his fist. "C'mon, lass. Climb on n'go fer a ride."

She gave the head of his cock one last kiss before she straddled him, knees on either side of his hips as she eased herself down onto his length. Donal looked at her with half-closed eyes, watching her slide down slowly until they were joined completely, as one. Kirstin felt him buried deep in her womb, the crown of his cock so far inside her she ached. It was a delicious sort of pain and she moved her hips, grinding, feeling him rock back and forth inside her.

"That's it, lass," he urged, his hands moving to try to span her waist as she undulated on top of him. "Ride me. Mmm, faster."

Her hips rocked, finding their own rhythm, her body in control. Donal reached up to cup her breasts, heavy and swaying, her nipples hard, the flesh around them pursed as if they were asking to be touched. She moaned when he pinched them, that delicious pleasure-string between her breasts and sex zinging like a plucked lute strung, making her ride him faster, harder.

Donal wrapped his arms around her, pulling her in for a kiss, the velvet tip of his tongue stroking the roof of her mouth, sending hot tingling sensations through her limbs, all the way to her fingers and toes. He began to thrust from underneath, faster and harder than she was able, making her moan into their kiss, carried away by the sensation.

"Sit up," he urged, pushing her back, hands on her hips. Kirstin sank down fully on him again with a low moan, her head going back, hair grazing his thighs as they rocked together.

"Look," he urged, grasping her hips, pushing and pulling her, back and forth, rocking himself deep inside her. "Look at yerself, m'love. See how beautiful ye're."

Kirstin caught a glimpse of herself in a looking glass on the bureau across the room and stopped for a moment, blinking in surprise. She saw herself, full-breasts and hips, hair falling over her shoulders like a midnight waterfall.

"D'ye see what I see?" His hands moved up over her curves, cupping the full weight of her breasts.

"Aye," she whispered, looking from her reflection back down to him again.

"She's mine," he reminded her, tracing a finger down the center of her body, between her breasts, dipping briefly into her navel before traveling further south. "Yer mine, Kirstin. I'll ne'er let another man look at ye, let alone touch ye. No other man or wulver'll e'er claim what's mine. D'ye ken?"

"Aye," she whispered, nodding, feeling tears pricking her eyes. She wanted to drown out all the voices in her head—Raife and Sibyl, Laina and Darrow—everyone who had said it was impossible, that her being with this man couldn't be.

But it was.

She had seen it for herself in the mirror, the two of them joined, connected in a way she'd never been with any other man before. He was changing her, day by day. Her body was transforming, becoming fuller and rounder, her breasts heavier, her sex fuller, always moist and ready for him. She was nearer her estrus with every passing moment.

"C'mere." He pulled her down to him, cupping her face in his hands and kissing the tears that had spilled down her cheeks. "Do'na cry. N'matter what happens, I'll let nothin' come b'tween us, m'love. I promise ye."

She nodded, swallowing past the lump in her throat, wanting to believe him.

"Shhh." He slid her off him, rolling and spooning her from behind, wrapping his big arms around her completely, drawing her body against his. His erection slipped between her thighs, riding up and down the seam of her sex.

"I love ye, Donal," she whispered, leaning her head back against his shoulder, seeing their vision in the looking glass, her expression of pleasure crossed with pained surprise when he impaled her on his length, settling her deep in the saddle of his hips.

"And I love ye," he murmured, kissing her lips as he began to move. He rocked into her from behind, keeping her caught against him, completely contained, her arms crossed over her breasts, his hands cupping them, restraining her from any movement.

She could thrash and writhe and squirm, but to no avail. She was his.

"Donal," she cried, feeling him throbbing inside of her, filling every available bit of space. "Oh Donal, m'love, aye, aye..."

"Tell me," he whispered, his lips against her ear, hips moving, their bodies slapping together. "Tell me yer mine."

"Aye," she panted, surrendering, knowing it was truer than he might ever know. Even if she had to be parted from him, she would belong to him, always. "Aye, Donal, aye, I'm yers, always, always..."

Her words made him drive in deeper, the wet sound of their bodies moving together filling the room. Donal kneaded the flesh of her breasts in his big hands, pinching her nipples, making them pucker and ache.

"Please," she pleaded with him, the sensation between her legs almost unbearable, something coiled tight in her belly, waiting to snap. She couldn't stand much more. "Oh Donal, I beg ye, please, please..."

"What do ye want, m'love?" he asked softly, his teeth capturing her earlobe, biting down gently, making her cry out. "Tell me what ye want."

"I want ye," she cried, writhing in his arms on the bed, undulating her hips, trying to take more of him, all of him, swallow every bit of him up. "Och, please, I want ye, I want to feel ye fill me. I want yer seed. I need it, please, give it t'me!"

She felt his body tense, both of his hands sliding down from her breasts, over her belly, reaching between her legs to cup her mound. Kirstin gasped when he rolled to his back, taking her with him, parting her legs as he thrust up from underneath. She saw the four posters of the bed, the high ceiling above, as he drove her upwards toward it, his fingers playing between the wet, swollen lips of her sex.

"Ahhhh! God!" She shuddered as he made fast, furious circles against the sensitive button at the top of her crevice, sending shooting stars through her body.

"Give it t'me," he growled, bucking his hips up fast and hard, pounding into her, an impossible rhythm. "It's mine, Kirstin. Yer mine. Give it t'me."

"Aye!" She howled and shuddered, arching on top of him as her climax overtook her. Her body shook on top of his, both of them slick and slippery with sweat, her sex clamping down hard around his throbbing shaft.

"Och, lass, yer cunny!" he gasped, and she cried out again when he rolled her once more, this time all the way over to her belly, crushing her with his weight as he spread her velvety thighs with the hard, muscled press of his own, opening her completely to the incessant, aching pound of his cock.

"Donal!" she gasped, breathless, unable to say anything else as he grabbed her shoulders, giving two last, hard thrusts and then collapsed on her completely with the force of his trembling weight. His seed burst deep and hot in her belly, white, pulsing rivers of the stuff, so much it spilled out of her. She could feel it sliding down her slit, soaking the bedding beneath them. The maids would know what had happened there, she knew.

And she didn't care.

"Yer mine." Donal wrapped himself around her, still stroking his half-hard member in and out of her slick slit, as if he couldn't stop the primal motion. "I will'na let ye go. I will'na e'er accept another woman in m'life, as m'wife. I can'na."

She nodded, closing her eyes, feeling tears slip down her cheeks onto the mattress coverlet. He eased himself slowly off, a moment she lamented, every time, before pulling her close against him again, spooning her. She saw their reflection in the mirror, Donal's leg over both of hers, thick arms cradling her, making her seem small in them, as if he might be able to hide her, keep her from the world.

But it was out there, just past the locked door. They couldn't deny it forever.

That made her remember Sibyl and Raife and she chuckled to herself at Donal's simple solution. Why had they not done it before?

"Do ye think they're still locked in yer chancery?" Kirstin asked, knowing he'd understand who she meant.

"Probably." Donal grinned, brushing her hair away from her face and kissing her flushed cheek. "Not that they'll care. I'll likely have t'send in Aiden and Angus t'drag 'em out in the mornin'."

"They're leavin' in the morning." Kirstin's heart ached at the thought. Her family was going home, back to the den. Her pack would be complete again. Except she wouldn't be with them. It felt as if she were being split in two.

"Aye." His hand played in her hair, taking a strand between his fingers and twirling it idly around her nipple. "Are ye sad yer not goin' wit'em?"

"No." It wasn't quite true—she was sad, but not regretful, and the latter was what he was really asking about. She didn't regret her decision to stay, even not knowing what would happen.

"I'm expectin' a dispensation from King Henry wit'in a fortnight." He kissed her shoulder, rubbing his stubble there, making her shiver.

"Yer also expectin' yer bride t'arrive wit'in a fortnight," she reminded him softly. "Will't be a race t'see which gets 'ere first?"

"She's n'bride o'mine," he growled, brow knitted. "I did'na choose 'er. I chose ye."

"She did'na get t'choose either," she murmured, thinking of Sibyl, who had come to Scotland to find herself betrothed to a cruel tyrant. "Remember, she's an Englishwoman, comin' into a strange land, to marry a man she does'na know."

"You've an awful lotta sympathy fer a woman who wants t'take yer place?"

Kirstin shrugged. "We do'na know what she wants."

"Well I know what I want." He moved a hand down to cup her mound and she let out a soft sigh of pleasure, turning her face to his and snaking an arm behind his head to pull his mouth to her.

This man was hers. She didn't know if it would be forever, or just for now, but however long it lasted, she intended to make the most of every single moment.

Chapter Seven

"She's goin't'need a shave!" Giggles ensued, the high-pitched sort of laughter shared by women whose intentions were both wicked and cruel. "Wanna bring 'er a blade?"

"Hush!" Moira waved the young maidservants out of the room, closing the door behind them after ushering them through. Gayle gsve Kirstin a wicked, gap-tooth grin before the door slammed shut.

Kirstin didn't move from her place by the fire, still rolled in her plaid, staring into the flames. The room was warm, but she shivered, as if from fever. She knew the signs. Her time was coming, and soon. She would change then. She had no choice. The giggling maidservants who had laughed and poked fun weren't wrong, after all. She was abhorrent, a monster, something sick and twisted and wrong.

She couldn't blame the girls for being disgusted by her.

She wouldn't blame Donal for not wanting her.

What man would?

"Pay'em n'mind, lass." Moira picked up a poker to stoke the fire. "D'ye need anythin'?"

"Nuh." Kirstin sat, pulling the ends of her plaid up around her shoulders and glancing out the window at the setting sun. The moon would rise soon, full and beautiful—and she would be trapped. Trapped by her body, by her own nature. Trapped into her life as a wulver woman.

She should just return home, as Sibyl had begged her to before she left, and find a wulver warrior to settle with, to love and raise pups with—even if no other man besides Donal could ever be her one true mate.

But she knew, there was no wulver warrior who could make her feel the way Donal did. She didn't understand it, nor did she question it. Her nature might have been at odds with her heart's desire, but she trusted her instincts, and every fiber of her being told her that Donal was the man she was meant to be with. It was the only reason she had stayed here in this castle with the MacFalons, willing to withstand all the whispers and jibes.

To be with Donal, her one true mate, her only true love.

She'd said a tearful goodbye not too long ago once Darrow was ready to travel. Sibyl hadn't yet told Raife her secret, even though he'd stopped being a stubborn fool and had finally forgiven her. Too many things could go wrong before she started to show, Sibyl insisted. She'd wait until Raife noticed the physical changes in her body before telling him she was expecting his bairn.

"You'll come to me, when it's my time?" Sibyl had whispered to Kirstin as they hugged goodbye.

"A'course, *banrighinn*," Kirstin assured her, not knowing if she would be able to make it to the den to attend the birth of the wulver heir or not. She didn't know anything for sure—except that she was going to change, and there was nothing she could do about it.

"I have the book." Sibyl kept her voice low. "Laina's excited about something Moira told us about the silvermoon. I have some of it transplanted in a pot, and a gathered a great deal of it to take home and dry. Mayhaps the book will give us the key to the change..."

"Mayhaps," Kirstin had agreed, hugging Laina too, who was anxious to get back to her bairn. She truly hoped Sibyl would be able to translate the book they'd found in the first den well enough to find something useful, something that would allow wulver women to gain some modicum of control over their bodies during estrus and birthing, but she couldn't count on it.

Her own change was coming, and she would have to deal with it.

"'Tis almos'time." Moira said, sounding reluctant to mention it, and Kirstin knew she was. This wasn't the first time they'd had an unpredictable wulver woman in their midst.

"Aye." Kirstin sighed and stood, tucking her plaid into her belt as a knock came on the door.

"I'm 'ere fer t'she-wolf." Gregor stood in the doorway, sneering at Kirstin as she straightened her shoulders and tried to put on a brave, public face, prepared to face this horrible humiliation. He took a leery step back as Kirstin approached and she almost laughed. It was true, she could have torn the man's throat out in an instant, the moment she turned.

"Nuh, I'll take 'er down." Moira insisted, linking her arm with Kirstin's and leading her out of the room. "T'isn't fer t'likes'o'ye."

"Lock 'er up good!" Gregor called after the women as they made their way down the hallway. "We a'ready lost one laird—not gonna lose another!"

As if Kirstin ever would have hurt Donal, in any form, human or wolf. But she didn't say anything as she and Moira made their way down the stairs. She expected to be led to the dungeon—where else would she be locked up? But Moira turned and led her down the hall, stopping outside the door of Donal's chancery.

"He wanted t'see ye... a'fore t'change..." Moira knocked softly on the door and Kirstin's heart broke when Donal opened it.

"Nuh, I can'na..." Kirstin took a step back, but Donal already had her in his arms, pulling her into the room and locking the door, shutting Moira out.

"Aye, lass, ye can and ye will..." Donal buried his face and hands in Kirstin's long, dark hair. "I want ye, I *need* ye..."

"Aye," she whispered, knowing just how he felt, unable to hide her own feelings, not here, in his arms. "Time's almos'up, ye ken?"

"Aye." He lifted his face to look into her eyes, searching there for some answer, some solution to their strange dilemma. "Lemme look at ye."

"I'm sorry," she whispered, feeling tears stinging her eyes, swallowing around a lump in her throat. "I wish I was someone else fer ye, some*thin'* else..."

"Nuh, lass. Do'na say't." Donal groaned, wrapping thick, strong arms around her waist, pulling her body in tight to his. "Ye're e'rythin' I've e'er wanted."

Kirstin shook her head, but her throat was closed with pain and heartache—and her impending change. She couldn't speak. She would lose the ability entirely soon.

"You're m'only love, and if I can'na'ave ye..."

"Shhh." Kirstin couldn't stand any more words and she was grateful when Donal's mouth found hers. This was a language she understood. Her arms went around his neck, fingers playing in the hair curling at the nape, his big hands moving over her tunic and plaid as if he could memorize her with his palms.

She wanted him, was desperate for him. If only he would take her and make her his own, mark her—marry her. She was a wulver, and wanted his claim, more than anything, but she knew it was the one thing she might never have.

Kirstin knew she should have listened to Sibyl's sensible advice. If anyone knew what it was like to be caught between two worlds, it was Sibyl. Donal was laird of his clan, and now he was promised to another—Cecilia Witcombe, a highborn, English lady, a woman who would arrive this week, a "gift" from King Henry VII.

The contract, arranged by the English king so he could secure the border, was binding. Even if Donal had not signed it, his brother had already agreed to give part of his lands to the English king in exchange for an English bride. So it was an English bride Donal would have.

The king's logic was sound—if the Scots married the English, it seemed reasonable they'd stop killing each other in the borderlands. It was a plan that had been set in motion when Sibyl had come to Scotland to marry Alistair, and one King Henry seemed determined to carry through with. The woman he chose seemed to matter not as all, as long as she was an English lady. It was a perfectly rational solution—but the heart didn't always follow the logical plans set forth by the mind, even the mind of a king.

It had surprised her that King Henry had simply chosen another Englishwoman to take Sibyl's place, rather than forcing her to marry Donal instead of his brother, Alistair. But mayhaps he knew it would bring the wrath of the wulvers down on the crown, because Sibyl was Raife's, and their pack leader wasn't about to let anyone separate them, whether he was the King of England or the Pope.

Now that he'd finally stopped being angry with her for risking life and limb, at any rate.

While Clan MacFalon had welcomed Alistair's younger brother, Donal, as their new laird, and King Henry had made him warden of the Middle March—that responsibility came with more than just a title, she knew. Sibyl's heart had led her astray, from the life of a lady to living in a wolf's den, and her advice to Kirstin before they'd departed had been sensible, even if they both knew it was useless to argue with what the heart wanted.

"Come back with us," Sibyl had pleaded. "Find a wulver to love. They are all good, strong men. Any of them would make a good mate for you. Lorien has eyes for you."

Kirstin had nodded her agreement. In her head, she knew it was true. She should find a nice, wulver warrior and settle down, like the rest of the wulver women. Lorien was a fine wulver, and they'd been together a few times, before she'd left the den, before she'd met The MacFalon. She could return to the den and make a family with him. Every wulver had a true mate—but not all wulvers found them. Sometimes, Sibyl had told her, you had to settle for something else. That "something else" would be a mate that wasn't true.

She knew wulver women who had done just that. They lived comfortable, if a bit bland, lives. Other women, like Beitrus, had refused to settle. She had never found her true mate. An old woman now, she was unlikely to ever find him. So Kirstin knew she had choices. She could leave Castle MacFalon, try to find happiness with a wulver like Lorien, or some other wulver warrior.

There was just one problem with that.

None of them were Donal.

None of them were her one, true mate.

The man had found his way into her heart and she couldn't stop her feelings, no matter how hard she tried. And she had tried. She'd thrown herself into caring after Darrow—the reason she'd come to the MacFalon castle in the first place—until they'd gone back to the den. Then, she'd thrown herself into helping Moira and the rest of the servants, learning the daily workings of the castle. This is what she'd done at home, after all, and came naturally to her.

But none of it had distracted her from Donal.

He was everywhere she went, everywhere she looked, that devilish smile and those dancing eyes. She told herself—often—that the man was, well, just a man. He wasn't a wulver. He wasn't her kind. He would never be able to understand, let alone tolerate, her ways. Kirstin didn't have a choice, not like the wulver men. They could change at will, could even transform into half-man, half-wolf, but wulver women didn't have that luxury.

Wulver women's bodies were tied inextricably to their moon cycles. When they went into heat, they changed into their full wolf form, and when they did, they were unpredictable. Kirstin's life had always been ruled by the moon. Unlike Laina, who had hated that fact and tried her best to find a way to change it, Kirstin had always accepted her lot in life as a wulver.

Until now.

"We are what we are," that's what Raife always said, and it was true. You couldn't spend your life wishing you were someone, or something, else. It was a recipe for heartache.

But that was just what she'd done, Kirstin realized, clinging to Donal, wishing she could stop what was coming. She wanted to blame him, for being so kind, so generous, so damned handsome and irresistible, but she knew better. It wasn't Donal's fault. The man hadn't done anything untoward, hadn't made any advances. He had been honorable—until she practically attacked him at the spring in the first den.

It was, shamefully, all on her. It was her own wild heart that had betrayed her.

Now she was tied to him, utterly in love with him, and she knew it was hopeless. Kirstin knew Sibyl's logical advice would have been easier to follow a month ago, before she'd let herself fall for this man. Kirstin should have returned to the wulvers' den with her family. She should have ignored the calling of her heart to his, should have denied her feelings, should have turned and walked away.

Kirstin remembered her home fondly, with some measure of homesickness, but she knew, in her heart, she would miss this man more. But when Donal had taken his brother's place as laird of clan MacFalon, he had, in turn, assumed his brother's responsibility to "marry the border." To join the English and the Scots, as King Henry VII had instructed him to.

Even if Donal was in love with another woman.

Or, another wulver.

That clearly didn't matter to the heads of state.

What the heart wanted had to be second to what the crown wanted.

"I should go." Kirstin tried to disengage herself from him, but he held her fast in the circle of his arms. To be fair, she didn't try too hard to get away. She spent too little time in the man's arms, and could have spent an eternity there. Since that first morning at the spring when she had fallen into his arms like some lovesick teen and confessed her affection for him, she had found herself taking every opportunity she could to be with him.

"I do'na want ye t'go, lass," he murmured, hands lost in the thick mass of her hair. "I'm n'afraid of ye. Stay wit' me."

She wanted to, more than anything, but there was more than just his betrothal to an English bride standing in their way.

Every time she thought of Lady Cecilia Witcombe, the Earl of Witcombe's only daughter, on her way to marry the laird of clan MacFalon, it made her physically ill. Not that it mattered, Kirstin knew. The king would never approve a marriage between a man and a wulver woman, even if the king himself had once bedded one. There was a big difference between bedding a wulver and marrying one, Raife had said, and he was right.

She and Donal had talked in circles about it, and they kept coming around to the same point.

"Ye know I can'na stay." Kirstin lifted her face to look at him, at those stormy eyes, his brow knitted with worry. "Y'er t'marry another."

"Do'na remin'me." He groaned, his expression pained, as if her words had stabbed him in the gut.

Because King Henry had denied the dispensation Donal had requested.

Donal sent another, but Kirstin didn't hold much hope that it would be granted after the first had been turned down. They had to accept what was, as Raife always said.

She was a wulver. He was a man. A man set to marry another woman, upon order of the English king.

"She'll arrive soon," Kirstin reminded him, reminded herself. "In another day, mayhaps two."

Donal nodded miserably. They both knew it was true, even if they didn't want to think about it.

"Ye lead yer clan, Donal," Kirstin reminded him of this, too. "Ye mus' do what's right fer the greatest good."

"Ye're m'greatest good, lass." He cupped her face in his hands, searching her eyes. "Ye're m'vera heart."

His words broke her. How could she do this? How could she feel this way, knowing she couldn't be with him, and still stand? She didn't know.

"I can'na stay wit' ye," she whispered, her lower lip trembling, in spite of her self-admonition to stay strong. "I can'na stay."

"Then I'll come wit ye."

And there it was again. They went around and around, in circles. It was impossible. He couldn't live in the wulver den with her, and she couldn't live in the MacFalon castle with him.

"Yer family's 'ere," she urged. "Yer obligation's 'ere. Yer wife..."

They both winced at the word "wife." Kirstin didn't like to think about another woman coming anywhere near this man. Even in her human form, Kirstin's instincts turned animal at the thought.

"But me *mate* is *'ere.*" He kissed her cheek, the tear that slipped down it caught on his lips. "I want ye, Kirstin. I *claim* ye. D'y'hear me? Yer *mine.* Ye'll *always* be mine."

"I wish t'were true," she whispered as he kissed her other cheek, another tear.

"'Tis true! We can make a life together, lass."

"How?" she pleaded, wishing she could see a way around it. "If ye marry me, King Henry'll come down on all our heads. 'T'will be the end of t'wolf pact and the end of the possibility of peace in t'borderlands. I can'na be responsible fer that."

"Let me worry 'bout that," he insisted.

"And then what?" she cried. "Ye live wit' a woman ye hafta lock up once a month because she changes into a wolf?"

"'T'wouldn't be the firs' time a man had to deal with a she-devil once a month," he replied with a grin.

"Donal!" Kirstin laughed. She couldn't help it. He always made her laugh, took her outside herself. It was the first thing that had attracted her to him. That and those big, dancing, mischievous, blue-grey eyes.

"But m'love..." She turned her wet eyes up to him, hating herself for saying it out loud, but it was true, and it was the one thing she knew they couldn't change. "I told ye. There'd be n'children. I can'na give ye heirs. We could'na mate while I was... while..."

She flushed, feeling the heat in her face, in her limbs, at the thought of mating with this man, as woman or wulver. The look in his eyes told her he was thinking about it, too. Lately it was all she ever thought about. Her body was so close to estrus, she was aroused almost constantly.

"Nothin' would keep me from ye, lass." That dark, determined look had come into his eyes. The man could be stubborn. "Nothin'."

"Och, Donal." Kirstin sighed, shaking her dark head. "Ye can'na come wit me, and I can'na stay. 'Tis impossible."

"'T'isn't impossible," he insisted.

"When I change, then ye'll see." She lowered her head, not wanting to look at him, to see the expression on his face. She hated herself, hated her very nature. If she could have swallowed some magic potion in that moment that would have given her the ability not to change into a wolf, she would have done it in an instant. "Ye do'na really want me, Donal. Ye will'na, once ye see..."

"I *do* want ye." His grip tightened, rocking her in his arms. "I'll always want ye, whether ye're a woman or a wolf or a... mouse!"

That made her laugh through her tears, but it didn't erase the reality of what was.

The fact remained, Kirstin couldn't be this man's wife, no matter how much they both might want it. And she was sure that Lady Cecilia Witcombe was a beautiful woman who would make Donal the perfect wife. And most importantly, she wouldn't turn into a beast once a month on a whim. But if the woman had been in front of her, Kirstin would have torn her throat out without a second thought.

That made her an animal.

In fact, she was an animal.

And that was the problem.

"Nuh!" Kirstin choked, voice muffled against his chest, but she hardly had any breath left, and there were no more words, no more arguments to be made. She felt it happening, her strength leaving her limbs.

"Aye, lass," Donal insisted, his mouth finding hers, sparking a fire in her that was undeniable and unquenchable. They went to the floor, slowly sinking together, and Kirstin knew there was no stopping it. Donal would see for himself, and it would be soon. Far too soon.

"Open up!" Gregor pounded on the door from the outside.

Kirstin barely heard him. Donal's mouth crushed hers and she welcomed the weight of him as they tore at each other's clothes. He was shirtless, and then so was she, her plaid slipping easily off her body, leaving her naked beneath him, more than ready.

The pounding came again.

"G'way, boy!" Donal growled, nuzzling the soft hollow of Kirstin's throat before moving down to her breasts, making her moan when he grabbed handfuls of her hair, pulling her head back so he could get better access.

She wanted him, but she couldn't have him.

Her body burned for him, but it was impossible.

She longed to speak his name, but all that would come out of her throat was a plaintive, keening wail.

"Kirstin, m'love," Donal whispered, and she felt him, eager to enter her, almost as hungry as she was.

She howled when he slid inside her, nails digging into his back as he rutted deep and hard, speaking words into her ear that turned her blood to fire. He pounded into her with such force she could barely breathe, but she didn't care. There were no bodily functions more important than this one in the moment, nothing more compelling than the ache between her thighs.

"Och, Kirstin, yer *mine*," he said throatily, slamming into her again and again. She whimpered her agreement as he grabbed her leg, flipping it over in front of him, twisting her hips to the side, her torso still facing front. She gasped at the new position, how big he felt inside her like this.

"Ahhhh yer cunny is so tight!" he grunted, pumping faster, hips moving at lightning speed. Kirstin felt it happening. Her climax was rising as fast as the moon. Through the window, she saw the sun had sunk below the horizon, and the pale face of the moon was coming up in the sky.

She met his eyes in the dimness, the light from the window fading, no lamp lit. She wondered what he could see, but she didn't have to ask. She saw it in his eyes, the dawning realization, the slow shift from desire to horror. She was changing. There was nothing she could do to stop it.

Kirstin tried to run, but Donal held her fast in his hands, grabbing her hips as she rolled to her belly. He was on top of her, so close, rutting from behind, unwilling to stop. And so was she. Her body shuddered with both pleasure and her change as her sex spasmed around his length. Donal gave a low roar of surprise as her muscles milked his seed, drawing it up from his sack in thick, pulsing waves.

She trembled and howled, the sound filling the room, so loud it felt as if it could shake the whole castle. The steady pounding on the door outside went on and on. It sounded as if they were taking a battering ram to the door out there.

Donal collapsed on her, hand moving in her hair, and then, in fur. Her ears pricked, her hearing keener now, her vision, too. She saw everything her human eyes could not, the shadows fading, the edges of things growing sharp. She heard the sound of Gregor panting outside the door as they struggled to ram it open. She felt the heat of Donal's breath on her fur, the weight of the man who had previously been crushing her, now like nothing.

The pounding had stopped but now the whole castle seemed to shake with the blows as Gregor applied something to the door again and again.

"Kirstin," Donal whispered, his hands cupping her face, finding fur and jowls and soft, twitching ears.

She whined, rolling to her side, their eyes locked. Donal pet her gently, stroking her muzzle, her neck, his expression pained. She'd tried to tell him, but he hadn't believed her, not really. Who would believe it, unless they'd seen it with their very own eyes? He'd seen her as a wolf only once before—and never like this. He'd never actually watched her change.

Kirstin put a dark, grey paw up on the man's chest, seeing her own limbs gone, replaced with that of a wolf. No more hands to grasp with. It was as it ever was, as it had always been. There was nothing she could do to stop or change it, and she knew he would finally understand this now. He would turn away from her in horror and disgust, and she wouldn't blame him.

She braced herself for it. Her emotions were even more powerful now, as a wolf. Everything intensified. Even her love for him. Her desire, too. It broke her and she howled again, a sound full of pain and longing. The pounding against the door stopped for a moment. So did everything else. Donal stared at her like he was seeing her for the first time.

"Shhh," he urged, his fingers lost in her fur, trailing over her ribs. "Yer safe wit' me."

Safe? Kirstin showed him a canine version of a smile, dark lips drawn back from her teeth. He seemed to understand, a smile reaching both his lips and his eyes as he bent his dark head to touch hers.

"Och, yer so beautiful," he whispered. "Yer t'most beautiful creature I've e'er seen."

A great cracking sound shattered the moment, and Gregor spilled into the room, dragging a set of chains behind him.

"He's wit' t'wolf!" Gregor called over his shoulder.

"Do'na touch 'er!" Donal roared, protecting Kirstin's body with his own as Gregor grabbed the wolf by the scruff of its neck.

The man's hand sank into her flesh and Kirstin howled and snapped at him.

"Let 'er go!" Gregor insisted, pulling the chains behind him.

Kirstin heard the sound of them and winced. She couldn't bear it. Even the thought of being locked up now made her growl and buck. When she was human, she would have gone docilely, but now that she was wolf, there would be none of that. Her freedom was paramount.

"Kirstin, listen t'me," Donal insisted, trying to control her scrambling limbs and snapping jaws. "We'll nuh hurt ye!"

But she knew better. Every fiber in her being knew she had to escape the man with the chains and the locks, even if another part of her understood Donal's pleas. Donal loved her—she felt it emanating from him in waves. There was no escaping the feeling, no misinterpreting it. That was the one thing about turning wolf—there was no more room for error when it came to things like that. The world became far more black and white, easy to negotiate.

For weeks, Kirstin had waffled, torn, not knowing what to do. For weeks, she had cursed herself for loving this man, wishing things could be different. Now, as she looked into his beautiful blue-grey eyes, things became suddenly, incredibly clear.

"Hold 'er so I can get this collar on!" Gregor insisted, dragging the chains close. "We've gotta cage t'bitch!"

Donal hit the man. It happened fast. One moment, Donal's arms were around her, his hands in her fur, and the next, he'd stood and brought his fist hard across the man's face. Gregor howled and fought back, and the men tussled, wrestling each other to the floor.

It was the only opening Kirstin needed and she took it.

There were more men in the hallway, but she was faster than they were, by far. One of them nearly clipped her tail with his sword, but she sidestepped, escaping through the breezeway. She used the bench in the garden to launch herself over the wall. It was an eight foot drop and she took that too, whimpering as she landed, feeling the whistle of an arrow beside her ear as she ran for the forest.

It was full dark now but she saw everything. The world was hers at night, full of scent and possibility. She stopped at the edge of the woods, seeing the castle being lit up, room by room. The alarm had been sounded. They would be looking for her.

Donal would be looking for her.

Kirstin threw her head back and howled, hoping he could hear her, hoping some small part of him understood if he did. She couldn't tell him, not like this. It was all she could do.

She turned and ran through the forest, heading toward home. Toward hope.

Her heart pounded, and she howled again, thinking only of Donal. There was no way to convey her message except through the plaintive, keening wail of a wolf.

A wolf, she prayed, she would no longer be, when she returned to him.

If only he would wait for her.

Chapter Eight

"Bloody wulvers," Lord Eldred swore. "This she-wolf is the most evasive one I've ever run across."

Kirstin took some pride in his words as she padded silently behind the trees. She could see the light of their fire from this distance and smell the roasting rabbit. They'd burnt it, which wasn't too pleasant. Her ears picked up their words floating downwind to her.

"How're we supposed to know if it's a wulver or a wolf again?" One of Lord Eldred's captains asked. It was the one called William, she remembered. She'd met him that first day. The day she'd met Donal. Thinking of Donal made her ache and she tried to shake it away, venturing closer to them, careful to avoid making any sudden movements or noise.

"All wulvers have blue eyes," Lord Eldred replied. "Real wolves are born with blue eyes, but adult wolves don't ever have blue eyes."

"How do you know so much about them?" the other captain asked, gnawing on a burnt bit of rabbit. Kirstin's stomach growled but she ignored it. That one was named Geoffrey, she remembered. Seeing them all together made her remember that first day, when she'd been trapped up in the tree and Donal had come to her rescue. It hurt to think of Donal, all the way to her bones. She was still in heat, and her whole body felt swollen, aching for him.

"I've been hunting wulvers since before you were born," Lord Eldred snorted, poking the fire with a long stick. Sparks flew up into the night.

"There are wulvers in England?" Geoffrey asked, chewing thoughtfully. "I've never seen one."

"To my knowledge, this is the last pack of wulvers in existence," Lord Eldred told him.

"So this female we're looking for—she can't turn into one of those half-wolf things?" William mused, stretching his boots toward the fire.

"No, females cannot turn into halflings." Lord Eldred sighed. "Have you not paid attention to anything I've said? You two are woefully unprepared to hunt these animals. You could learn a thing or two from Salt and Sedgewick."

Kirstin wondered about the two Lord Eldred spoke of, the men with the funny, unlikely names. Were these two also wulver hunters?

"So what do we do with her when we find her?" Goeffrey threw a bone into the fire, picking up another piece of meat to gnaw on.

"Sometimes I could swear you're deaf, young captain." Lord Eldred sighed, running a hand through his salt and pepper hair. "I already told you. After she leads us to the wolf den, we kill her. Then we send word to King Henry to call up his waiting army from the borderlands so we can kill them all."

Kirstin froze, staring at the man poking a stick at the fire, her hackles up out of her control. She felt a growl rising in her throat and swallowed it down. The urge to attack—to protect her pack—was overwhelming. She sat back on her haunches, teeth bared, but no sound come out of her. She made sure of that. She wouldn't dare let them find her, not now.

She'd always had a bad feeling about Lord Eldred Lothienne, and now, she finally knew why.

"What about the wolf pact? The MacFalon thinks it's still in effect." Geoffrey spit a piece of gristle into the fire. "If he hears we've killed a wulver..."

"Especially *his* she-wulver..." William's face clouded at the thought.

"Who's going to tell him?" Lord Eldred sneered, looking between the two young captains. "You?"

"No, m'lord..." William held up his hands in a warding off gesture, looking genuinely scared and Geoffrey affirmed his sentiments, assuring his Lord that he wouldn't tell anyone either.

"Besides, even if word did get back to him," Lord Eldred said with a shrug. "By the time he found us, it would be too late. The wulvers would be dead."

Kirstin's body went cold. Her paws felt numb. She could barely feel the forest floor. King Henry planned to kill the wulvers? She had to warn her pack. She had to tell Donal that he'd been deceived.

"So this she-wolf, she'll turn back into a woman?" Geoffrey mused. "A real woman? With woman parts?"

"Once her estrus has ended." Lord Eldred glanced up at the sky, cloudless, the moon high above. "Another day perhaps. You've seen her for yourself, Geoffrey. She's exceptional."

"Yes. I was just wondering..." He cleared his throat, glancing over at William across the fire. "Maybe we could force her to change into human form? Chain her up and uh, have a little fun—before we get rid of her?"

"After she leads us to the wolf den, of course." William interjected.

Kirstin's breath caught, her eyes flashing at the two English captains. She could have bounded into their camp and ripped them to pieces—and she wanted to. The two young men she wasn't worried about. She would have both of their throats torn out before they knew what was happening. It was Lord Eldred she had to concern herself with. She didn't dare attack while he had two free hands and was able to face her.

"You like to live dangerously, my young friends." Lord Eldred chuckled. "And if she turned back into a wolf in the middle of your 'fun?' As a wolf, she outweighs you by a hundred pounds and could tear your throat out with her teeth in less than a second."

Bloody well right, Kirstin thought with a low snarl. She caught herself, hoping no one had heard it. She often forgot how little humans paid attention to the things their senses told them.

"So, no fun then?" William sighed. "I'd like to say I bed a wulver."

"You'd be in good company. King Henry himself has indulged." Lord Eldred grinned. "Unfortunately, you can't rape a wulver woman in human form. She can turn back into a wolf at will. So if it was a woman's hot cunt you were looking to fill, you'd be out of luck."

"So King Henry bed a wulver... when she was... uh..." Geoffrey looked at William and the realization dawned on both of them at once.

"In wolf form?" Lord Eldred's grin widened. "Yes, indeed he did. The issue from that union runs the wolf den she'll lead us to. If we can find the bitch. I hope Salt and Sedgewick are having better luck than we."

Lord Eldred scowled into the woods. For a moment, Kirstin thought he was looking directly at her and she shrank back behind a tree.

"Do you think we've really lost her?" William mused.

"Mayhaps she's back at the den already," Geoffrey speculated.

"No. I believe she's still actively evading us," Lord Eldred's gaze scanned the woods—Kirstin looked at him from behind her tree. He hadn't seen her then. But he sensed something. "I think she knows we're on her trail."

"Mayhaps Salt and Sedgewick have found her," Geoffrey said with a shrug. "They may already know where the den is."

"It could very well be, but they haven't sent my hawk." Lord Eldred's brow lowered as he looked between his young captains. "You did remind them to send my hawk, if they found the bitch or the den, didn't you?"

"We told them," both Geoffrey and William exclaimed at once, like lads reassuring their father their chores were already done.

Kirstin didn't remember Lord Eldred bringing more than his two captains to the MacFalon castle. He had more men working for him, then, she mused. This Salt and Sedgewick. In secret. Behind Donal's back, working all along for King Henry, who *did* want the wulvers dead, it turned out. Just like Alistair had claimed.

She remembered Lorien bringing word back that the king was upholding the wolf pact. He had been lied to, she realized. They'd all been lied to.

"They're amazing creatures, if entirely unholy," Lord Eldred's gaze still scanned the tree line, making Kirstin sink even further back into the darkness. "Both more than men and more than wolves."

"But the women!" William gave a little grunt, shifting in front of the fire. "Hotter than the blazes."

"I'd still like to get my cock in that one's mouth." Geoffrey sighed, tossing the last bone into the fire and taking out a flask.

Lord Eldred laughed. "She'd snap it off and eat it as a treat."

That was true enough. Kirstin would have been happy to oblige. It took all her energy to resist it, even now.

"Get some sleep, lads." Lord Eldred tossed his stick into the fire. "Tomorrow we meet with Moraga."

"Again?" William frowned.

"I'd like to get my cock in *that* one's mouth, too." Geoffrey took a long swig from his flask.

"She's a witch." William shuddered. "I'd be afraid she'd turn it to stone."

"Could do worse." Geoffrey chuckled. "At least you'd always be hard and ready to please, eh?"

"She wouldn't touch either of you with a Maypole," Lord Eldred scoffed, shaking his head.

"Do we have to meet up with her?" William asked, hurrying on to explain when Lord Eldred gave him a speculative look. "I mean, can't you go alone? We're supposed to meet up with Sedgewick and Salt the day after tomorrow at the old well."

"Scared, young William?" Lord Eldred's eyes flashed, the corners of his mouth curving into a sly smile. "You know, lads, we wouldn't even have to be out here tonight if you hadn't lost the wulver party when they left with that book."

He knows about the book? Kirstin's heart raced in her chest, faster than when she was chasing rabbits. *How?* But of course, he'd been spying. She'd been so busy falling in love with Donal, she hadn't paid any attention to her instincts about Lord Eldred Lothienne. She'd done nothing except avoid Lord Eldred, when she should have acted on her feelings. She realized, now far too late, that she should have insisted Donal be wary of the man. At the very least, have him watched.

"I have to get my hands on it," Eldred muttered, glowering into the fire.

"What's in it?" Goeffrey asked. "More witches magic?"

"I don't know. That's why I need to get my hands on it, you dolt," Lord Eldred snapped. "But mayhaps Moraga knows of it. At the very least, I can warn her they have it. Mayhaps she can counter whatever they learn from it, if it hinders our plans."

"Your plans, you mean."

"My plans are your plans, Captain." Lord Eldred gave Geoffrey a cool smile, standing and stretching. "Sleep well, lads. We'll see if we can find the she-bitch's trail in the morning. Then we'll meet up with Moraga."

"G'nite, m'lord," called Geoffrey and Lord Eldred slipped into his tent.

Kirstin watched the two captains until the fire burned low. They talked late into the night, about nothing important. She wanted to know more of how they planned to destroy the wulvers, needed to know as much as possible to relay it to Raife when she went back to the wulver den.

It was a dangerous gamble, but she decided she would have to follow them. At least until they met up with the other two men. She needed to know if the wulver den had been discovered. Once she knew that, she would return home and tell her pack they were in danger.

Kirstin shouldn't have expected Moraga to be an old woman, given how the young captains had talked about her, but for some reason, the sight of the shapely blonde shocked her. Moraga welcomed Lord Eldred alone—he'd sent the captains out to wait for Salt and Sedgewick. They weren't due until the morrow, but Eldred had set camp quite a ways from Moraga's cave, near the old MacFalon well. It wasn't until Kirstin saw the woman that she realized why.

The witch wrapped her arms around Lord Eldred's neck and the two of them kissed deeply. The man's hands roamed her English gown. He shoved one of them roughly down the front of it, but the woman didn't protest. Instead, she gave a loud moan, her hips bumping up against his.

Kirstin considered going back to Lord Eldred's camp to wait for Sedgewick and Salt. She had to know if they'd discovered her pack's den. If she was going to be subjected to nothing but the sexual escapades of Lord Eldred and his concubine by staying here, she would rather listen to the bragging and bravado of the two captains while they waited for their comrades to return.

"I take it ye missed me?" Moraga gave a low, throaty laugh when they parted. Her brogue was thick—she was clearly a Scotswoman, and not English, in spite of her dress. Eldred's hand was still stuck down in her cleavage, massaging her breast. Her eyes narrowed as she leaned back slightly in his arms, giving him better access down the front of her dress. "Ye weren't beddin' any wulvers, were ye?"

"Do I look like I have fleas?" Lord Eldred bent his head to kiss the tops of her breasts.

"Good." She gasped when he yanked the front of her dress down, exposing her to him. His mouth fell to suckling her nipple and she moaned. "Ye know I do'na mind ye sleepin' wit' other wenches—as long as ye bring me the good ones so we can share."

Lord Eldred chuckled, moving his mouth to her other nipple, his fingers working the first one. Kirstin's lip curled in disgust. She didn't want to see this. Her gaze skipped around the encampment, looking anywhere but at the kissing, petting couple. There was a pack horse and a riding horse tied nearby. Kirstin had been careful to stay downwind of them both. The woman's camp was surprisingly sumptuous and comfortable. She had a tent up outside the cave, along with a fire pit in front with an iron tripod, a cooking cauldron and table.

"Did ye find the wulver den, then?" Moraga asked. "Are we celebratin'?"

"Not yet." Eldred made a face. "We lost the first party over the creek. And that damned she-wolf has given me the slip all three times I've found and followed her trail."

"I thought ye were a famed wulver hunter?" She gave a throaty laugh when he bit her nipple.

"Mayhaps Sedgewick and Salt have had more luck," he said morosely. "There are no men alive who can track a wulver better than they can—except mayhaps myself. Most men don't even know the wulvers exist, let alone know how to follow them. And if a wulver doesn't want to be tracked, likely the Lord of the Great Hunt himself couldn't track them."

"So ye say." Moraga pulled away from him, covering herself.

"I do have something that will please you, mayhaps, even if I didn't get my hands on that book." Lord Eldred reached into the pack over his shoulder, pulling out a handful of silvermoon. Kirsten could smell it, even from where she stood at the edge of the wood.

"Silvermoon!" Moraga's eyes lit up with delight and she took the bunch from him. "I've ne'er seen it grow anywhere! And what book?"

The witch missed nothing. Kirstin watched the woman expertly bundle the silvermoon for hanging and drying on the little table.

"There was a book." Lord Eldred sighed. "The she-wolf found it snooping down in the first den."

"What first den?" Moraga's blonde head lifted as she looked up from her work.

"There is an ancient wulver den under the MacFalon tombs," Eldred informed her.

"The grotto of Asher and Ardis?" Moraga frowned, her hands slowing in their work. "Ye found the grotto? Where the silvermoon grows?"

"That's where this came from." He nodded at the leaves and branches in her hands. To Kirstin, it looked like he'd pulled a whole plant up by the roots! "That's where she found the book. Some ancient wulver text?"

"Not the Book of the Moon Wives?"

"Yes, that's it."

The witch hissed something under her breath. From a distance, even with her incredible hearing, Kirstin could only make out the word "prophecy," and something about a king with the blood of dragons in his eyes. Was she talking about the red wulver? It was an old prophecy, one that had been passed on to her from her mother, but Kirstin didn't know all of it. Beitrus called him "the devil's savior," but she didn't know what that meant either. Who would want to save a devil?

"They have the book," Lord Eldred said. "But I don't think they know what it really is—or what to do with it."

The witch frowned. "Ye better hope they do'na find out."

"Why?" he asked. "What's in it?"

"The cure fer their curse," she said simply. "Or so I'm told."

If Kirstin had been in human form, she would have gasped out loud, giving away her position. Instead, she just whined, a low, pained sound, even to her ears. She waited to be discovered, but Lord Eldred had his arms around the woman, massaging her breasts again through her gown, and the witch was too busy with the silvermoon to be paying attention to anything else.

The book held the cure to the curse? Kirstin could barely breathe. Was it really true?

She'd almost forgotten why she'd run away from her lover's arms in the first place, given everything she'd discovered in the past day or so. She'd escaped with the bleak hope that Laina and Sibyl had found the cure. Something that could give her control over her change once a month.

"Something that will turn wulvers to men?" Lord Eldred asked. "Permanently?"

"Aye." The witch agreed, working with the silvermoon again. "If'n ye b'lieve the legends. I did'na e'en think the book actually existed."

"Oh, it exists," he assured her.

"Did ye see't fer yerself?" the blonde asked, looking over her shoulder at him.

"No." He shook his head. "But my little bird did."

"Oh, was she a pretty lil bird?" The blonde inquired throatily, abandoning her work and turning in the man's arms to put hers around his neck.

"She sang very sweetly," he agreed with a grin. "Buxom little blonde. Reminded me a bit of you, but she was only about this tall, and had a fetching little gap between her teeth."

Gayle.

So that was who had been spying for him. Kirstin tried to remember what she'd said around the woman. She had definitely been there when Kirstin showed Laina the book. And she'd run straight to Lord Eldred Lothienne to tell him about it, the spying little wench. If Gayle had been in front of her, Kirstin would have torn her throat out without a second thought.

"And ye did not bring 'er to me?" Moraga pouted, disengaging herself from his embrace and turning back to her work on the table. "Ye know I hate't when ye do'na share yer toys."

"Mayhaps when this is done." He watched as she took out a curved-bladed dagger. Kirstin cocked her wolf's head, looking at its new-moon shape, the silver glinting. "And I'm sitting on the English throne, with you beside me. We can have any woman we want between us then."

"Aye." Her eyes glittered in the firelight. "And ye still 'ave t'king's trust?"

"I have them all eating out of the palm of my hand." Eldred chuckled, sounding quite pleased with himself. "King Henry's so distraught over Arthur's death, he's afraid of any threat to his throne. He even considered marrying Catherine of Aragon himself."

"She's jus' a child!" Moraga complained. "And she was a'ready married t'his son."

"He may still be considering the match. I don't know," Eldred replied. "But it was easy to convince him that the king of the wulvers was a threat to his line. Raife is his bastard, after all. He does have a claim."

"And The MacFalon?" The woman sharpened the blade on a whetstone. "He still trusts ye?"

"King Henry told him what I advised," Lord Eldred said. "The MacFalon believes England will honor the wolf pact. He has no idea how many wulver traps I've armed, hidden in his woods. I'm surprised the wulver party didn't run into one. Or that damned she-wolf I've been tracking..."

"And t'English king?" she asked, testing the sharpness of the blade on the side of her thumb. Bright red blood bloomed there. Kirstin could smell it. "He still b'lieves ye wanna kill t'wulvers?"

"Why would he think otherwise? That's what I told him," Lord Eldred scoffed. "Besides, no one hates the wulvers more than I do."

"I wish I could be there t'see't." She chuckled. "T'English king's goin' t'get quite a surprise when an army of wulvers kills 'is men and ye take 'is throne. "

"All of England will rejoice when the rightful heir to the throne sits upon it again." The man's spine straightened, making him even taller in the moonlight.

"Aye, the Tudors used the wulvers and stole the throne," the witch agreed, sucking on her thumb, licking off the blood. "Seems fittin' it'll be taken back t'same way."

"They're all conniving thieves, from the first Arthur on—first king of England, pulls a sword from a stone!" Eldred scoffed. "He had no right to it. Why do you think Henry's so afraid someone's going to take it from him? He knows it isn't his. It's mine."

"Aye," she agreed softly. "Ye fight fire wit' fire, enchantment wit' enchantment."

"I thank my ancestors for the day I met you, my devilish little witch." Lord Eldred put his arms around her waist from behind, pushing her long, corn-colored hair out of the way to kiss her neck.

"Ye've done good wit' the silvermoon, I mus' say. It'll do well to bind the spell," she said, tilting her head to accept his kisses. "As soon as I have t'wulver king's blood, we'll be able t'enchant the wulver army fer yer purposes. Then, they'll follow ye anywhere."

"Good." Lord Eldred slid his hands up to cup the woman's breasts again.

"The she-wolves will'na let them go so easily, ye know," she warned. "They're not warriors, but when they're changed, they're formidable. And I can'na compel t'females."

"I have no need for the women or the pups," he sneered. "My first order will be to have the warriors slaughter them all."

"Ye'll wanna keep one," she suggested. "T'continue t'line?"

"No." He frowned. "Once I have the throne, I'll have no need for the wulver army. We'll dispose of them."

"Ye do not wanna keep them locked up somewhere at t'ready?" she asked. "T'defend yer right to the crown?"

"Mayhaps," he mused, thoughtful. Then he chuckled, dipping his head to gnaw at her neck. "You are an evil wench. I love the way your mind works."

Kirstin watched the woman waving her blade over the silvermoon, incanting something softly in Gaelic. Then she turned in his arms, arching her back, knife still in hand.

"Bare m'breasts, Lord Eldred."

He grinned. "As you wish."

He yanked her already low-cut gown down, letting her large breasts spill free. His mouth went to them immediately, but the witch was impatient.

"Now ye," she insisted. "Take off yer shirt."

Lord Eldred complied, pulling his shirt over his head and tossing it aside. The man was still heavily muscled and the blonde eyed him greedily. Kirstin cringed, knowing she was going to have to witness their lovemaking. But what happened next surprised her.

The witch expertly used the curved blade, tracing the edge over her skin, a line of blood swelling between her breasts, over her heart. She did the same to Lord Eldred. The man didn't even wince.

Kirstin watched as Moraga tipped the blade with their mingled blood, letting it drip onto the bundle of silvermoon that shone, luminescent, in the moonlight. Then she hung it over the fire, the blood falling in fat droplets, sizzling into the flames.

Eldred grabbed Moraga to him, the red liquid on their chests mingling as they kissed in the firelight. Kirstin could smell their blood, coppery and bright. It made her hungry and she considered making a meal of them both. Who would know? She could end Eldred and his line right here, prevent any magic, if there was such a thing, that might compel the wulvers. But it was possible the other two, Sedgewick and Salt, already knew the way to her den.

And Moraga's knife was still close, on the table. Even distracted, Lord Eldred was a formidable foe. What if he managed to slip the blade between Kirstin's ribs before her teeth grazed his neck? If she was dead in the forest, she couldn't warn Raife and her pack of Eldred's arrival. No, she couldn't risk it. She would have to wait for Sedgewick and Salt to arrive on the morrow to find out if they'd discovered the wulver den.

Then, and only then, could she go home.

Kirstin curled her lip in a snarl, although no sound came from her throat, as she watched Lord Eldred put the naked woman up on the table. She had a beautiful body, lush curves and big breasts. Moraga reclined, wrapping her full thighs around him as he stood between them to enter her. Even this sick, twisted display made her think of and miss Donal and their lovemaking. Her estrus was fading, like the waning moon above their heads, but she still wanted him.

Moraga cried out, arching as Lord Eldred began to move, thrusting hard and fast. He leaned over to kiss her, his chest wound, just a scratch, rubbing against hers. Again, Kirstin smelled their blood, still dripping into the fire from the luminescent silvermoon, and from the open gashes on their torsos.

"Taste me." Moraga brought the man's face down to her breast and Eldred gave a low moan as she rubbed his cheeks over her wound, spreading blood like war paint. Their fingers played in the sticky liquid, and they left bloody fingerprints on one another, wherever they touched or grabbed.

Moraga's fingernails raked over the man's chest, making him hiss and cry out. She opened the wound, which had begun to coagulate, watching rivulets of blood run down his ridged abdomen.

"You witch," he growled, quickly withdrawing. He grabbed her hips and rolled her onto her belly on the table, entering her again, this time from behind. He began to rut into her, deep and hard, grunting with every thrust.

Kirstin cringed, watching the woman licking the curved blade still sitting on the table, cleaning it of their blood. She could plainly see the witch's face, her eyes glittering in the firelight.

"M'Lord," Moraga murmured, putting the knife down and gripping the sides of the table. Her voice came in a staccato, broken by Eldred's pounding thrusts. "We're bein' watched."

Kirstin froze. She was right across from them, at the edge of the woods, but surely, she was in the shadows. The witch couldn't possibly see her!

"I don't care," he sneered, but his gaze moved up from his lover's body to scan the tree line. "You should be used to it by now. Besides, my men have their hands to keep them company, if they want to watch—or they can buggar each other for all I care."

Moraga moved so quickly Kirstin barely saw it happen. One moment she was splayed on the table, helpless on her belly, being plundered by Lord Eldred, and the next she was up. Her nude body was sheened with sweat in the firelight as she stood beside the bewildered man who had been so recently inside of her.

"Look," Moraga hissed, turning Eldred's face in Kirstin's direction. *"See."*

She can't see me. Kirstin was sure of it. Neither of them could. But the witch sensed something.

And then, so did Kirstin. She caught their scent. Two men—not Geoffrey and William, she knew their smells by now. It had to be Salt and Sedgewick. She didn't know, not for sure, but she wasn't going to stick around to find out.

Lord Eldred made some bird call, signaling with his hands, and she felt them moving in on her, one from each direction, on either side. It scared her that she hadn't heard their approach. She should have been able to track them.

Kirstin froze, paralyzed, hearing a branch crack to her left, the barest rustle of underbrush on her right. She didn't know if they had arrows pointed at her.

She heard an arrow being knocked. Her heart hammered in her chest and she crouched, low to the ground. That's when she saw the silver glint in the moonlight. Her mind didn't want to see it, didn't want to accept that she was watching the curved, silver blade, still stained with blood, spinning in the light of the fire, two feet above the table it had been sitting on.

The witch was whispering something. Incantations. Kirstin couldn't hear the words, but it was clear, Moraga was controlling the blade. Before she knew what was happening, the knife was sailing through the air, all on its own, heading for Kirstin in the woods.

Lord Eldred made that sound again, more signals to his men, but the blade was faster. She knew she couldn't avoid it, although she'd already turned sideways to run along the tree line, thinking she'd take her chances with whatever archer was trying to shoot an arrow at her in the dark.

The blade was enchanted, and it was headed straight for her.

Kirstin went low, as low as she possibly could, nearly flattening herself against the dirt, limbs splayed. The blade was traveling so fast it whistled past her ears. The curved half-moon grazed her fur, and she felt it zing across her back, piercing her flesh. She could smell her own blood, but she didn't have any idea how bad the wound was.

The knife hit a tree somewhere behind her with a sick thunking sound, quivering like a tuning fork. That sound didn't stop, though—in fact, it got worse—and that's when Kirstin realized… *the blade was trying to pull itself free.* And once it did, the enchanted knife would come for her again. Follow her until it found its mark.

Terrified, Kirstin heard the archer's arrow whistle past her, just as she rolled deeper into the woods, shaking herself to her feet. But it didn't pierce her flesh.

The knife was singing in the tree, its hilt wiggling back and forth like the back end of a fish. Kirstin heard the archer cock another arrow, but she was gone, running faster than she ever had in her life, before he could draw his bow.

Chapter Nine

Lorien was one of the scouts on duty, and Kirstin was relieved to see his big, hulking black form as she neared the edges of the familiar forest. She was exhausted from running. Her sides ached with it. But still, she followed him in with a new burst of speed. Two more scouts caught their scent—must have smelled her urgency—and followed them to the hidden entrance of their mountain den. Lorien growled at the sentry, but the half-wolf, half-man standing guard knew her well. She'd been at the birth of two of his mate's pups.

Once they were free in the tunnels, Kirstin ran again, Lorien loping along beside her, giving her concerned, sidelong glances. She knew he could smell her fear. She could smell it herself. She'd never been so scared in all her life. She meant to head straight for Raife—it was early morning, and he was likely already out in the valley, starting the day's training exercises—but when she heard Sibyl's voice, she stopped.

"Laina, I will not allow it. No! Do not ask me again!" Sibyl cried. The voice came, not from the rooms her *banrighinn* shared with Raife, but from the one Laina shared with Darrow.

Kirstin stopped at the doorway, nosing the door all the way open, and saw Laina sitting by the fire, nursing her bairn. Garaith waved his chubby fist in the air, kicking his bare feet, suckling happily. Sibyl sat opposite them in a chair of her own, and she glanced up as Kirstin appeared at the entrance.

"Yes, Lorien?" Sibyl asked, glancing down at Kirstin, and for a moment, she saw her *banrighinn* didn't recognize her. But Laina did.

"Kirstin!" Laina cried, jumping up, her nipple popping out of a very unhappy Garaith's mouth. She quickly gave the protesting baby to Sibyl, covering herself as she rushed toward her sister-wolf. Laina grabbed a blanket off the bed, wrapping Kirstin in it as she began to change. She hadn't tried, not since her estrus, but it wasn't any more difficult than ever before.

"Thank you, Lorien." Sibyl smiled at the dark wolf who stood behind them. "We'll take it from here."

He gave a short bark and a whine, but then turned, and headed back toward the tunnel entrance. Back to sentry duty, no doubt, Kirstin thought. She'd have to thank him later, for bringing her in. If she got the opportunity. She shivered at that thought, putting her newly formed arms around Laina and letting her help her stand.

"You're a mess." Sibyl bounced the hungry Garaith on her hip, trying to quiet him. "Are you hurt? Is that dried blood?"

Kirstin glanced behind her, where the blanket had dropped low on her back, and saw where the blade had streaked across her skin.

"Aye." She had her voice back. What a relief that was! "Sibyl, ye hafta t'take me t'Raife. They're coming. They're goin' t'kill us all."

"Who? What?" Sibyl put the baby up over her shoulder, patting his back.

"Lord Eldred's a traitor to the king," Kirstin accepted the long shirt Laina put over her head. "He plans t'use some sorta witchcraft t'compel t'wulver army t'take t'English throne. I heard 'im. And I saw 'er. The witch."

She shuddered at the memory.

"You're not making any sense." Sibyl handed Laina the baby, who was happy to be back with his mother. "Witchcraft? Kirstin, why are you here? I thought, you and Donal—"

The mention of his name made Kirstin burst into tears. She was exhausted, panicked, grief-stricken, and so afraid, she wasn't sure anymore which way was up. For all she knew, she'd been tracked to the wulver den. She didn't think so—and the scouts were always watching—but she'd been

- 159 -

in such a hurry to get home. She couldn't be sure. And, mayhaps, Sedgewick and Salt had already found the den. Mayhaps they were following, even now.

"Ye've t'listen t'me," Kirstin sobbed, pulling the blanket Laina had given her more fully around her. She was cold, hungry, tired, but those things could wait. "Please. Take me t'Raife. Take me t'Darrow. I'll tell 'em everythin'. But I do'na wanna t'have t'say it twice."

"A'righ', we'll take ye to 'em," Laina soothed. "But firs' let's get ye cleaned up and dressed, mayhaps feed ye, and we can talk—"

"There's no time!" Kirstin howled, tears streaked down her face. "They're goin' t'kill ye all. The women, the children—they're goin' t'kill them first. Yer baby, Laina. They're goin' t'kill yer baby. Yer son, Sibyl, the one ye carry in yer belly. They'll cut it out and gut ye like a fish."

She made her language as horrible and her images as vivid as she possibly could. It worked. Sibyl went pale, her hand moving to her still flat belly.

"Kirstin, you're scaring me," Sibyl whispered, meeting Laina's big eyes and they both looked back to Kirstin. Garaith was wailing now, as if he'd picked up on the energy in the room.

"Ye should be scared. I'm terrified. And the wors' part is—I do'na know if we can stop them," Kirstin confessed hoarsely. The weight of her words felt like an avalanche of rock falling over her head, burying her. "Where's yer mate? Where's Raife? Where's my *righ*?"

Righ—her king. If anyone knew what to do, how to keep them safe, it would be Raife.

"He's in the kitchen," Sibyl said. Her lips barely moved. It was like she was frozen. "They're restringing the bows today..."

With that, Kirstin was off, tearing down the tunnels barefoot, wearing just a shirt, the blanket wrapped around her shoulders trailing behind her like a plaid cape. She didn't even stop to see if they were following her.

Raife was far easier to convince than Sibyl and Laina had been.

He and Darrow listened to it all without comment, her whole story, from the time she'd run away from the castle, to the time Lorien had scouted her and brought her into the den. Sibyl sat beside Laina on one of the long kitchen benches, the two women grasping hands. Sibyl was so pale by the time Kirstin was done with her story, her freckles stood out on her cheeks like constellations. She sat with her hand over her belly, and Kirstin knew she was thinking about the bairn she carried. Kirstin was thinking about all of them—all of the bairns, and their mothers.

Her pack. Her family. The last of their kind.

They all stood, gathered around, to hear Kirstin's story, and they all looked to Raife to see what to do. Their leader was quiet, thoughtful, and it was Darrow who spoke first.

"We hafta barricade ourselves in," Darrow urged. "Seal off both exits."

"If we do that, we're sealin' our own tomb." Raife shook his head.

"Donal will protect us," Kirstin insisted. It was the only thing she could think of—and not just because she wanted to go back to the MacFalon castle. "If we go t'him, he'll protect the wulvers. I know he will."

"The wolf pact doesn't exist," Darrow scoffed. "We can'na trust The MacFalon."

"He loves me," Kirstin assured him. Even though she'd left him, she knew this was true. "And he'll honor t'wolf pact wit' his life, no matter what t'English king says."

"Ye said his bride is on t'way," Raife reminded her, frowning. "And King Henry did'na grant the dispensation."

"It will'na matter," Kirstin assured him. "He'll do it, because he loves me. He'll do it because he cares about all t'wulvers. He will'na wanna see anythin' bad happen t'any of us."

Raife considered this.

"There's plenty of room at the castle... or..." She bit her lip, the idea just coming to her. "Raife, we could go down into t'first den. Our numbers aren't as great as they once were. We don't take up half this mountain anymore. There's enough room in t'first den t'house e'eryone..."

"If we can'na barricade ourselves in, we can face 'em," Darrow countered. "Whoever comes—no man can stand against a wulver warrior."

"Can a wulver warrior stand in the face of magic?" Kirstin asked softly, glancing between Raife and Darrow.

"Nuh magic spell can compel me," Darrow sneered, rolling his eyes. "D'ye really think we'd follow anyone, simply because a witch said some silly words over some silvermoon? She threw a knife at ye and scared ye, 'tis all..."

Kirstin swallowed, looking at Sibyl and Laina, seeing a knowing in their eyes. Men were always doubtful of witchcraft, either afraid of it because they didn't understand or like its power, or distrustful and doubtful. Darrow had always been the latter, even though Laina's belief they could break the wulver-woman's curse was dependent on the idea of magic.

Raife looked at his brother, frowning, then at Kirstin, who stood as tall as she could in her plaid blanket, speaking up so everyone could hear her.

"I assure ye, there *is* a witch," she insisted. "She did'na throw a knife at me, Darrow. She ne'er touched it. It wasn't in 'er hand. It jus'... flew."

Raife was listening—and that was good.

"It grazed me, *Righ*. Look." Kirsten turned, dropping the blanket, pulling her shirt down in back to reveal her wound. "But it did'na stop there. The knife wobbled back and forth in the bark, like this."

She showed them with her hand, mimicking a fish's movement through the water.

"If it had'na hit the tree with such force, I think it would've pulled instantly free and found me heart." She swallowed at the memory. "I'm tellin' ye, Darrow—that blade was tryin' t'pull itself out so it could finish the job..."

"It was enchanted, *Righ*." She turned her pleas back to Raife's receptive ears. Darrow just scoffed and rolled his eyes. He was a man who could turn into a half-wolf, and yet he doubted the existence of magic? The strangeness of it almost made her want to laugh.

"It would take days to gather everyone, to pack them all, and at least that long to reach the MacFalon castle," Sibyl said, putting a hand on her husband's arm. "We'd be giving Donal no warning and—"

"We do'na have time." Kirstin interrupted her with a shake of her dark head. "We need t'go. *Now*. We can'na wait. We can'na stay. We hafta go, and we hafta go *now*."

"Raife, we can't just leave everything..." Sibyl glanced nervously at Kirstin, and then back at her husband. "Aren't we safe here, in the mountain?"

Kirstin saw doubt pass over Raife's face, and he looked at Sibyl. He wanted to tell her they were safe, that they could stay. Kirstin saw that much in his eyes. He wanted to give his mate what she wanted, and Sibyl didn't want to leave. This was the place she called home now, and the fact that she was with child made her all the more protective of her territory.

"Aye." Raife nodded slowly, touching Sibyl's cheek.

"No!" Kirstin cried, ignoring the dark look in Raife's eyes at her protest. "D'you know what yer sayin'? What yer riskin'?"

She'd thought of nothing else, on her run through the woods. She'd seen images in her mind of slaughter and death, the wulver warriors slaying their own mates, their own children, the tunnels in the mountain running with rivers of blood. She couldn't let that happen.

"Kirstin, we're glad ye told us," Darrow said, sighing. "Now we can be prepared if they try t'get in. But y'know nothin' of—"

"Raife, please," she pleaded, ignoring Darrow's words, ignoring the way the wulver warriors agreed with him, nodding their heads. Had the witch's magic already started to work, then? Were they already being compelled? That thought made her blood turn to ice in her veins. "She's powerful, this Moraga. I do'na think her name's any accident. It was Morag who killed Ardis, the first she-wulver. Do ye n'remember the legend?"

"More legends, more magic!" Darrow threw up his hands.

"She's goin' t'compel ye." Kirstin knew it was hard to believe. She wouldn't have believed it herself if she hadn't seen the witch's blade fly through the air all on its own, if she hadn't seen it struggling to free itself from the tree. What could she do to convince them? "Jus' like she did the blade. Lord Eldred's goin' t'use e'ery one of ye to his own ends. But first, he's goin' t'have ye kill yer women, yer children."

"Yer goin' t'draw yer sword on yer mate, Darrow." Kirstin couldn't keep the tears from falling down her cheeks as she looked at her sister-wolf, Laina, and little Garaith, happily suckling at her breast once more. "Yer gonna slit yer own bairn's throat. Is that what ye want?"

"Enough!" Raife said roughly as a small sob escaped Sibyl's throat, her hands low on her belly. "Kirstin, enough! I know y're afeared, but—"

"The wulver mountain'll run wit' blood," she choked. "Ye think ye can'na be compelled, ye think y're invincible, that ye'd ne'er hurt the ones ye love—but I swear t'ye, if'n we do'na act now, e'ery woman and bairn here'll fall under yer own swords."

"Kirstin, please." Laina's voice shook as she looked down at the baby in her arms and then at her sister. "Ye've been traveling long, ye're wounded, mayhaps feverish—"

"No." She shook her head, realizing her arguments were falling on deaf ears. They couldn't believe it, couldn't imagine it. Darrow's doubt was feeding all of them, she could feel it, and they were all going to perish because they thought their mountain den was safe harbor.

The problem was, the danger would come from within, not without. Every wulver warrior would take up a sword and hack his family to bits before mounting a war horse and riding out of the mountain to fulfil Lord Eldred's demands.

Then, she realized—there was only one wulver she had to convince.

She turned to Raife, her mouth trembling. It was hard to talk through her own, choked sobs. Kirstin sank to her knees before him, taking his big hand in both of her small ones.

"*Righ*," she whispered, kissing the brown, scarred knuckles, tasting the salt of her own tears. "Please. Think of yer mate. Think of Sibyl."

She turned her tear-streaked face up to his, seeing the love in his eyes, not just for his mate, but for all of them. His pack. His family. She said the only other thing she could think of that might motivate him to action.

"Think of yer unborn child," she pleaded. "Do'ye nuh wanna see 'im grow into a man?"

Raife stared at her, unblinking, but she saw the confusion pass over his face, saw the realization dawn slowly in his eyes as he shifted his gaze to his wife. Murmurs went through the wulver crowd gathered around them, and Kirstin understood what she'd just done.

"Me... what?" Raife asked, his lips barely moving.

"Ye didn't tell 'im yet?" Kirstin bit her lip, glancing at her *banrighinn*.

Sibyl sighed, giving Kirstin a dark look and shaking her red head.

"Yer wit child?" Raife grabbed his mate's shoulders, turning her fully to him.

"Aye," Sibyl admitted with a small smile.

The wulvers around them cheered. It was a brief moment of celebration in what had been a dark morning.

"How long've ye known?" Raife murmured into her hair, pulling her into his arms.

Kirstin stood, smiling through her tears as she watched them together. She would never have this moment with the man she loved, and that cut through her, sharper than the half-moon blade could have ever pierced her heart.

"Since before we left MacFalon land. But I didn't want to tell you then, you were so mad at me," Sibyl confessed, laughing when Raife pulled her into his arms, right off her feet.

"If ye'd told me, I would'na been mad anymore!" he exclaimed.

"But I wouldn't have known that it was me you really wanted, then, would I?"

"Och." Raife rolled his eyes. "I should spank ye right here and now."

"Can we postpone the spankings until we get to Castle MacFalon?" Kirstin asked, looking between her *righ* and *banrighinn*.

"Aye." Raife had Sibyl pulled so close to him, he was nearly crushing her. Not that she seemed to mind. "Ye win, Kirstin. We'll go."

Murmurs went through the crowd, some doubt. Darrow groaned and smacked his forehead. But he relented. Raife had made a decision, and they would follow him.

"I'm sure Donal would be happy t'schedule a public floggin' fer me and another fer Sibyl if ye wanted one," Kirstin said happily, grinning at him. "I do'na really care, as long as we're all away from 'ere when that witch and 'er consort show up."

"Aye," Raife agreed, speaking now to the whole pack. "Take only what ye can carry. We'll go on horseback. We'll take the horses through the mountain—it's faster—women paired up wit' men. Strap your bairns and wee ones to yer back or yer belly. We leave in one hour."

They were the last to leave the den.

Raife had to make sure every wulver was on a horse or had a traveling companion, every last bairn strapped in. The younglings rode in front of or behind their parents. They strapped what they could to the horses and left the sheep in the valley. The last time they'd brought the horses through the mountain, the wulver warriors had been riding them in full armor. They'd thundered down the high, wide mountain tunnels, the sound of the horses' hooves echoing off the walls, trembling the earth, leaving their mates and young behind. That's when the wulver army had gone to confront the MacFalons, to rescue Laina and save Sibyl.

This time, the war horses whinnied and pawed the ground as they plodded along, impatient to be off, weighed down not by armor but blankets and women and children, as well as their wulver warriors. Once out of the mountain, they rode slowly into the woods, single file. There were too many of them to travel too fast, although Kirstin's heart raced with urgency, her body trembling. She wanted them to be off, to ride fast and furious to the MacFalon castle, to be safe, already.

"The den's empty." Darrow rode toward them—Raife and Sibyl, Lorien and Kirstin—where they waited at the den entrance, Laina on his saddle in front of him, little Garaith strapped across her front. "'Tis time t'go."

Raife stood by his steed, holding the reins. Sibyl was already seated in the saddle. Raife gave Darrow a nod and mounted his horse, sliding in behind Sibyl, who had tears streaking down her freckled cheeks. Raife tenderly kissed the top of her head, slipping an arm around her waist, his big hand covering her belly, rubbing gently. "We'll make a new home, lass. T'will be a'righ'."

Kirstin was the only one left on the ground. She mounted Lorien's steed, allowing him to give her a hand up, settling in front of him. Laina had loaned her a plaid and a pair of boots to go along with her shirt. She felt Lorien's steadying arm go around her. The top of her head only came to the bottom of the big man's chin.

They rode slowly, silently, out of the den for the last time. Kirstin leaned back against Lorien, feeling sad, deflated. What if she was wrong? What if Lord Eldred's men hadn't found the location of the den after all? What if Darrow was right, and they were safer staying, instead of running? She doubted herself, but she also trusted her instincts. Something had told her she had to get home, she had to warn them. They had to go—now. Before something horrible happened.

The tail end of the wulver riders were out ahead of them by a ways. Kirsten glimpsed a toddler strapped to his father's big back. The little towhead was smiling, waving at them, and Kirstin waved back, her heart lightening. Even if she was wrong, it was better to be safe than sorry. All of the wulver women she'd tended, all the bairns that had been born, would be safe at Castle MacFalon before nightfall. They would all be under Donal's protection, and she knew he would defend them, no matter what the English king had in mind. She had no idea how many men Donal could call in from the surrounding clans, but if it meant war... would he go that far? She thought he would.

For her, he would.

The thought of seeing Donal again made her heart race even faster. He would be furious with her for leaving, of course, but he'd forgive her. Raife had forgiven Sibyl, in the end, hadn't he? She wondered if Lady Cecilia Witcombe had arrived at Castle MacFalon yet. That thought made her hackles rise. She'd almost forgotten the reason she'd left the castle in the first place.

The book...

Sibyl had it, strapped to her, across her breasts, like a baby. It was that precious, Kirstin supposed. It contained the cure to their curse, somewhere inside of it. Mayhaps, when they were at the castle, Sibyl could work more on a solution. Kirstin hadn't had the time to ask her about it, in the hurry to get everyone ready to ride.

Kirstin straightened as three riders came barreling toward them, doubling back.

"'Tis jus' the scouts," Lorien assured her softly when she stiffened in the saddle. "Comin' in t'report t'Raife."

She nodded, seeing them pull up next to his horse, turning and riding alongside him, one on either side, another slipping in behind. Raife consulted with both wulvers, nodding at their report. Kirstin could only see him in profile as he turned to talk to them and she tried to judge if he looked worried, but his face was impassive.

Raife said something to the three scouts and they dropped back, letting him ride into the lead. Kirstin relaxed. Nothing to worry about then. She was so exhausted, she thought she might collapse and fall off the horse, if Lorien didn't have an arm around her waist. But she couldn't sleep. She was too tense, too wired.

They weren't fifteen minutes out from the den when it happened.

The only warning she had was that Kirstin felt Lorien straighten in his saddle.

"E'erythin' a'righ'?" she asked, but it happened so fast, the wulver didn't have time to answer her.

Someone dropped from a tree above, right onto Raife's horse. He wasn't a big man, but he had the advantage of surprise. And he had a knife. The man jabbed it into expertly into Raife's side, between his ribs, unseating the big wulver. The horse bucked and nearly threw Sibyl and the stranger, but the man was able to hang on, grabbing the reins and urging the animal forward.

Kirstin screamed. She heard Sibyl screaming, calling for Raife, but the war horse was already tearing through the woods. Kirstin was shocked by the horse's behavior—but then she realized the man was wearing something on his boots, something sharp he dug into the horse's flanks.

Raife had already transformed to wulver warrior, and behind her, so had Lorien. They barked orders, snapped at each other, the scouting warriors already racing after the runaway horse, with Sibyl and the stranger atop.

Darrow barked something to Lorien about keeping the women safe, leaving Laina and his bairn with him. Kirstin climbed down from the horse, putting her arms around Laina and Garaith, still not understanding what was happening.

Darrow and Raife wasted time fighting, snarling at one another, and Lorien threw Kirstin the reins of his horse, stepping in to help Darrow restrain their wulver pack leader. It took the two of them, snapping and circling, to keep the big wulver from going after Sibyl straightaway.

Raife howled, a sound so full of anguish and pain it echoed through the woods, and Kirstin knew it had nothing to do with the wound in his side.

The rest of the pack had heard and were doubling back toward them.

Kirstin realized, far too late, screaming at Raife, "No! Ye can'na go after 'er! Yer what they want! They need yer blood!"

But they already had it, didn't they?

The man had slipped a knife between Raife's ribs and had run off with Sibyl.

It wasn't Sibyl they wanted, though, Kirstin realized.

It was the book strapped to her chest.

This is my fault, she thought, watching in horror as Raife got free and pulled his sword, threatening his own brother with it if Darrow kept him from pursuing their attackers.

This is all my fault.

They'd been waiting for them, she realized. Mayhaps they knew Kirstin would run straight back to the den with her escape plan, leading Raife out into the open where they could get what they needed to take back to the witch. But Darrow was right after all. They would have been safer staying in the den.

Raife took off—Darrow and Lorien couldn't hold him—running after Sibyl. Lorien stayed, on Darrow's orders, but Darrow went after his brother. Kirstin looked at Laina, tears streaked down her face, and felt her own tears wetting her cheeks. Little Garaith howled between them.

"'Tis all m'fault," Kirstin sobbed against her sister's shoulder as the wulver pack began to gather around them on horseback. "They've got 'is blood, Laina. 'Tis all they needed."

"Shhhh." Laina stroked her hair, comforting both Kirstin and her bairn at once.

Kirstin couldn't bear it. She'd led them straight to the wulver den, had put everyone in danger in the hopes of trying to save them. She sobbed in Laina's arms, wishing the earth would open up and swallow her whole. If anything happened to Sibyl, or Raife, or any of her family, because of what she'd done, she knew she could never forgive herself.

"Kirstin," Laina whispered, shaking her gently. "Look!"

Kirstin lifted her head, blinking through her tears, seeing Raife carrying Sibyl in his arms. Darrow followed on foot, and Laina broke away from Kirstin to meet her husband, putting her arms around him. Both wulvers were men again.

"Is she hurt?" Kirstin barely got the words out as Raife approached. Sibyl was, at the very least, unconscious, her body limp.

"He took the book." Raife blinked down at the woman in his arms. "Then he pushed 'er off m'horse."

"No," Kirstin whispered, her hands already moving over Sibyl's inert form, looking for broken bones. "She's alive, Raife. She'll be a'righ', here, put 'er on the ground, I'll—"

And that's when Kirstin saw the blood. Sibyl's plaid was all greens and blues, but there was a dark spot on it that was growing by the moment. She didn't say anything it about to Raife as he knelt, gently depositing Sibyl's body on the forest floor.

"Where's t'attacker?" Lorien growled as Darrow approached. Raife and Darrow were transformed into men again, but Lorien was still half-man, half-wolf, prepared for battle.

"They went after 'im." Darrow jerked his head toward the woods, Laina and his bairn drawn into one arm, his sword drawn in the other.

Lorien, now freed up from having to protect Kirstin and Laina, took off on his horse, barking to three more scouts to join him, so there were now seven out pursuing the man.

"She was thrown from the horse," Kirstin told Laina as the two women bent over Sibyl. Kirstin was sure there were no broken bones, at least any she could feel. Raife watched them work over her, his eyes full of fire.

"I think she may be losin' the bairn," Laina whispered to Kirstin. They both saw the blood on her thighs, the way her plaid was twisted, high up on her legs.

Raife heard them and closed his eyes, his head going back with a long, sustained howl. It made gooseflesh rise all over Kirstin's body as Laina ran to Darrow's horse, unpacking blankets and what medicine she could find.

"I've got black haw and cramp bark." Beitrus made her way to the front of the crowd. The old woman, who had taught Kirstin everything she knew, held out two vials. "It may save the pup."

"Thank ye." Kirstin uncapped one and poured it past Sibyl's lips. The woman coughed at the sudden introduction of liquid into her mouth and Raife grabbed her to him, ignoring their protests.

"Sibyl," he whispered, holding her close. "Can ye hear me? Are ye a'righ'?"

"I'll be fine," she gasped, her eyes opening wide. "If you quit crushing me, you beast!"

Raife chuckled at that, rocking her against his chest, bringing her face to his so he could kiss her.

Sibyl sobbed when she realized she was bleeding. Laina, Kirstin and Beitrus all worked to reassure her that the bairn was likely fine, that bleeding happened sometimes, and they'd done everything they could to help them both.

Kirstin hoped their reassurances turned out to be true. The bleeding did seem to be ebbing, and Sibyl was awake, and coherent. Laina tended Raife's wound—it was superficial, not deep at all. Whoever had slipped the knife in had known exactly what he was doing, and hadn't been aiming for anything vital.

Of course, not—they want him to be able to fight.

They only wanted his blood...

Sibyl finally calmed, but didn't want to get on Raife's horse, when Lorien returned with him. But without the attacker. Or the book.

"What if it hurts the baby?" Sibyl sobbed. "What if I start bleeding again?"

They spent time reassuring her, giving her sips of water, waiting for the tonics to work. It helped stop the blood, and that was a good sign, Kirstin assured her.

Darrow and Raife talked together, low and out of earshot, with Lorien.

"Can't we stay here now?" Sibyl suggested, as Raife came over to get her, lifting her easily off the ground. "In the den? Isn't it the safest place? We can block the exits, like Darrow said, we can—"

"No, lass." Raife pressed his lips to her forehead. "'Tis no longer safe, if they know where the den is. We have to ride to the MacFalon castle."

"I'm scared," Sibyl told him, burying her face against his neck.

"Aye." Raife mounted his horse, pulling Sibyl with him, settling her side saddle. Lorien had tended the animal's wounds, from whatever the stranger had been digging into its sides, with a balm Kirstin gave him.

"I haven't ridden side-saddle in years," she told him, pressing her cheek to his chest.

"Aye, but Kirstin says 'tis safest for t'bairn." He kissed the top of her head. "We'll go slow."

Raife sent the rest of the pack on ahead, toward the castle. They would bring up the rear.

"D'ye want me t'stay 'ere and wait fer t'scouts?" Lorien asked them.

"Ye should ride wit' us," Darrow told him, getting on his horse behind Laina and the baby. "We may need ye if they return fer Raife again."

"They won't," Kirstin said miserably as Lorien gave her a hand up onto his mount. "They a'ready 'ave e'erythin' they need."

She scanned the woods as they began to ride, taking it slow, as Raife had promised, hoping, praying, the scouts would catch up to the thief before he could make it back to his camp to give the book and the knife to the waiting witch and her wicked consort.

Chapter Ten

"Where is she?"

Kirstin heard his voice before she saw him. She was leaning back against Lorien, his arm the only thing keeping her from falling face first out of the saddle, drifting in and out of nightmares that would occasionally jolt her awake with a start. It was full dark by the time their little party reached the castle—they'd had to travel much slower than the others—but a large bonfire had been lit out front to guide them in.

Donal's voice came to her out of a dream. She thought she must be dreaming when he lifted her down from the saddle, scowling at the wulver who held her close, and kissed her so long and deeply she could barely catch her breath.

"I do'na wanna wake up," she whispered against his shoulder as he put an arm under her knees and carried her into the castle.

"Shh." Donal's arms tightened as he took the stairs with her in his arms, two at a time.

Moira followed them, clucking over Kirstin as Donal put her on the bed. Now she was sure she was dreaming, because nothing had ever been so soft. She must be in heaven, in the clouds, warm under the sun.

"Sibyl!" Kirstin came awake, sitting bolt upright in the bed. "Raife! Where is e'eryone? Donal, ye hafta keep 'em safe! You hafta—!"

"Easy, lass." Donal undressed her like a child. "E'eryone's safe as they can be."

"Sibyl's bleedin'." Kirstin tried to clear the fuzz from her head. She was so tired. She must still be dreaming, she reasoned. "Someone attacked Raife... they stabbed him. Donal, oh, 'tis all m'fault."

"Shhh." He eased her shirt over her head. Someone was knocking hard on the locked door. "'Tisn't yer fault. None of it."

He picked her up, completely nude now, and carried her over to a bath in front of the big fireplace, placing her into the warm water. He looked at her for a moment, dark hair floating, and she stared at him as if in a dream. Surely, it was. He couldn't be here, touching her, undressing her, leaning in to cup her face and kiss her like he thought he might never see her again.

"MacFalon!" It was Raife, pounding on the door.

"Keep her 'ere," Donal told Moira, who knelt beside the tub with a washing cloth. "Do'na let 'er outta yer sight. I'll be righ 'back."

Donal unlocked the door and slipped out into the hallway, closing it behind him.

"Moira, 'tis all m'fault," Kirstin lamented, as the old woman began to wash her hair. "I led them straight to t'den. I was such a fool. Are t'wulvers all 'ere?"

"Oh, aye, lass," Moira assured, rinsing her hair with a bucket of warm water. "Most of 'em have camped out on m'kitchen floor in front of the fireplace."

Kirstin smiled at that, but it faded as soon as she remembered.

"He got away. He stabbed Raife, and took t'book, and he got away..." She covered her face with her hands.

"The wulver scouts brought 'em in an hour ago," Donal told her as he came back into the room. "We've got t'book."

"And the knife?" Kirstin gripped the edge of the tub, looking up at him with big eyes. She'd been able to think of nothing else since, memories of the witch flitting through her mind. "With Raife's blood?"

"Aye, m'love." He stroked her hair away from her face. "The wulver scouts brought back four men. Geoffrey, William, and two others."

"Salt and Sedgewick." She shuddered, remembering the way they'd tracked her in the woods, how they'd come up on her out of nowhere. She was sure, now, that they'd been the 'poachers' who they'd come upon in the forest that very first day. They'd been Lord Eldred's men all along, hiding and doing his bidding. "What about Lord Eldred and the witch, Moraga?"

"Moira, lemme finish up 'ere," Donal said, taking the soap and washing cloth from the old woman. "Can ye bring us up some food?"

"Aye," she agreed happily, getting up from the floor and heading to the door.

"Did they catch 'em?" Kirstin asked again, desperate for an answer.

"N'yet." Donal shook his head, rubbing soap over the washing cloth and pushing up his sleeves as he knelt near the tub. "I've got me men out lookin'—and the wulvers are lookin' too."

"It's Raife they want." She met his eyes—oh how she'd missed looking into those blue-grey eyes—pleading with him. "Donal, ye hafta keep 'im safe. He's t'one they want. If they capture 'im, if they get a drop of 'is blood…"

"Shh." He turned her chin to him and kissed her quiet. His first kiss had been like something out of a dream, not possibly real. This kiss was like coming home. She wrapped her soapy, wet arms around his neck, feeling grateful tears slipping down her cheeks.

"They've told me e'erythin'," Donal assured her when they parted. "I should've listened t'ye from the beginnin' about Lord Eldred, lass. If I had…"

"Ye couldn't've known."

His face darkened in a scowl. "We'll find 'em. We'll find 'em both and we'll bring 'em t'justice."

Kirstin searched his face, seeing new lines there, dark circles under his eyes. He smelled of whiskey, and there was a good four days' stubble on his face.

"I missed ye," she confessed. "Did ye miss me?"

"Did I miss ye?" he repeated, blinking at her as Moira carried in a tray weighed down with food. She put it on the

- 177 -

little table in the corner. "I had e'ery available man at m'service out lookin' for ye. I've been in me cups for days. I can'na sleep. I can'na eat. I can'na breathe wit'out ye, lass. Did I miss ye? What d'ye say. Moira, did I miss 'er?"

"He put a huge reward out fer yer capture," Moira informed her. "Alive, a'course."

"Ye did?" Kirstin raised her eyebrows in surprise.

"He also had Gregor flogged," Moira told her, pouring cups of mead. "An'banished. If any man dares ever harm a wulver on MacFalon land again, they'll be put t'death. Publically."

"Painfully," Donal agreed, glowering.

"D'ye need anythin' else?" Moira asked, looking at both of them, a small smile playing on her face.

"Jus' tell 'em not t'disturb me," Donal replied, his gaze raking Kirstin's nude form. "Unless it's urgent."

"Aye." Moira grinned, opening the door. "Ye better lock in behin' me, though, jus' in case."

"I will," Donal said, nodding as she went out.

He paused in his bathing of her to go lock the door and Kirstin smiled at that. They were good at locking out the world. She remembered the time they'd spent in the first den, laughing, eating, making love, swimming in the cold spring and drying themselves in front of the fire. She'd known, even then, that their time was limited.

"Is she 'ere yet?" Kirstin asked softly as Donal came back to tend to her.

"Who?" His hands moved over her under the water, big, rough, calloused, they scrubbed her far better than any washing cloth.

"Yer bride," she reminded him.

"I'll not be marryin' anyone else but ye, lass." He leveled her with a cool look. "Not now, not e'er."

"Ye didn't answer me."

"Nuh." He sighed." She's not 'ere yet."

"But she will be..."

And what then? Kirstin wondered.

"I can'na stop 'er from comin'—her party will be welcomed 'ere." Donal scowled. "But I will'na be marryin' her. I intend t'be married t'ye by then."

She looked at him in the firelight, the shadows playing on his handsome face. What woman wouldn't want this man? Lady Cecilia Witcombe would take one look at him and fall instantly in love. Why not? Kirstin had.

And she wouldn't blame her.

"Donal, ye can'na start a war," Kirstin told him. "We were all deceived. King Henry wants t'wulvers dead. All of us. Includin' me. He'll ne'er let ye marry a wulver. We hafta go into hidin' somewhere..."

"If t'English king wants t'go t'war wit' Scotland, then let 'im see if he can take t'border against the Scots *and* t'wulvers." Donal's eyes flashed and she gasped when he roughly scrubbed the cloth over her back.

"I do'na want any more war," Kirstin whispered, feeling tears stinging her eyes. "N'more bloodshed."

"Och." Donal sighed, tossing aside the cloth and reaching for her. His front was soaked from bathing her, his white shirt see-through, clinging to his thickly muscled chest and abdomen. "I'm sorry, lass. I jus'...I will'na let ye go again. I'll fight fer ye. I'll die fer ye."

"No fightin'," she said, frowning. "And mos' definitely, no dyin!"

"Jus' do'na e'er leave me again." He pulled her close, burying his face in the wet skin of her neck, his stubble hard and prickly, making her squirm, but she didn't let him go.

"I'm so tired." She sighed, trying to keep her eyes open, but it wasn't easy in the warm water, in the heat of the fire.

"Let's get some food in yer belly."

He had her stand, shivering, while he rinsed her with a warm bucket of water.

"I'm sorry," she said when he had her step out and wrapped her in a cloth that had been warming by the fire. "For leavin' ye..."

Donal chuckled. "When I saw ye, I didn't know whether to kiss ye or spank ye."

"Ye could do both..." She bit her lip when his gaze swept over her as he patted her dry.

"Do'na tempt me," he growled, wrapping her with a dry cloth and leading her over to the table.

"It must've been a shock, the wulvers ridin' up to the gates..." She sat across from him at the table, the smell of the food hitting her, and suddenly, she was ravenous.

"The scouts on t'walls said the entire wulver army was headin' our way." Donal chuckled, watching as she started eating, not bothering with utensils. "I'd been in me cups for days. No one could find ye... and I was... well, let's jus' say, I missed ye."

She smiled, chewing on a bit of buttered roll.

"But when ye have an entire den full of wulvers ride up t'yer gates, it tends t'sober ye'up," he told her, handing her a napkin to catch the drip of gravy on her chin.

She giggled at that, trying to picture it, her whole pack riding up to Castle MacFalon and begging entry.

"But ye took 'em in?"

"They're yer kin," he said simply, which made her heart swell. Then he said something that made tears come to her eyes. "And mine. A'course I took 'em in."

She was so hungry, she felt faint. Donal watched her eat the salt pork Moira had brought up with her fingers, tearing off thick pieces of dark bread in between bites. He hadn't taken his eyes off her since she arrived, like he thought she might disappear, just an apparition. When Kirstin's belly was full, she sat back with a satisfied sigh. She was still exhausted, and could have fallen asleep right there in the chair, but she didn't want to close her eyes.

She didn't want to stop looking at the man across from her.

"What're we gonna do?" she wondered aloud.

"I'm goin' t'take ye to bed." Donal stood, pulling her up, into his arms. The cloth he had wrapped around her dropped to the floor, leaving her nude. "And I'm ne'er lettin' ye outta m'sight again, lass."

"Ye know what I mean," she whispered, and he nodded, but he didn't answer her with anything but a kiss.

Kirstin woke sometime in the middle of the night, not sure where she was. Then she heard Donal's soft, even breathing beside her, felt the weight of his arm over her, and knew. She was home. Sighing happily, she snuggled back against him under the covers. There was no place on earth she wanted to be more than in this man's arms.

Her mind drifted as she started to fall asleep again. Her body was exhausted, but her mind was on overdrive. Every time she woke, it was with a panicked thought or new fear. Donal helped dispel those, although even now, she had a sinking feeling, like there was something she was forgetting, some little bit of information she'd forgotten to relay that would be the downfall of everything.

She knew it was ridiculous. There were MacFalon and wulver sentries on the castle walls. There were more out looking for Eldred and Moraga. In fact, they'd probably captured them already and put them down in the dungeons with Eldred's four trackers, she told herself. The castle was quiet, asleep. The windows were dark, so it was still night. Kirstin closed her eyes and drifted again, comforted by the sound of the man sleeping behind her.

She'd almost drifted off, finally content, when her eyes opened wide, staring into the fading embers of the fire.

Gayle.

That was what she'd forgotten. Eldred's little spy.

Her heart felt like it was beating in her throat. Could the little maid let him in? Get him a message? Or… worse?

She didn't want to think about worse.

She considered waking Donal and telling him about the maid, but she knew he'd get up and wake the whole damned castle looking for her. Besides, she wasn't sure she was still here. Moira had brought up the food, and she hadn't seen anyone else, but maybe… maybe the maid had left, afraid she was going to be discovered? She didn't want to worry Donal for nothing.

Kirsten was used to moving around at night without waking anyone. She'd extracted herself from a wulver pile often enough to be able to move silently when she wanted to. Donal slept through her slipping out of bed and getting dressed in a clean shirt, plaid and boots. She left him still sleeping as she unlocked the door and slipped into the hallway.

The maid's quarters were off the kitchen, and that's where Kirstin headed. She crept silently down the stairs, heading across the hall. No one was awake yet, she was sure of it, although looking at the windows, they were lighter than they had been a few moments ago. Perhaps it was nearing dawn, after all. She was so exhausted and had missed so much sleep, her internal body clock was off.

Kirstin heard voices at the other end of the hall. She cocked her head. Her hearing was keen and she recognized them both. It was Moira and Sibyl talking. Kirstin's heart leaped in her chest. Was everything all right? The memory of her *banrighinn* bleeding filled her mind and she padded down the hall, heading toward the light coming from a room at the end of it.

"Thank you, Moira," Sibyl said. Her voice was soft, low. "I didn't know who else to ask…"

"Ye can ask me fer anything, lass," Moira assured her. "Where's yer husband?"

"Raife insisted on going to check on the sentries." Sibyl sighed. "Darrow went with him."

Kirstin stopped outside the door, listening. She should have knocked, but she didn't.

"I'm sorry to bother you," Sibyl said again. "You're so busy, with all the wulvers to feed, in addition to the MacFalons."

"Aye, 'tis a handful." Moira agreed with a sigh. "And I'm short maids. Gayle and Shona ran off and I haven't had time t'go into t'village t'hire anyone new."

Kirstin blinked in surprise. So Gayle wasn't at the castle anymore. That was a relief. She almost turned around and went back upstairs. Bed was calling, and she was admonishing herself for eavesdropping, when Sibyl said something that stopped her cold.

"Moira, do you have a good hiding place here in the castle?"

"Fer what, lass?" Moira chuckled. "T'family jewels?"

"No, for this."

Kirstin couldn't see her, even through the crack in the door. She leaned in closer, wondering what in the world Sibyl could want to hide.

"What's this?" Moira asked.

What, indeed. Kirstin held her breath, waiting.

"It's the cure."

She thought her heart would stop beating entirely. The cure? *The* cure? Could it be?

"Fer t'wulver curse?" Moira asked. She sounded as shocked as Kirstin felt. "Ye did it?"

"Yes, thanks to the silvermoon, and the book, and you." Sibyl sighed. "Laina wants to take it and I... I'm afraid she'll find it, if I keep it anywhere near me. She knows I have it. And she knows it works. The problem is, it works too well."

"What d'ye mean?" Moira asked. "How d'ye know it works?"

"Because I tested it," Sibyl told her. Kirstin gaped at the door, blinking in surprise. *Who?* But Sibyl went on to say. "The old midwife, Beitrus. She volunteered. Said she'd lived a long life, so if it killed her, she was ready to go—and if it turned out to be permanent, well, she didn't need to change anymore..."

"Ye let her take it?"

"No, of course not," Sibyl scoffed. "I told her no. I wanted to come up with a safer way to test it. But... she did it anyway."

"Wha' happened?" Moira asked. Kirstin leaned even closer, eager to know herself.

"Well, she's still alive," Sibyl said. "And... it worked. She can't change anymore, even at will."

"Oh no..." Moira clucked at that and Kirstin's heart sank.

"Laina keeps trying to take it," Sibyl explained. "And I can't do that. I can't possibly let her."

"Let me hide it fer ye," Moira said. "I'll keep it safe while yer here, at least."

"Thank you so much."

So Sibyl had done it. She'd found the cure for the wulver curse—but it had turned out to be permanent. Kirstin could hardly believe it. There was a substance that existed that could keep her from changing when she went into estrus. But it would keep her from ever turning into a wulver again...

She couldn't think of anything but Donal, sleeping upstairs, and the woman who would arrive any day, expecting to marry him.

What would it mean, to take such a remedy?

Kirstin wouldn't ever have to worry about changing. There would be no need to lock her up once a month. She could live in the MacFalon castle, side by side with the MacFalons, not as an outsider, but as one of them.

As The MacFalon's woman. His wife.

And... she could have his children.

So what if it was permanent? She wanted to be with Donal. Now and forever.

Permanently.

She'd already decided that. Sibyl's cure would make that possible.

She had to get her hands on it.

"Try t'get some sleep, Lady Sibyl," Moira said softly. "G'nite."

"Thank you," Sibyl called. "Good night."

Kirstin panicked, looking for somewhere to hide. She slipped under the legs of a table that held a vase filled with flowers, crouching in the darkness as Moira came out of the door, closing it behind her.

Did she have the cure? And if she did, what was she going to do with it?

Kirstin watched the old woman carrying her lantern through the hallway. She was heading toward the kitchen. When she saw Moira push open the kitchen door, she slipped out from under the table and followed. The door opened silently and she saw Moira standing with her lantern near the shelves where they kept all the flour and oils she used to cook.

The old woman took down a canister from a high shelf, putting something inside it. Then she put it back up there, standing on her tiptoes and pushing it all the way to the back. Kirstin held her breath, waiting for Moira to turn and discover her. She would say she'd come down for something to eat, she decided, getting her explanation ready, but Moira didn't turn her way. Instead, she headed toward the back of the kitchen.

Kirstin breathed a silent sigh of relief, seeing Moira lift the lantern, looking down at the floor. Kirstin saw many of her pack mates sleeping in a pile on the kitchen floor in front of the low fire burning there, and smiled. It would be the place that most felt like home, she realized, as Moira looked at them, shaking her grey head.

"Wulvers," Moira said with an exasperated sigh, and then she chuckled, heading past the wulver pile, toward the servant's quarters.

Once she was gone, Kirstin made her way over to the shelves, reaching up and finding the canister. Inside, was a tiny vial of dark liquid. She stood there holding it in the palm of her hand, looking at it in the dim light of the fire. Was she really going to do this?

She looked at the wulvers sleeping by the fire, realizing if she did take it, she'd never be part of them again. She would live wholly in the human world.

But she would have Donal. And he would have her.

That convinced her.

She had to find a place to take it, a place away from everyone, because she didn't want anyone to interfere.

Kirstin slipped the vial into the pocket of her plaid to keep it safe.

It was her future.

Hope in a bottle.

She fell asleep in the first den, rolled up completely in her plaid by the spring, the empty vial beside her. The potion had been sweet, tangy, not bitter, as she'd expected. Her last run as a wulver had been through the MacFalon lands, down into the tombs, and had ended in the grotto of Ardis and Asher. She thought of them as she drifted off, not sure if she was sleepy because of the cure, or because she was just plain exhausted.

Donal shook her awake, swearing in Gaelic when her eyes opened to meet his in the early morning sunlight. It came in through the grate above, making the spring look dappled and inviting. Kirstin smiled, remembering the night, putting her arms around his neck.

"I tell ye not t'leave me," he snapped, pushing her away so he could frown at her. "And what d'ye do? Ye run away again?"

"I did'na run away," she protested, stretching and yawning. She felt rested for the first time in days.

"Ye left t'castle! I had n'idea where ye were!" Donal exploded, grabbing her to him and shaking her again. Her plaid fell away and he looked down at her nude body. "I swear, lass, if ye e'er do anythin' like that again, I'll take ye over m'knee and—"

- 186 -

"Spank me?" A smile played on her lips. "Aye, I think, mayhaps, I deserve t'be spanked..."

"Och, yer gonna be t'death'o'me," he groaned, pulling her to him and kissing her. It was a hard, punishing kiss and she whimpered, but she clung to him as they parted, feeling his body against hers, the cool air on her skin. She'd never felt so alive.

But was she different? She couldn't tell.

"Do I look different?" she asked, cocking her head at him.

"Ye look delicious." His hands moved down to cup her breasts. They had made slow, easy, sleepy love the night before. The memory of it made her feel warm all over. But she was rested now, and ready for more of him.

"I took the cure." There was no sense keeping it from him, she decided. Besides, if it worked, it meant they could be together. At least, that was her best hope.

"What cure?" Donal blinked at her, distracted from her breasts by her words.

"This." Kirstin picked up the vial, shaking it. There was a tiny bit of liquid left in the bottom. "Sibyl did it. She made the cure. It works—Beitrus took it, and she can'na change anymore."

"What're ye talkin' about?" Donal looked from her to the vial and back again, as if trying to make sense of her words. "What cure? A cure for...?"

"A cure fer t'curse." She laughed at his dumbfounded expression. "Donal, this means I'll ne'er change again. It means I can marry ye. It means I can have yer bairn..."

Her eyes filled with tears at this last.

"How d'ye know it worked?" He took the vial from her, holding it up in the light. "How d'ye know what else it might do t'ye?"

"I do'na know." She frowned, looking down at her body, then back at him. "I guess I should try t'change and see—"

Donal frowned, looking up at the grating above.

"What?" Kirstin asked, frowning.

He cocked his head, shushing her. "Ye do'na hear that?"

"Hear what?" She blinked at him in surprise. Her wulver ears were far better than his human ones at picking up sound. If there was something to hear, surely...

But I'm not a wulver anymore.

The realization dawned on her as Donal stood, pointing an angry finger in her direction.

"They're soundin' t'alarm." Donal glowered at her. "Ye do'na follow me. Stay put, ye ken?"

"Aye." She nodded, pulling her plaid around her. "What is it?"

"I'm gonna find out." He made his way over the rocks, glancing back at her before he slipped out the exit. "I mean it, Kirstin. Ye'll be safe 'ere. *Stay put.*"

"Aye," she agreed again, nodding. "I'll wait fer ye."

She intended to do as he asked. She really did. She knew she'd scared him, taking off to the first den. She hadn't meant to fall asleep. She just wanted to make sure the cure had worked before she went back to the castle to surprise him with her news.

But the more she sat there, shivering on the rock, the more worried she became. Why had they sounded the alarm? Had Eldred and Moraga somehow managed to complete their spell after all? The thought of Donal riding back to the castle to face an army of enchanted wulver warriors left her choked with fear.

She washed her face and hands in the spring, trying to keep the latter from trembling. She got dressed, sitting back down in the slant of light from above, to wait. Mayhaps it was good news, she told herself. Mayhaps Eldred and the witch had been found. Donal would come back and tell her, and they would celebrate. They would make love in the grotto. Mayhaps they would even make a baby.

That thought made her smile.

That's when she heard it.

She didn't have wulver's ears anymore, but her human ones couldn't mistake the sound.

It was the high, panicked scream of a terrified horse.

Kestrel? Donal's big, black war horse? Could it be?

Fear clawed her throat, but she willed herself to wait, to be still. Donal had told her stay put. But what if he was hurt? What if he was up there, right now? Hurt? What if he needed help?

Kirstin couldn't stay put.

She ran across the rocks and out through the kitchen. Once she reached the tunnels, she changed to wolf form, just because it was faster. But instead of paws and claws clicking on the rock, she looked down at the soft leather of her boots.

Because while she expected to change, while she did what had always come naturally to transform her into a wulver, she didn't change at all.

She *couldn't* change.

Her lungs hurt by the time she got to the stairs and she groaned as she started up them. Her thighs burned when she reached the top. Donal's horse wasn't tethered anywhere. And she didn't have a horse at all.

It was the first time in her life she cursed not being able to turn into a wulver when she wanted to.

She heard it again, the high scream of a horse in pain. Kirstin ran for the woods. Nowhere near fast enough on human legs. She tired far too quickly. She reached the edge of the forest and stopped, listening. Her ears were faulty, she was sure of it. It was almost like going a little deaf.

In the distance, through the trees, she saw Donal's big, black charger.

She made her way through the brush, approaching the animal carefully from the side. It wasn't until she was almost on top of it that she saw the other, now dead, horse on the ground. Its neck was broken. Had this been the horse screaming?

"Easy, boy." Kirstin soothed, taking Kestrel's reins. The horse's head bobbed, but he didn't seem afraid of her. She saw that he had two arrows in his hindquarters and winced at the sight of the animal's blood. "Where's yer master, hm?"

She blinked as she looked around the forest, wishing for her wulver's eyes to see with. It wasn't light enough to see much with human ones. The sun was just casting its first, early morning orange glow over the land, but here in the forest it was still like dusk.

Kirstin squatted, touching the flank of the dead horse. Whose? She wondered. No identifying marks on the saddle. But she had a strange feeling that she'd seen this horse before. If only her sense of smell were working—she'd know it in an instant.

Kestrel pawed the ground nervously, shaking his big head. Kirstin stood, patting his neck. She'd have to take him back to the castle to tend him. But first, she had to find Donal. Kestrel whinnied and nudged her. Kirstin stumbled, grabbing onto the horses reins, but the big horse had knocked her hard enough to make her fall to the ground.

She sat there for a moment, the wind knocked out of her, and that's when she saw him.

Donal was swinging from a wulver net, trapped high up in the tree.

"Donal!" she called, but he didn't answer.

Kirsten checked her boot for her dirk, making sure it was there, before she began to climb. It didn't take her long to reach him—or to find that, while unconscious, he was, thank the Lord, still breathing. She didn't want to cut him free—the drop to the ground was too far. She'd have to pull the rope and lower him, she realized, although she wasn't sure if she had enough upper body strength to do it.

"Donal?" she whispered, nudging him in the net with her foot as she inched out onto the branch. She realized, from this vantage point, that this was the very same tree, the very same trap, she had been entangled in when she met him. Kestrel had moved closer to the edge of the forest, as if the big animal knew her plan to lower Donal to the ground and had gotten out of the way.

Donal gave a little groan and she leaned over to look more closely at him.

"It's a'righ'," she assured him softly. "I'm gonna get ye down."

"Kirstin." Donal's eyes came open, wide. "No, lass!"

"Make a move to lower that trap, she-bitch, and I'll shoot an arrow through your heart."

Kirstin froze at the sound of Eldred's voice from below.

"Do'na touch 'er!" Donal growled, twisting in the net, trying to see the man who had an arrow aimed in their direction. Kirstin couldn't see him. He was somewhere in the trees. But she could hear him. "I'll kill ye!"

"You're not exactly in any position to be making threats, MacFalon." Eldred chuckled. "I think I'm going to have a little 'fun,' as my captains liked to say, with your wulver-bitch, before I kill 'er."

"I'll kill ye," Donal said again through clenched teeth. "If ye lay one hand on 'er, I'll kill ye!"

"Blah blah blah." Eldred sighed, then he snapped, "MacFalon, you touch that knife in your boot, I'll put an arrow right through her eye."

Kirstin saw Donal's hand stop moving downward and he winced.

"Sad, what's happened to your family," Eldred called. "You're all dirty wulver-lovers now, aren't you? Your father would be appalled to know you had wulvers sleeping in your castle. And your grandfather must be rolling over in his tomb."

Kirstin met Donal's eyes, seeing the anger and fire in his. She could only feel fear, knowing Eldred had his bow aimed at them. She couldn't think of what to do. The animal instinct she'd come to count on had seemed to dry up and disappear overnight. Her limbs felt paralyzed.

"But don't worry, the MacFalon name will die with you this day, Donal." Eldred chuckled. Kirstin felt tears coming to her eyes, panic clawing up her throat. She leaned over, edging just a little closer to Donal, hugging the big branch with her limbs. "There won't be much of your family left to carry on the name after the wulvers are done with them anyway. And you let them walk right into your castle. Foolish."

Donal swore, twisting and turning in the net, going mad, tearing at it with his bare hands, making them bloody. Eldred just laughed. The motion caught Kirstin's eye and she glimpsed him through the trees. She knew where he was then, at least for the moment. Donal looked at her, his gaze moving from her to the rope, and she knew what he wanted her to do.

But could she?

She wasn't sure she had the strength. Or the courage.

Donal gave a slight nod, urging her, and Kirstin grabbed the rope. She pulled it, hard, and then let go. The length of rope ran quickly through the pulley, Donal's weight taking the net toward the forest floor. It happened very fast. One moment, Kirstin was leaning over the tree branch, the next, her shoulder was on fire, and she was falling, following Donal down toward the ground.

She screamed. She heard herself, landing on her hurt shoulder with a sick thud, the wind knocked out of her completely. The world went gray. Everything was a blur. She heard Lord Eldred drawing his bow again and opened her eyes to see Donal cutting himself free of the net with his dirk, his face a mask of horror and concern at the sight of her with an arrow through her shoulder.

She heard the zing of the second arrow and prepared for it, knowing it was aimed at her.

Donal heard it, too, and he roared, turning to face it and covering her body with his.

She screamed again, but she couldn't hear herself. The scream was coming from the inside, from the sight of the tip of the arrow that had pierced Donal's left shoulder appearing just inches from her eye.

Then Donal was on his feet, charging at the man in the underbrush, drawing his claymore, one-handed, a Herculean feat. Eldred screamed. Like a woman, he screamed, high pitched and frightened. He managed to draw his longsword at the last minute to stop a rageful, deadly swing that would have split him from the top of his head to his heart—even one-handed.

She tried to call out, to warn him, but she couldn't seem to find her voice. She was still screaming. It was just all in her head. Both men had their longswords out—Donal had abandoned the heavy claymore. It had been an impossible feat the first time he'd lifted it one-handed, and she didn't think he could do it again.

Donal was tiring quickly. She could see that much from her forest floor vantage point. Her shoulder screamed too, when she tried to move, but that was also on the inside. Eldred drove him back toward her, toward the net. It was disarmed now, useless. Then she saw it, glinting silver in the early morning light. Donal's dirk, the one he'd used to cut his way out of the trap.

The sound of their swords clashing filled the air. It hurt her ears, made them ring. Kirstin reached her good arm out, groping in the dirt. The knife felt like it was ten feet away, although it was probably only inches from her hand.

Donal yelled in pain when Eldred knocked him into a tree, his hurt shoulder up against the bark. But he didn't stop swinging his sword. Now she could see Donal's face, as they circled, Lord Eldred's back to her. Kirstin's fingers touched the hilt of the knife. Just barely. Almost there.

Swords clashed again, the men grunting, breathing hard. Kirstin winced and rolled, her shoulder burning with pain, but she grasped the dirk in her good hand. She had it!

Now, what was she going to do with it?

"Is this bitch really worth it?" Lord Eldred panted, using both hands to block a one-handed blow from Donal.

"You're The MacFalon. You deserve better than to lie with the dogs."

"I'm goin' t'take great pleasure in runnin' you through," Donal growled, driving the older man back another step. "And draggin' yer corpse behind m'horse back to the castle, jus' like m'grandfather used t'do wit' t'wulvers."

"You're not going to win this fight." Eldred grunted and ducked, blocking another blow. "Even if you kill me. The wulvers are already doing my bidding."

Was it true? Kirstin trembled at the thought. Had the enchantress found a way to compel them, without using Raife's blood?

Or had Raife's blood already been spilled?

"Ye lie." Donal brought the sword, one-handed straight at the man's side, but Eldred blocked it, taking another step back. "Yer the lyin' dog 'ere."

"You won't make it back to the castle to see for yourself." Eldred was breathing hard as he lifted his sword to strike a blow that Donal had to ward off one-handed. "More's the pity. They'll all be dead by the time I ride your horse back to Castle MacFalon, and my wulver army will be ready to march."

"Ye talk t'much." Donal jabbed his sword at the man, who side-stepped, but just barely.

"But first, I'm going to rape your little she-wolf." Eldred laughed in triumph as Donal charged him, and Kirstin knew, it was a mistake. Eldred was baiting him, and it had worked.

Kirstin screamed. This time on the outside. It hurt so much she thought she was going to pass out, but she managed to struggle to her feet, the knife in her hand. Her scream had alerted the huntsman and he turned far enough around to see her holding the dirk up high.

"Ye touch me, and I'll be the last dog ye e'er lie wit'." Kirstin brought the knife down sideways, overhand, into the soft flesh at the side of the man's throat.

Eldred gurgled. He didn't say anything, but blood filled his mouth as he sank to his knees, his sword falling to the forest floor. Donal didn't hesitate. He ran the man through. Eldred gave one last, strangled cry, and then fell, taking Donal's sword with him as he collapsed into the dirt.

"Are ye a'righ'?" Donal pulled her against him with his good arm and she cried out, feeling dizzy and nauseous for a moment.

"Aye," she agreed, mustering enough energy to smile at him. "Would ye look'a'that? I saved ye this time. Now it's ye who owes me yer life."

"Ye have m'life, lass." His arm tightened around her as he pressed his lips to hers, and murmured, "Ye've had it since the moment I met ye."

Donal called Kestrel so he could put her on the horse. But first, he broke off the fletched part of the arrow, and pulled it through the exit wound.

"'Tis gonna hurt," he warned before he did it.

Kirstin saw stars and thought the world had gone gray for a moment.

"I'm sorry, lass," he murmured, doing the same with the arrow that had found its way into his shoulder.

He mounted behind her, but only after he'd resheathed his sword and tied Eldred to the back of his saddle with a length of rope, like he'd promised.

She heard the man groan and she looked at Donal with wide eyes.

"He's not dead?"

"He will be," Donal said grimly as he took Kestrel's reins.

Kirstin didn't look back, but there was something quite satisfying, knowing the man who hated and wanted all wulvers dead was being dragged behind them through the dirt.

They didn't talk about it, but she knew Donal was thinking the same thing she was.

It wasn't until they arrived back at Castle MacFalon that they knew for sure.

Lorien met them on horseback, and Kirstin felt Donal's good hand move to his sword as the wulver rode up.

"'Tis the witch," Lorien told them, pointing to the center of the field, where a shapely woman had been lashed to a tall post. "And I see ye found Lord Eldred."

"What's left of 'im." Donal's jaw tightened as he looked at the woman struggling against her bindings. His hand wasn't on his sword hilt anymore. Lorien was clearly not enchanted. Nor were any of the other wulvers in the yard. "Not much of a threat anymore, is she?"

Donal rode toward the post, drawing close—but not too close.

Moraga looked up, fire and hatred in her eyes, and she screamed at them in Gaelic.

"What's t'matter?" Kirstin asked, narrowing her eyes at the woman who had once sent an enchanted blade after her. "N'blood fer yer magic, witch?"

Moraga snarled like an animal. Her dress was dirty and torn, face streaked with dirt.

"Mayhaps ye wanna use his?" Kirstin jerked her thumb behind her and the witch turned her head and saw him for the first time. Lord Eldred was still recognizable by his clothes, if nothing else.

"Noooooooooo!" The witch wailed, railing against the post, trying to escape her lashings, but whoever had tied her had done their job well. Besides, she had three MacFalons, two of which were Aiden and Angus, and four wulver warriors standing guard. The woman wasn't going anywhere—except the dungeons.

Moraga sobbed, real tears, screaming Eldred's name over and over.

"Donal, I'm feeling nauseous," Kirstin confessed, although she wasn't sure if it was her wound or the witch's display that had done it.

"Aye." He kissed the top of her head. "Let's get ye t'Laina and Sibyl, so they can patch ye'up."

He slid off his horse, glancing back at Lord Eldred's body, now bent and broken from being dragged behind the horse. It was a horrible sight and Kirstin turned her face into Donal's chest as she slid off the horse into his waiting arms.

"Send what's left of 'im t'King Henry." Donal tossed Kestrel's reins to Angus.

"Donal," Kirstin warned, shaking her head, feeling dizzy. "Do'na start a war."

"When he finds out what t'man was plannin', he'll give me an honorary knighthood," Donal scoffed, and Lorien laughed. Donal grinned back, then leaned in closer to whisper in her ear, "Or mayhaps m'choice of a bride."

She thrilled at his words, in spite of the pain in her shoulder, the nausea in her belly, and the dizziness in her head. She lifted her face to his, smiling, and let him kiss her. For a moment, she didn't feel anything but pure bliss. She didn't hear the witch screaming, she didn't feel the pain of her wound.

There was only Donal. The only man in the world. In her world. She felt dizzy with him, filled with him. She was his, and he was hers.

Finally, completely.

"Uhhhh, MacFalon..." Lorien interrupted, clearing his throat.

"What?" Donal snapped, annoyed at being interrupted. Kirstin clung to him, close. She was so dizzy she could hardly stand.

"Yer bride..." Lorien replied, glancing over at Angus. "She..."

"Aye?" Donal prompted, looking between the two of them.

And Kirstin knew. She just knew, by the way they looked at her, with that little bit of guilt in their eyes.

Aiden rocked back on his heels, clearing his throat. Then he pointed at the front of the castle, where a carriage was parked, led by four big horses.

Lorien sighed and announced, "Yer bride's arrived."

And with that, Kirsten fainted.

"I'm goin' to run ye through wit' an arrow e'ery month, jus' t'keep ye in bed wit' me." Kirstin snuggled down under the covers, resting her head against Donal's shoulder—his unbandaged one. Thankfully, their arrow wounds were mirror images of each other, so they fit together, as always, perfectly.

"Ye do'na hafta shoot me t'keep me in bed wit' ye, lass." Donal chuckled, kissing the top of her head.

"I'd usually say yer betrothed might object," Moira called, grinning over at Laina as she readied their breakfast on trays on the table. Laina had been called in to play nursemaid—because Moira was so shorthanded and Raife insisted Sibyl stay in bed and rest for the bairn's sake, even if there'd been no more bleeding—and she sat at their bedside, tearing cloth to make dressings. "But Lady Cecilia Witcombe's been spendin' s'much time wit' the handsome Lorien, I do'na think she'd care a bit."

The mention of Donal's intended still made Kirstin wince, no matter how much he reassured her that he was, never, under any circumstances, going to marry the woman. They'd both been laid up in bed for almost a week with their wounds. Donal's was healing quite nicely, but Kirstin had broken out into a fever on the second day and was just now, finally, starting to feel human again.

Which made her laugh to herself, because that's all she was now—human. Her wulver side had been banished by the mix of herbs Sibyl had prepared. Kirstin still felt a little bad about stealing it and secretly taking the mixture. Laina had been beyond angry when she found out, but now that they had two instances of proof that the "cure" was permanent—and Darrow had been informed of its effects—

Laina had come to her senses and had decided to stay a wulver, in spite of her deep desire to control her change. At least, until Sibyl could develop something that wasn't so permanent.

"Too bad yer not a wulver anymore," Laina grumbled, pulling back the covers to check Kirstin's bandage, as if she'd read Kirstin's mind. "Ye'd mend faster."

"I'm glad I'm not a wulver anymore." Kirstin winced when she pulled the dressing away. She was going to have an ugly scar there, she knew. "How's Sibyl?"

"She's doin' well." Laina couldn't help the smile that spread over her face. She stood, holding her linked hands out in front of her middle. "Startin' t'show."

"And the cure?" Kirstin knew it was a sensitive subject, but she was too curious not to ask. "Has she recreated it yet?"

"She's workin' on it. Silvermoon's plenty in the first den, but now we have to travel for the huluppa." Laina helped Moira bring their breakfast tray over to the bed.

Moira was still shorthanded, but at least she didn't have all the wulvers to feed anymore. They'd all moved into the first den, and from what Laina said, they'd made a home there in a very short amount of time. The space was the perfect size, and The MacFalon had no problem instructing his men to fix up the old barn to house their horses or build a fence in the field to keep sheep.

"'Tis always somethin'." Kirstin sighed, cracking her hard-boiled egg and beginning to peel it.

"Sibyl a'ready sent somma t'wulver scouts back t'gather the huluppa fer her," Laina said, pouring water into a cup and putting it on Kirstin's bedside. "They also herded t'sheep to t'first den, so they would'na starve. I was glad they brought home some more of our things."

"Laina!" Darrow's voice echoed through the hallway, floating into their room. Kirstin wasn't surprised to hear him. The wulvers and the MacFalons had been going back and forth, between the first den and the MacFalon castle.

Darrow and Raife had been in to see them at least once a day, sometimes together, sometimes separately. They had a lot to discuss with The MacFalon, who was doing business from his bed, which Laina and Moira insisted he not leave. This made Kirstin happy, because the longer they kept the real world at bay, the better, as far as she was concerned. She liked having Donal all to herself in their own little world.

"Here!" Laina called back.

Darrow poked his head in and grinned at Kirstin and Donal sitting up in bed together. "There's t'love birds. Ready to go ridin' yet, MacFalon?"

"I'm quite happy wit' t'mount I've got righ 'ere," Donal replied, sliding an arm around Kirstin and pulling her close. She giggled and flushed, but didn't object. "I trust ye and Raife 'ave e'erythin' handled, Darrow?"

"Oh aye," Darrow agreed, grabbing his wife to him one handed and planting a kiss on her cheek as she passed. "E'erythin' except the witch."

Kirstin shivered at the mention of her. She couldn't get the memory out of her mind of the woman screaming, sobbing, cursing all of them in Gaelic at the sight of Eldred's mangled body being dragged behind the horse. When they had unlashed her from the pole and taken her to the dungeons, she had been put in a cell alone, away from Eldred's four men. When one of the servants had gone down to bring her bread and water the next morning, the cell had been empty. Neither the bars nor the lock had been tampered with. She had simply vanished.

"I told ye she was a witch." Kirstin couldn't help ribbing Darrow a little about that.

"Mayhaps." Darrow shrugged. He was still reluctant to believe, even now. "Although I think it more likely someone who had access to the keys set 'er free."

"But no sign of 'er?" Donal asked, frowning. "Ye haven't found 'er?"

The missing witch had been the main reason Raife had decided to keep the wulver pack on MacFalon land, in the first den. With her on the loose, there was at least one person in the world who knew exactly where the mountain den was located, and that made it too dangerous to live there. At least, at the first den, they had the MacFalons at the ready to watch their backs. Mayhaps they would find another place, in time, but for now, it was a good solution.

And it made Kirstin so very happy, to have her family close, even if she was no longer a wulver.

"Ye sent Eldred's body t'King Henry, along wit' me message?" Donal asked, taking the egg Kirstin had just finished peeling and popping the whole thing into his mouth. He asked this question every time Darrow or Raife or any of his men came in, and they always gave the same answer.

"Aye," Darrow agreed.

"Nex'time, I bite yer finger off," Kirstin growled, nudging Donal with her elbow for stealing her food.

"Yer not a wulver anymore, luv," he reminded her with a reciprocal nudge. "I'm not afeared a'ye. Bite away."

She turned and nipped at his shoulder, feeling him jump, but he grinned down at her, a dark light in his eyes that made her feel warm from head to toe.

Another knock came on the open door and the two MacFalon brothers, Aiden and Angus, who seemed to go everywhere together, appeared. Kirstin saw that Lorien was behind them, a head taller than both of the big men. He smiled over their heads at her and she smiled back. She wondered if it was true, what the women were saying about him and Lady Cecilia Witcombe.

Donal's intended had arrived, terrified of the Scots, afraid she was going to be raped and murdered the moment she stepped out of her carriage. It had taken her party a great deal of extra time to arrive, because according to castle rumors, Cecilia had sabotaged their trip on more than one occasion, including "accidentally" shooting the captain of her guard in the thigh with an arrow.

She had stepped out of her carriage to find a witch lashed to a pole in the yard, guarded by half-men, half-wolves and bare-kneed, bearded Scotsmen in kilts. She had screamed at the sight, attracting the attention of the wulvers. Lorien, who had forgotten he was in warrior form—half-wolf, half-man—had rushed to her aid, always the gentleman. She had taken one look at his face and screamed again.

And when he'd remembered, and changed back to a man?

She had simply fainted dead away

Kirstin's feelings for the woman had been nothing but venom at first, but the more she heard, the more she realized, Lady Cecilia Witcombe wasn't any more interested in marrying Donal MacFalon than he was in marrying her. But if the rumors were true, she had become quite enamored with the wulver who had caught her when she fainted and carried her into the castle. And Lorien had been spending a lot of time at Castle MacFalon, if Laina and Moira were to be believed...

"What's yer business?" Donal asked with a sigh as Aiden and Angus argued their way into the room, Lorien following close behind. "'Tis startin' to feel like a circus in 'ere."

"Ye were drunker than I was, man," Aiden protested. "Why d'ye think I won at dice?"

"Ye did'na win, ye cheated," Angus snorted. "An' I wan'me money back."

"Nuh, I would've known if he was cheatin'," Lorien replied. "A wulver can spot a cheater a mile away, at least."

"'Tis true," Darrow agreed, leaning against the door frame. "We're also vera good at cheatin', if we wanna be."

"T'was ye then!" Angus pointed a finger at Lorien. "Ye were cheatin' fer 'im! How much did he pay ye outta d'winnin's?"

"Do'na lookit me!" Lorien laughed, holding up his hands. "I do'na need yer worthless coins. I'm a wulver, remember?"

"Face it, Angus, ye're jus' not a winner." Darrow grinned at the man, who glowered at all of them. "Let's g'back out on the archery range, eh? I'd be happy t'beat ye again. This time we can wager on it…"

"I would'na lost if I was half-wolf either," Angus snorted over his shoulder at the wulver, pulling something from the pocket of his plaid, handing it to Donal. "This came fer ye."

"Yer half wild boar, but that does'na seem t'help ye." Darrow laughed.

"Sounds like wulver-human relations are improvin' a'ready," Kirstin giggled, looking over Donal's shoulder at the scroll.

Her heart stopped when she saw it had the king's seal. Moira glanced at it and saw too.

"Mayhaps ye should go along wit' King Henry and nullify t'wolf pact," Angus joked. "So I can drive these dogs back t'their kennels where they belong a'fore they give all the MacFalons fleas, eh?"

"The only flea-bitten dog 'ere is ye, Angus MacFalon," Moira said with a laugh, already shooing the two big, bearded men out the door. "Now, out wit' ye!"

Darrow snickered at that and Moira, who had no qualms about who ran the castle, smacked his bottom with a tray.

"Ye, too, dog! Out!" She threatened him with a tray over the head and he backed away through the door, still laughing. "I do'na care if yer a wulver or the Lord of the Wild Hunt 'imself, ye'all need to clear out. I've got patients t'heal before I'm called t'me own death, ye ken?"

"A'righ'!" Darrow agreed, pulling his wife into his arm. "But I'm takin' m'wife wit' me!"

"Take this one, too!" Moira waved Lorien out with her tray and he avoided being smacked by it—just barely—as he slipped out, all the men snickering at Moira's dramatic, but effective, display. She shut the door behind them with a sigh.

"That's that, then," she announced, fanning her red face with the tray. "I'll leave ye alone t'eat yer breakfast. Call if ye need me?"

"Aye, thank ye," Kirstin said, meeting the old woman's smiling eyes. Moira knew what was in the scroll, just as well as they did.

At least, she hoped.

When Moira had gone out Kirstin looked at Donal, feeling a lump in her throat that was hard to swallow past.

"From t'king?" she asked and he just nodded.

She noticed Donal's hand shook slightly as he broke the seal and she felt cold, in spite of the fire in the fireplace.

"Wait." She put her hand over his. "Donal... what if...?"

"I told ye, lass." His blue-grey eyes were clear, shining with love. "Yer mine, n'matter what. I'll fight for ye, I'll die fer ye, I'll—"

She kissed him, feeling the soft, full press of his lips against hers, a promise more powerful than any king's proclamation.

Kirstin covered her face with her hands as Donal opened it and began to read. She couldn't read the words anyway, and even if she could, they meant nothing.

Nothing except freedom or death. Nothing except peace or war. Nothing except her love or pain. Nothing. And everything.

"Kirstin..." he whispered her name, trying to peek through her fingers.

"Nuh. I can'na." Her voice was muffled, her tears—they seemed to come so easily lately, now that she had no wulver left in her—stinging her eyes.

"Kirstin, look a'me." She dropped her hands, feeling her mouth trembling as he cupped her face. "Yer mine. I do'na need any man's permission."

"He denied it again," she whispered, feeling a heavy weight tugging on her heart.

She had visions of war, King Henry's men marching to the borderlands, facing off against her whole family, all of them, the MacFalons and the wulvers, the green, velvet hills of her homeland running with blood. She could lose them all, in one horrible, bloody battle, simply because the English king was afraid a wulver might claim the right to his precious throne.

"Nuh, lass." Donal pressed his mouth to hers and a fat, salty tear slipped between their lips. "King Henry's granted the dispensation. As a thank ye fer exposin' Lord Eldred's treason, King Henry's given up all rights to the MacFalon lands."

"Ye do'na hafta marry an Englishwoman?"

"Accordin' t'this, James IV of Scotland's s'posed t'marry King Henry VII's daughter, Margaret Tudor some time this year."

"Looks like t'king's gettin' serious 'bout marryin' t'border." Kirstin's eyes widened. "What else does it say?"

"This says I'm free to choose me own bride."

"Free." She repeated the word softly, saying it out loud, hardly believing it could be true.

"Aye." He pressed his forehead to hers. "Free t'choose—and I choose ye, Kirstin MacFalon."

Kirstin MacFalon. Hearing him say it out loud gave her a little thrill of pleasure.

"Are ye sure?" She swallowed, feeling doubt now that there were suddenly no barriers at all between them. "Even if I'm... not quite a woman, and not quite a wulver?"

"Och! Ye've always been all woman, lass." He laughed, grabbing their tray of food and setting it aside on the bedside stand. He moved his body over hers, stretching her out beneath him, and she welcomed his delightful heat and weight, wrapping her arms around his neck.

"I told ye, nothin' could keep me from ye." His mouth claimed hers, hands roaming over her body, carefully avoiding her wound. They'd slept in the same bed for a week, but had been warned not to engage in any 'strenuous behavior' by Laina, their resident nursemaid, and Donal had taken her at her word, no matter how much Kirstin begged him to take her.

"E'en if ye were a star up in the heavens, I'd reach ye," he whispered against her throat, his big, calloused hand moving over her hip. "And make ye mine."

"I'm much closer than that." She took his hand and pressed it between her legs, rocking against it, moaning softly. "And I burn hotter, too…"

"Aye, ye do." He slipped two fingers into her heat and she gasped.

"But e'en if I was a star…" Her hand traced over the sloped hills and valleys of his belly, tracing that dark line of hair down from his navel to find him oh-so-hard and ready for her. "Ye could still reach me wit' this…"

He chuckled as he shifted his weight fully onto her.

"Yer a thousand times brighter and more beautiful than any star, m'love," he murmured. "And I'm t'luckiest man in the world, because I don't have to look up into t'sky to see ye."

"Nay, ye jus' have t'look in yer bed," she laughed, putting her arms around his neck. She would never, ever tire of this. Making love with him was the deepest, best expression of who she was.

"Nay, lass." His breath was hot in her ear, and she realized with a little thrill that this was the first time they would make love as man and woman, free and unencumbered. "T'only place I'll e'er have t'look fer ye is in m'heart."

She met his gaze, smiling.

He was such an extraordinary man, who said such extraordinary things.

And he was hers.

Kirstin gave a little cry as his mouth laid claim to her first. She felt him, throbbing against her, seeking entrance, their hearts beating hard and fast together.

She knew she would burn for this man forever.

Kirstin parted her thighs to welcome him home.

The End

But the Story Continues…

I hope you enjoyed reading Kirstin and Donal's story as much as I enjoyed writing it!

The world of the wulvers and the MacFalons has really come alive for me, and there is one more book in the series left to see where things end up. I know you all remember the mention of the prophecy and the red wulver from the epilogue in the first Highland Wolf Pact—and it's time to find out just what happens with Raife and Sibyl's son, Griffith!

In the meantime, I just wanted to let you know that you can get five free reads from me if you subscribe to my newsletter. Don't worry, I always message responsibly. I never send spam—only great deals! So take a moment to click below and subscribe to get your free reads.

Then go ahead and read about the next book…

GET FIVE FREE READS!
Selena loves hearing from readers!
website: selenakitt.com
facebook: facebook.com/selenakittfanpage
twitter: twitter.com/selenakitt @selenakitt
blog: http://selenakitt.com/blog

**Get ALL FIVE of Selena Kitt's FREE READS
by joining her mailing list!**

**MONTHLY contest winners!
BIG prizes awarded at the end of the year!**

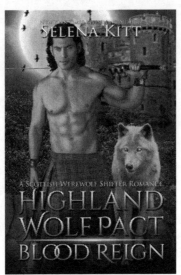

**HIGHLAND WOLF PACT
Blood Reign**

Bridget was an orphan raised by wulvers in a secluded wilderness temple to be its priestess and guardian, but now the outside world has found her and her world will be changed forever. Being suddenly swept up in ancient prophecies and ancestral blood feuds is bad enough, but fighting off the desire ignited in her heart by the proud and arrogant wulver warrior, Griffith, the only man who has ever defeated her in battle, may prove to be her greatest battle yet...

When you're the son of the wulver pack leader, and your father isn't about to roll over and show you his belly, life is tough enough. But when you're the Red Wulver, future King of the Blood Reign Prophecy, it's hard to know your own heart, let alone who to trust while trying to be the liberator of your people. Just as you finally take your fate into your own hands you've got your father, the pack leader, hot on your trail and you run headlong into a deadly ancient enemy you never even knew you had.

And in the midst of the chaos you crash into the aggravating, infuriating and impossibly beguiling, Bridget, the one obstacle in your path you're not sure you want to overcome…

ABOUT SELENA KITT

Selena Kitt is a NEW YORK TIMES bestselling and award-winning author of erotic and romance fiction. She is one of the highest selling erotic writers in the business with over a million books sold!

Her writing embodies everything from the spicy to the scandalous, but watch out-this kitty also has sharp claws and her stories often include intriguing edges and twists that take readers to new, thought-provoking depths.

When she's not pawing away at her keyboard, Selena runs an innovative publishing company (excessica.com) and bookstore (excitica.com), as well as two erotica and erotic romance promotion companies (excitesteam.com and excitespice.com).

Her books EcoErotica (2009), The Real Mother Goose (2010) and Heidi and the Kaiser (2011) were all Epic Award Finalists. Her only gay male romance, Second Chance, won the Epic Award in Erotica in 2011. Her story, Connections, was one of the runners-up for the 2006 Rauxa Prize, given annually to an erotic short story of "exceptional literary quality."

She can be reached on her website at:

www.selenakitt.com

YOU'VE REACHED

"THE END!"

BUY THIS AND MORE TITLES AT
www.eXcessica.com

eXcessica's YAHOO GROUP
groups.yahoo.com/
group/eXcessica/

eXcessica's FORUM
excessica.com/forum

Check us out for updates about eXcessica books!

38085114R00134

Made in the USA
Lexington, KY
04 May 2019